Also By Kimberly K Fox:

A Distant Star Volume One
A Distant Star Volume Two
To Be A Star
Shattered Star

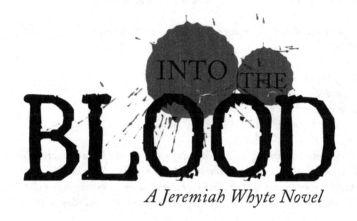

INTO THE BLOOD

A Jeremiah Whyte Novel

Kimberly K. Fox

INTO THE BLOOD
A JEREMIAH WHYTE NOVEL

iUniverse books may be ordered through booksellers or by contacting:

iUniverse
1663 Liberty Drive
Bloomington, IN 47403
www.iuniverse.com
1-800-Authors (1-800-288-4677)

Because of the dynamic nature of the Internet, any web addresses or links contained in this book may have changed since publication and may no longer be valid. The views expressed in this work are solely those of the author and do not necessarily reflect the views of the publisher, and the publisher hereby disclaims any responsibility for them.

This is a work of fiction. All of the characters, names, incidents, organizations, and dialogue in this novel are either the products of the author's imagination or are used fictitiously.

Any people depicted in stock imagery provided by Thinkstock are models, and such images are being used for illustrative purposes only. Certain stock imagery © Thinkstock.

ISBN: 978-1-5320-3064-2 (sc)
ISBN: 978-1-5320-3065-9 (hc)
ISBN: 978-1-5320-3063-5 (e)

Library of Congress Control Number: 2017916234

Print information available on the last page.

iUniverse rev. date: 11/13/2017

For: Mom

With All of My Love and Gratitude

Your,
KK

PROLOGUE

The long hallway was white and seemed almost cylindrical. Everywhere he looked, the hallway seemed to pulse with light. He looked down briefly at the two bleehs on either side of him. They came up to maybe his thigh. They were white blobs, with two very bright blue oval eyes, which were their only prominent features. The bleehs silently marched beside him, leading him to his destination.

His destination. His destiny. He had been trained all of his thirty years for this particular moment. All of the knowledge he had gleaned, all of the martial arts training, hand-to-hand combat, and use of weapons from every era were indelibly ingrained in his mind, body, soul. He knew he had been born for this, but had no idea why. That would be one of the questions he would be asking today.

*He turned his gaze to stare straight ahead at the end of the long corridor, which featured a massive golden motif door with the intricate seal of the **Razzifi** on it. He drew in a deep breath as the double doors slowly opened, leading into the massive chamber beyond.*

*This was a chamber few people ever saw. With an absolute secret location, there were only a handful of elite who were even aware of its existence. He himself certainly would never have known if not for being trained for one of the highest purposes of the **Razzifi**.*

As the doors slowly opened, he stepped through the entrance, his gaze moving around curiously. The bleehs beside him disappeared, and he was alone.

The room was massive, but seemed to have no substance. Everything was white, and it felt like he was walking on a cloud—ethereal and all-encompassing. As the feathery light parted, he could finally make out a high pearlescent pedestal high above his head, maybe twenty feet or so. There were six glowing shadows on either side of the bench. In the middle sat an elderly bald Asian man. He sat robed in white with gold trim, his cherubic face marked by a beard and spiked mustache.

He was the only other human being in the room. Jeremiah had no idea what the shadowy light forms on either side of the Master of the **Razzifi** represented.

Jeremiah moved closer to the high bench and kept his gaze directly on the Master. He was also dressed in white. The only vibrant colors in the room were Jeremiah's raven black hair and sapphire blue eyes. He stopped at the center of the bench, looking directly at the master.

"Jeremiah Whyte, welcome," the Master slowly and clearly intoned.

Jeremiah bowed his head and rose slowly. "Thank you for summoning me, my master."

The Master waved one hand, his fingers filled with various rings. "We may dispense with the formalities." He paused. "You are aware of why you were summoned?" The Master arched one black brow in question.

Jeremiah was silent for a moment, mulling over his answer. "Not exactly," he finally replied.

The Master was silent a moment, clasping two fingers to his lips as he regarded the man before him. Finally he spoke. "You know you have been trained throughout your life for a special purpose. The time has come."

Jeremiah asked the question he had wondered his whole life. "Why me?"

The Master smiled slowly. "Because you are the son of the One."

A very enigmatic answer.

"You have been trained for a special purpose that will be revealed to you now. You are to be sent back in time and history to change an event, or save a person who perished who should have lived, or to change a person's circumstances, or to protect a certain individual. These are assignments you will be given through a certain chip that, as you are aware, was inserted into your brain to give you needed information for each assignment. You will be given a new identity and name with every task. Each one will occur in a different part of history." He held up one finger to emphasize a point. "The reason you are being sent back is to change the course of history. In the history of mankind, there have been many events should not have happened, or certain people were meant to do things they did not have a chance to accomplish. Your whole purpose will be to steer mankind to a better path. To a better future. As you were born in 2057 we can send you back as far as 2055 or earlier." He paused. "Do you have any questions?"

Jeremiah glanced up into the Master's eyes. "Again, why me? I understand I have prepared my entire life for a certain purpose, but how can I, merely a man, change the course of history? How is that possible?"

The master leaned back in his ornate chair with a pleased smile. "Ah, I am *glad you are asking questions. Asking questions gains one knowledge. Ignorance is not bliss." He was silent for several moments, assessing Jeremiah.*

Finally he spoke again. "I have told you that you are the son of the One. I cannot tell you more except that you have a special skill set and a special knowledge set most humans do not possess, even in this year of 2087. You have within you the empathy and the strength to be a protector and a builder. You can do what others cannot. You can feel what others cannot. Have you never noticed this about yourself?"

Jeremiah's life flew quickly before his eyes. All of his training, all of the stunt work, all of the many tomes ancient and modern that he had read. It had all coalesced to this one moment. However, he did not feel special. He mostly felt alone. Separate. Apart. Maybe that is what the Master meant. There had never been anyone special in his life. No woman. No family. No children. Only the studies and the skills to be learned for a future purpose. Now he knew what that purpose was.

He looked up at the Master. "I think maybe deep somewhere inside myself I knew. But I pushed it away- ignored it."

"Hmmm…" the Master replied.

"I don't feel special in the way you described. I'm just a man with special skills that any other man could have been trained for."

"Do you really believe that?"

Jeremiah shrugged slightly. "Since I am here, I guess there was a purpose. I just did not know until now. When I am back in history, will I remember my true identity? Will my new identity supplant my own?" His bright blue eyes searched the Master's.

"Ah, a very good question! Yes, you will retain your original personality and self in a certain section of the cell implant. You will always know you are from the future, but that will be set aside until you complete your assignment and return. Your new identity will be the prominent one — so as not to put yourself in danger. You will need special skill sets in each new environment, and that will be your primary focus. And, of course, to finish your assignment to a successful end."

"Can I lose my life in the past?"

"That is a question I cannot answer for you. It would jeopardize your assignment and the person or event you are sent to change." He paused, drumming his fingers slightly on an ornate golden arm-rail. He was silent for several moments and Jeremiah waited.

"The only assurance I can give you is you are the son of the One. If he chooses to protect you, this may happen. However, YOU, and only you, are responsible

for the success of your mission. Is this understood?" The black eyes were deep and dark, probing Jeremiah.

"I understand. Once my assignment is complete, how will I know?"

"The computer chip cell in your brain will give you that information. If you are successful, you will return here for your next assignment. All knowledge you need to complete your new mission will be installed in the chip so that you know the language, the customs, the couture of the times, and the events of the world at that time period. Any questions you may have while there, you can access from this chip. If it does not give you the information you seek, that means you are not privy to it." Another long pause. "Do you understand your mission and your purpose now?"

Jeremiah bowed his head. "I do, my Master."

"I wish you much success Jeremiah Whyte, and may the One be with you. Always."

The bleehs reappeared at each of his sides. One by one the shadowy twelve lights blinked out, leaving only the Master watching as Jeremiah was escorted from the large white chamber.

July 1, 1863
Gettysburg, Pennsylvania

The moaning of soldiers echoed through the air, caught on the hot July wind and thrown back at the rocks and trees. Bodies were scattered for miles, strewn throughout the rocky landscape. Blood splattered rocks, grass, and bodies brightly lit by the full moon. The scene was devastating, ugly, and bitterly foul. The stench of death permeated everything.

Slowly, Trevor Tompkins lifted his head. He had a slight headache. He examined himself quickly. He was wearing a Union uniform and armed with a bayonet rifle. He seemed to have lost whatever headgear he had been wearing. His face had been buried in the dirt and he wiped a sleeve across his face, clearing the mud off of it. He seemed to be without injury but as he glanced around, he realized he was probably one of the few. Dead bodies were everywhere, some alive and badly wounded; there was a chorus of thousands of men moaning and crying in pain. Some wore grey uniforms, others the blue of the Union. The American Civil War.

He slowly stood, grabbing his weapon. Squinting, he glanced around carefully at the bloody scene spread out before him. Nearby, a dead Rebel soldier gazed sightlessly at the summer moon, both of his legs blown off. Others were scattered nearby. Trevor took a moment to assess his situation and determine his mission. The cell chip in his head clicked and he focused internally.

Your mission is to ensure a woman named Miriam Klark is not killed in the Civil War. She perished sometime during or after the Civil War. Her burial remains are unknown. It is imperative that this woman survives the conflict. Your mission is to protect her at any and all costs.

So, he had to somehow find a missing woman in the middle of this bloody battlefield? Grunting, he pushed several bodies away and started to pick a path through them, trying to ignore some hands that were reaching out for help. He had a mission and needed to stick to it. Slowly, he made his way up a slight incline and looked about from a higher angle.

Again, as far as the eye could see, dead and bloodied soldiers. Most of them seemed to be wearing grey, so maybe the Union Army had held this ridge. He needed to get his bearings and find out exactly where he was. Most importantly, he needed to find a human being alive who he could speak to.

"Hey, you!" he heard someone shout.

He turned quickly to his left and he saw a young man heading up the embankment toward him. Trevor waited for the man to head up before grabbing his arm and hauling him up the last few feet.

The guy was young, in his early twenties maybe, with thick brownish red hair and hazel eyes. He wore a bloodstained Union uniform and by the stripes on the side, Trevor determined he was a private foot soldier. He seemed to be alone.

The boy looked at the stripes on Trevor's shoulders before quickly straightening and saluting awkwardly. "Sorry, sir. Didn't know ya was a Major and all, bein' so far away."

"What's your name, Private?"

Wiping his hand across his grimy face, the kid answered. "It be Toby. Nice to meet ya, Major-?" he stuck out his hand, waiting for the Major to identify himself.

Trevor took the hand and shook firmly. "Trevor. Trevor Tompkins." He looked out over the battlefield and sighed deeply. "Looks like a helluva battle went on here."

"Yeah, we kicked the Johnny Rebs back for tonight, but they'll be gathering on Cemetery Ridge tomorrow, trying to rutt us out. You're kinda far afield, Major." He said it as a question, trying not to disrespect an officer.

Trevor glanced around as the kid studied him, taking in his appearance. The Major was relatively unscathed from battle and he was as *tall* as a mountain! Heck, even General Meade was big, but this man would dwarf him. Toby knew he was not short either at five foot ten, but he had to look up to make eye contact with this man, and his eyes were shadowed.

The Major noticed his stare and Toby quickly glanced away.

Finally the Major replied. "I don't know how the hell I got thrown out this far. Where the hell are we?"

"Well, right now, we be at Cemetery Ridge, trying to hold it from the Rebs. They'll probably attack at dawn, leastways that's the word comin' down. Since I'm pretty much in one piece, I've been trying to get some of the wounded here into the cart nearby." He motioned down the ridge on the left.

Trevor glanced over and could see it was overloaded with wounded men, many trying to staunch their wounds.

"I had me some help from some fellas, but they ran off, seeing all the blood and guts. Bunch of girlie chickens," Toby said snidely.

"What is your destination with the wounded?"

Toby waved into the distance. "There's a field hospital nearby set up for the wounded. At least, those we can help. Heading that way right now."

Trevor shouldered his weapon. "I'll give you a hand with that."

Toby's eyes widened but he grinned. "Mighty obliged."

He started down the ridge in his torn shoes and Trevor followed in his tall boots. He glanced down as they walked and noticed the full military uniform he was wearing, with MJR.Tompkins knitted in black above his front pocket and golden braid riding on his broad shoulders. He moved down the slippery slope behind the kid, joining him at a crude wooden vehicle. There were maybe twenty or so men and the thing was already overloaded. They would only be able to pick up ten or so more or they wouldn't get the damned thing to move at all. Together they would need to push it to the hospital.

"How far away is the field hospital?" Trevor questioned.

Toby gestured. "Not far. About a good stone's throw that-a-way," he pointed to a stand of trees further on the right where Trevor could now see a white tent with lanterns moving inside, shadows bouncing as people moved about.

"Well, let's get as many as we can here and head there as quick as we can. These men need medical assistance immediately."

"Yes sir," Toby replied.

As they gathered up more wounded men, grunting, Trevor turned to Toby. "Got a last name, Toby?"

"Sure do. It's Klark, sir. With a "K"".

At this response, Trevor went motionless. Casually, he hopped into the back with Toby as they loaded the last of the wounded in. "Got any siblings, brothers fighting in this hellhole, Toby?"

Toby shook his head. "No brothers. Do have a sister. She's a nurse at the hospital we're heading to. A bit older than me. Miriam. She tries to mother me, boss me around. Our folks are gone. It's just the two of us. But she is a great nurse. Should be able to help some of these poor fellows."

Target acquired. Now all he had to do was make it to the field hospital.

They finally got the creaking cart to the entrance of the white-sheeted hospital. It was clearly thrown up in a hurry and only gave cursory privacy. The rough cots were practically stacked on top of each other, piled with many badly wounded and a few superficially wounded men. Ages ranged from sixty to maybe six or eight. He was appalled to see children among those fighting for their lives.

There were several nurses, about five or so, moving among the soldiers. They were all dressed similarly with white bonnets, dark dresses with blood-splattered aprons, and black sensible shoes. The moaning from the battlefield had followed him into this field hospital. Toby had several others help him unload the men from the cart. As a Major, Trevor was not expected to do this.

He turned to Toby. "Point out your sister to me. I want to meet her."

Toby turned to him for a moment, then glanced around. His sister was one of the taller nurses. He pointed to a far corner. "That's her over there, in the far right bed." He went back to his chore.

Trevor left him to it and walked purposefully among the wounded. He found several clean white scarves and started bandaging gaping wounds, working his way down the aisle. He had medical training and if he could help alleviate some poor soul's pain here, he was damned if he wasn't going to try. He received many murmured "God bless you," but he ignored them until he came to a soldier who had lost his leg in battle. He was clearly going to bleed out and die. As he looked up into the soldier's eyes, he gave one last breath and said to Trevor "Go with God." He closed his eyes, sinking back.

Trevor tried to blink back tears as he slowly stood; only to confront a *very* angry nurse. It was the nurse Toby had pointed out. Miriam Klark. She had her arms crossed across her chest as she regarded him under her bonnet. She had deep chocolate brown eyes and he could see wispy sweaty blonde hair escaping in curls from her cap. She noticed his rank and immediately straightened but her frown did not leave. As Trevor turned to her, she spoke.

"Excuse me, Major, but what are you doing? Unless you have a medical license, you are not supposed to be administering to these men. Sir."

Trevor looked down into her eyes. "I just saw a soldier die right in front of my eyes, ma'm. Where were you?" he demanded.

She had the grace to blush but her backbone remained ramrod straight. "Attending to the other wounded here, of course. I am a nurse." She pointed out the obvious.

"Yes, I can see that, nurse--?"

"Nurse Klark," she identified herself.

"Well, Nurse Klark, to put your mind at ease, I do have medical training. I may be a Major in the Union Army, but I do practice medicine. I am fully qualified to help you in any capacity you may need. When I am not on the battlefield, of course. Which I guess qualifies for now," he informed her.

Miriam looked up at the very tall stranger. He was so handsome women probably swooned when they saw him. Tousled thick raven black hair paired with piercing deep blue eyes that seemed to reach into one's soul. Miriam discarded her thoughts. There were wounded to be attended to.

"Well then, Major, won't you please come and assist me in this corner? There are several men I feel we can save and as you can see, we are vastly overworked." She looked over his uniform. "You don't seem to be injured or wounded. Follow me, please."

Trevor followed her as he removed his heavy Union coat in the steamy, bloody hospital, as he prepared to help his new target save lives.

◆━━━━━●━●━━━━━◆

After working together steadily for two hours, Miriam finally put a hand to her back and slowly stretched.

"I think we've done all we can for tonight. We need a break and some sleep ourselves, but I'm too keyed up to sleep yet. Would you like some coffee?"

Trevor stood, his white shirt now sporting various bloodstains. He slowly unbuttoned it and shoved it away, wearing his white undershirt that showed off his muscular physique. "Whiskey would taste a whole lot better, Nurse Klark."

"We save whatever alcohol we have for hospital and medical purposes."

She moved over to a small coal-burning stove that had a tin coffee pot on a boiler. She poured them both a mug of the steaming brew. Trevor took a sip of it, then winced. It tasted like hot mud.

Miriam noticed the wince and smiled a bit, settling on a chair nearby, and he joined her. "I know it tastes awful, but anything to eat or drink after all of that," she waved her hand around, "tastes heavenly."

She sipped her coffee and watched as Trevor rummaged in his rucksack. "Well, ma'm, to add to this delicious brew I do believe I have a packet of biscuits."

Her lovely brown eyes widened. "Real biscuits? Not the salt biscuits infested with weevils?"

Trevor checked his memory chip for weevils. All food in the era was preserved with salt and in war time, even this was not sufficient. He grinned slowly.

"Yeah, real biscuits. The real thing. I brought them from home."

As she accepted a biscuit, she replied. "Where is home?"

"Yonder. Far away from here."

"You're not from Pennsylvania, are you?"

"No. I'm not."

"How did you end up in Gettysburg? Usually distant troops are sent to outlying areas, like New York or even Maryland."

He shrugged. "I got my orders and here I am. I believe I was sent to replace a Major who died in a previous battle."

She was silent as she enjoyed the biscuit, closing her eyes in bliss. She opened them, but not before he noticed the very long eye lashes fanned out on high cheek bones. Yes, she certainly was a looker, even dirty and bloody as she was. Cleaned up, she would be quite beautiful.

He looked away and took a sip of the awful coffee to try to chase away his thoughts. He was here to *protect* her, not to ogle her.

"I met your brother out on the field. He brought me up to the hospital."

She looked around. "Toby! Oh, I'm so glad you found him. In all of the fighting, I was hoping he would be all right. Do you know where he is now?"

Trevor pointed outside the tent. Some of the unharmed men had started a small campfire. "I believe he's outside with the other men."

She sighed in relief. "Good news. Too often, he gets into scrapes he cannot control. He's a bit hotheaded."

Trevor grinned. "Would he be anything like his sister in that regard?"

She smiled slightly. "Yes, Major. As you've probably already realized, I can also be quite hotheaded. But he has the reddish hair, not I." She finished her biscuit, licking crumbs off of her fingers daintily.

"Would you like another?"

"No. I'll save that pleasure for breakfast, if you don't mind. Speaking of which, we should get some sleep. The battle will probably begin at dawn. We need to be ready."

Trevor looked around. "Where do we sleep?"

She gestured at some crude cots that most of the other nurses were now occupying, sleeping soundly. There were two or three open. "Over there."

Trevor stood slowly. "I have a sleeping bag in my ruck. I'll just put it on the floor here. You take your cot. I'll see you at dawn."

She took their empty cups back to the stove and wiped them off. As she headed to her cot, she turned back to him.

"Thank you for your help today, Major. You helped save many lives," she said quietly.

"Just call me Trevor," he replied.

A tiny smile. "I think I'll stick with Major for now. Good night." She moved over to her cot and pulled a thin blanket over herself after removing her bloody apron and shoes.

Trevor turned to his rucksack to pull out his sleeping bag. He crawled inside and was soon asleep.

2

Trevor's mind slowly awakened to movement within the small sheeted tent. For a moment he was disoriented, then he remembered. It was July 2, 1863, and he was in the middle of the battle at Gettysburg. If he remembered his history correctly, some of the most vicious fighting would be fought on this day between the Confederate and Union armies.

Slowly he pushed up on his elbow and looked around. Nurses moved around the soldiers, tending to their wounds, feeding them whatever they could. It was barely dawn, but the day's activity had already begun.

He moved out of his sleeping bag and rolled it into the rucksack. Glancing around for Miriam, he saw her in a far corner offering a soldier a tin cup of water. She gently held the cup to the soldier's lips. The man had lost an arm. Blearily, Trevor wiped his eyes and decided to go out to the small pond nearby to clean up as best as he could manage. In this century, disease was prevalent and it was necessary to try to stay as clean as possible.

After splashing water on his face, neck, and arms, he retrieved his shirt. Noticing Toby over by the small campfire, he went to join him for more of the tacky coffee. Maybe it would taste better than before. His stomach grumbled, but he ignored that for now.

He approached the small group of men huddled around some coals still glowing from last night. As he sat on a rock next to Toby, the young man offered him a tin mug and Trevor accepted it. The coffee was hot, strong, and satisfying, helping to further clear his head.

"Morning," he said to the younger man.

"Sir," Toby replied, slowly drinking his own brew.

Trevor's steady gaze swept over the soldiers nearby who were quietly talking and drinking.

Toby's eyes searched the Major's. "What can we expect today, sir?"

Trevor didn't reply right away. He knew everyone was expecting General Longstreet to attack at dawn but something - gut instinct maybe - told Trevor it would not be that soon. So it was important to get everyone battle-ready and fed, armed, locked and loaded.

He finally answered the question. "The Rebel army will obviously attack. Longstreet is massing his army below and he will be heading our way." He paused. "I have orders from General Meade saying he is sending in additional Union troops, but they have yet to arrive." He sipped his coffee, idly kicking a stone by the fire with his boot.

Toby glanced away, his gaze on the rocky ledge leading down toward the strand of trees that helped to shelter the hospital and wounded. His eyes reflected pain and wisdom far beyond his years. A bloody war certainly made a man out of a boy very quickly. "I wish the Johnny Rebs would just get here so we can attack. Kill 'em! Kill 'em all!"

"Are you so ready to die, son?" Trevor asked quietly.

Toby's eyes flicked back to the Major's face. Major Tompkins' handsome chiseled features seemed hewn by stone. He exuded strength both physical and mental as his extremely blue eyes studied Toby carefully. Toby felt safe just being in his vicinity, although he could not quite figure out why. He barely knew this man that was his superior.

"Think I'll die today?"

"After what I saw last night, there's a good chance of it. Stay close; I'll have your back. As I told your sister, I have medical training. I'll be fighting, but I'll also be attending to the wounded. I'll need help with that." Trevor sipped at his coffee.

"Yes sir, I can do that," Toby assured him.

Trevor rose, dumping out the rest of his coffee. "Good. In the meantime, scavenge as many weapons as you can and make sure all of the men at least get some bread to eat, or whatever is available."

"I have some beef tacky I can share. And I'll be right on the weapons issue. Got a cache buried and stored."

"Good. I'm going into the hospital to help out your sister for now."

Toby watched as the tall man entered the tent, then turned to the tasks assigned to him.

The sun had fully risen and still no attack. Trevor entered the hospital and started administering to the wounded and dying. Many who had been alive last night were now being covered with sheets and taken to a temporary morgue nearby, where men were stacked like cordwood. Man's inhumanity to man never ceased to amaze him.

Putting his thoughts aside, he looked around for Miriam. Already, her apron had blood stains and she looked weary. Trevor approached her. He pulled her away from her task, nodding at another nurse to take her place.

"Hey, what are you doing-?" She looked up to see who had grasped her arm and remembered it was the new Major. Tompkins, she believed.

"You need a break. You were up several hours before dawn, weren't you?" He pulled her down to a stool and pulled over a nearby chair, straddling it as he studied her. She had yet to put her white bonnet on and her long blonde hair was tinged with sweat at her hairline. He filled a mug with cool water and handed it to her. She accepted it gratefully.

"Thank you… but we are very short-handed, and I can't take breaks."

"Well, you're going to have to. Because I have a feeling you're gonna be much busier later in the day."

"Later? We expect the Rebs to attack any moment."

"I was just outside. Nary a Reb to be seen. Take a minute or five. You need it." Sapphire eyes moved over her weary features.

Sighing, she took another drink of the cold water. It was delicious. Trevor produced a biscuit from his pocket and tore it into two pieces, offering her half. "As promised - breakfast."

She accepted it gladly, stuffing it into her mouth and chewing slowly, closing her eyes as she savored the flavor. "I don't know how you manage to produce such minor miracles, but it is wonderful," she said, wiping morsels off of her lips.

Trevor looked away for a moment, trying to ignore how beautiful the woman was in daylight. "Where do you and Toby hail from? Are you from around these parts?"

"Yes, fairly close. Chambersburg. About twenty miles west or so." She finished up her breakfast, looking up at him. "How about you, Major? You said you came a long way to fight here." She sipped her water, waiting for his reply.

You must never reveal you are from the future or your mission.

He sighed. "Out west. It's pretty much unsettled where I live. But it's north. As a doctor, I was commissioned as a Major and received new orders to return to the Union fighting, which brought me eventually here to Gettysburg."

Miriam accepted it for the non-answer that it was. She recalled the evening prior - how he had appeared to not even sport a scratch, although he had shown up in the middle of a bloody battlefield, seemingly from nowhere, according to her brother. She sat back a bit and studied him. He was extremely handsome; the deep blue eyes contrasted sharply with his jet black hair. How he had come to be here with her at this moment was uncertain, but somehow it felt fated, which was a very strange thought indeed. After taking several more sips, she handed the cup back to Trevor.

"Duty calls," she said, heading back to the makeshift cots.

He took the cup and drank the last few drops, watching the woman he was assigned to protect.

It bothered him that the hospital was on the frontlines of the fighting. It would be hard indeed to protect her, especially when he would be on the battlefield.

He flung off his thoughts, going to his rucksack to get his military uniform. He donned it, although it was already eighty degrees out.

<hr />

General Meade sent an additional twenty thousand soldiers to hold Cemetery Ridge. Cannons and additional artillery also arrived. The Confederate Army had been very quiet, and the delay in the attack gave Meade plenty of time to make sure he could defend the Ridge in order to push the Confederates back.

At about four in the afternoon, the soldiers stationed along Cemetery Ridge finally saw the grey of Confederate Uniforms - General Longstreet was sending his men to storm the ridge.

The fighting was fierce and bitter. Thousands of men in navy and grey clashed, killing each other with any weapon available- machetes, bayonets, knives and rifles.

The battle spilled out into Little Round Top, Devil's Den, and Peach Orchard. General Ewell from the Confederate Army joined Longstreet's forces and the Union Army fought back desperately to keep the Rebel forces from advancing. The Rebels did seize Culp's Hill, but were pushed back from Cemetery Ridge. The fighting lasted for two hours.

Finally Longstreet retreated to regroup with General Lee's forces, as did Meade with his reinforcements. The Rebels, led by Lee, charged Cemetery Ridge again. This time, the fighting lasted well into the evening. It was ten-thirty before the Union Army was successful at pushing the Rebels back for the evening.

However, the cost was deadly for both sides. The Confederates lost 23,000 men and the Union Army sustained losses of 28,000 men out of the 88,000 who fought.

Once again, as on the previous evening, the full moon shone down on the carnage, thousands of sobbing and wounded dying men's voices echoing off of the rocky ridges.

<hr />

Once more, Trevor helped in the hospital. He had sustained a minor arm wound in the fighting from a bayonet but he had dressed it himself immediately in the field so that infection would not set in. Toby had not been as lucky. He had been shot in the leg. Miriam tended to her brother's injury. The boy was lucky it was not too serious. In the background of the moaning wounded, Trevor could distantly hear the young nurse berating her brother as she tenderly dressed his wound.

Trevor was weary of the fighting already and it had only been his first day in this bloody war. The kaleidoscope of whirling color and flashing steel and bloody red flying through the air all blended together into one nightmarish blur. He kept slashing, firing, slashing with his bayonet, always trying to keep an eye out for Toby. Fortunately the kid did as he was told and never strayed too far away.

After the bloody battle ended in the evening, they both loaded up the wounded until they were too exhausted to move. Finally, the Major and eight other ablebodied men pushed the loaded cart up the hill to the makeshift hospital. It had sustained some cannon blasts from Confederate fire, but was mostly intact. One of the nurses did receive fatal wounds. Thank God it had not been Miriam.

After tending to the wounded, she joined Trevor outside at the campfire to rest with a cup of coffee. She was in the same condition as when he first met her- tired, dirty, and bloody. She wiped grime and blood from her face. He smiled slightly as he offered her coffee.

"Thanks," she murmured as she took a seat next to him on another rock. Several other men were gathered around the campfire. It was a hot night and very humid. Miriam removed her white bonnet, allowing the blonde waves to escape down her back and shoulders. She gazed pensively into the fire, no doubt trying to erase the memories of dying and wounded men.

"How are you?" he asked quietly.

Her eyes slowly raised to meet his. "I'm okay. Just tired. Thank God Toby only sustained a minor wound. But the fighting isn't over yet."

"Not yet. Hopefully soon."

Her smile was sarcastic. "Then onto the next battle. And the next. Until the Union can retake the South. IF it can retake the South. Sometimes I wonder what it's all for. What all the dying is for. Mothers losing sons. Daughters losing brothers. Men losing their lives," her eyes started tearing up.

Trevor gently touched Miriam's hand. "Don't lose hope. I know it's hard, but don't lose hope." His steady blue eyes caught hers and she took strength from his touch.

She sighed heavily and sipped at her coffee. "I should be sleeping. I am so weary, but I'm afraid I'll just have nightmares. I'd rather stay awake. I've never seen such horror and I've been a nurse many years-" she shuddered slightly.

Trevor moved closer to her. "Why did you become a nurse?"

She shrugged. "Daddy was a doctor. He caught an infectious disease from a patient that took him and Mama when I was about sixteen, and Toby maybe twelve. Fortunately, we survived, and I decided right then and there to go to nursing school in Harrisburg. Toby and I lived there until the war. We both enlisted when the Union went to war. I wanted to help others and Toby- well- he wanted to help too, I guess."

"He's a fine young man. You did a good job raising him on your own. That had to be difficult."

She laughed slightly. "Yes, at times. He is so hotheaded. But he knows I always have his best interests at heart. Not that we don't get into it from time to time. But-," she shrugged again- "that's the nature of siblings, I guess." She paused, looking at up him in the orange glow from the fire. "What about you? Have family? Married?" she asked curiously.

He snorted briefly. "No, not married. Very unattached. Literally. I don't have family back home. I just attend to my medical practice. In the wilderness, lots of people get injured. I was too busy to have any kind of personal life. Then I got caught up in this war." He paused, then gazed at her intently. "Miriam, whatever happens tomorrow, or the next day, I want you to promise me one thing."

"What is that?"

"You HAVE to stay alive. You must!" he stated emphatically.

She smiled slightly. "I have every intention of doing so, Major. But it is war and I am a nurse. No one knows their fate. I'm doing what I was put on this earth to do."

He leaned forward, locking his eyes with hers. "You were put on this earth for a very important reason and it is not just for nursing. You must always guard your personal safety. It is imperative."

With that said, he rose and walked away, flinging back the sheet and entering the hospital.

Miriam watched him leave, a curious quirk in her brow.

Trevor woke abruptly. Moonlight flooded the tent, pulling Trevor
from a deep sleep. He was in his rucksack on the floor. Quickly he
glanced over to Miriam and saw her asleep in her cot alongside the
remaining nurses. He sighed slowly and rubbed his forehead.

Flashes of light and explosions echoed through his brain from the day
before. The moans of the wounded and the stench of death permeated the
tent. He couldn't stand this. He needed some fresh air, now!

Flinging off the sleeping bag cover, he reached for his undershirt to slip
over his head, then pulled on his military-issued navy pants. He decided to
head out to the campfire. Maybe if there were still a few embers burning
he could get a slight fire going.

He picked his way carefully and silently through the tent until he
reached the sheeted entry. He parted the cloth gently, his gaze chasing
downhill a bit toward the campfire. To his surprise, he saw a lone soldier
sitting there with his hands stretched toward the fire as if trying to take
solace from the few remaining embers. By the moon, Trevor judged it to
be the middle of the night, maybe three in the morning.

Trevor moved toward the campfire. The soldier looked up as he
approached. He recognized Toby. What a perfect opportunity! He needed
more personal information on his charge to help protect her, and who
better than her brother to give it to him?

Toby watched silently as the Major approached and then hunkered
down next to him. The Major took a stick and stirred up the coals,
throwing more sticks on the embers until a slight flame licked and curled
around the wood, creating a tiny fire. Toby glanced up, smiling.

"Couldn't sleep either, sir?"

"Yes. I mean, I was- until I woke up." He rubbed his forehead, recalling his nightmares. He glanced at Toby. "What keeps you up, soldier?"

Toby shrugged. "Can't sleep. Too many demons chasing me tonight, I guess. With more to follow, I'm sure…" his voice trailed off.

Trevor glanced at the flames. He understood the other man's feeling. Idly he stirred the coals, then glanced over at Toby.

"Tell me more about your history, son, and your sister. I'd like to know more about you two."

"Why? Why are we so special that a Major would want to know about us?" Toby asked skeptically, deciding to be honest since it seemed, at this particular moment, that Major Tompkins was not his superior. Just another man haunted by battle.

Trevor met his eyes. "Just curious is all, I guess."

Toby was silent for a while. Then he started to speak. "Nobody in my life is as special as my sister. See, we lost our folks a long time ago. Once-" he gulped, then continued, "once there was someone special to me. A girl. I loved her, but she died. They said it was some kind of food poisoning, I'm not sure exactly." He shrugged and went silent again.

Trevor waited him out, poking the stick in the flames and coals.

Toby sighed heavily. "Since then, it's just been my sister and I. We look out for each other."

"Tell me more about your sister. Does she have anyone special in her life? A man, a husband?"

Toby met his eyes. "Why? Are you interested in my sister?" He arched a brow, meeting the shadowed blue eyes.

Trevor decided to tell some of the truth; he probably would get more out of the kid. "I'm asking because I want to keep her safe. I don't want anything to happen to her. So, I was just wondering about her life." He shrugged slightly.

Toby ruminated on this for a moment. Sighing, he answered the Major. "Miriam's always been first the mama for me, then the dedicated nurse. In her life, she's dedicated herself to helping others. First me, then others through nursing. She never had time for a man, though there were plenty who were interested. I'm not blind. My sis is a beauty. Is that why you're asking about her?"

Trevor met Toby's gaze directly. "As I've said, I'm concerned for her safety. I don't have any romantic interest in your sister, if that is what you're implying."

"What about you, Major? You got family in this war?"

"Nope. As I've already told Miriam, I'm single, unattached. Like her, I pretty much kept busy with my medical practice. No time for women."

Toby's brows rose. "No time for women?! *Ever?*" He questioned, finding this hard to believe.

"Yep. It was always the mission, the job."

Toby again was honest. "Handsome doctor like you, think women would be swarmin' all over ya."

The Major snorted briefly. "There have been women here and there, nobody ever serious like you had." He paused. "Tell me more about that... since I've never experienced it." *At least, not that I can remember.* "What does heart break feel like?"

Toby grimaced, glanced away, lost in the memory. He spoke quietly. "It feels like someone reached into your chest and tore your heart out-physically and mentally. Here and here," he gestured to his chest, then to his head. "You feel like you're going to die, but know you aren't. That you're going live to see another day when the one you want most in the world is gone from it." He sighed heavily. "So one day blends into the next and sometime, somehow, somewhere- it starts to become bearable. You start to have a life again. You may never love again, but you carry on." He paused. "That about answer your question?"

Trevor contemplated everything Toby told him. He knew he had never felt that way, neither in the future and probably would not in this particular century. Briefly his thoughts went to Miriam. He was here to protect the woman and she was attractive, but other than that he had no real feelings towards her other than completing his mission successfully.

He answered Toby's question. "Yes, I guess it does. Never experienced that... and sounds like I don't want to," he grinned briefly at the younger man.

Toby smiled slowly. "Being in love isn't all bad. Don't want make it sound that way. It is one of the most uplifting experiences you can ever imagine. Just being next to that one special person is- I don't know- can't find the right word-"

"Exhilarating?" Trevor tried to help out.

"Yeah, that be the right word! You feel like you can fly. You feel like you can accomplish anything because you have such a special feeling and it races from the top of your head to the bottom of your toes. Nothing compares to it." He shook his head. "Yeah, I went through a lot of pain but the ride was definitely worth it." He gazed at the other man. "Never been in love, huh?"

"Nope. Not ever."

"Too busy? Or just not interested?"

"Try both."

Toby shook his head negatively. "Can't wrap my head around that one, sir. That's being half alive. 'Course, where we are now-" he gazed around at the battlefield and the hospital close by, "we may not live much longer. So my advice, sir, if I may be bold enough to give it is, live now. Tomorrow isn't guaranteed."

The boy glanced over at the man next to him.

Again, Trevor was amazed that one so young had lived so much. The average life span of a male in this century was far shorter than his would be in the future. But Trevor discovered kernels of truth in the younger man's words, things that his teachers and masters had never spoken of. Love. A difficult concept to grasp when you were trained to think only of others, protect others, become separate and apart from yourself to accomplish that. Introspection would not help him to accomplish his mission. Or maybe it would. He should never rule anything out.

He knew tomorrow they would both be on the battlefield, his mind constantly divided between fighting and defending Miriam. To stay alive, he needed to concentrate on one issue at a time.

The sound of marching soldiers had their heads abruptly jerking up. Union reinforcement forces were arriving in droves with many more cannon and artillery. General Meade himself rode by and dismounted, coming towards the two men. He noticed the stripes of a Major on the older man's pants.

The General was tall and gruff-looking with a bushy beard. He was in full dress uniform, his hand resting on his elaborate sabre as he looked down at the two soldiers.

"What are you two soldiers doing up this late? We're attacking the Rebs in about an hour and a half." He gestured behind him. "I've brought in several more regiments and we're going to pound the hell outta Lee until he runs back to Virginia. Got one hour to get prepared. Wake everyone!"

With that said, he left to return to his regiment as they scattered across the ridge. Cemetery Ridge.

"Well, I guess reminiscing is over," Trevor said, standing. "Get your weapons and get your regiment up and battle ready. I'll alert the hospital."

"Yes sir," Toby was back to soldier mode as the two men parted ways.

General Meade's plan quickly changed. He decided to take several thousand men to Culp's Hill at four-thirty that morning, a spot which the Confederate Army had seized the day before.

Union cannons pounded the Rebel forces holding the Hill, but the Confederates did not retreat. Heavy fighting ensued until about eight, when the Rebels finally retreated, only to re-group and attack again at about eleven in the morning. The Federals counterattacked with their additional forces and finally drove the Rebels down and off of Culp's Hill.

After fighting all morning, an eerie silence now descended over the whole battlefield.

With the loss of Culp's Hill, the Confederate forces decided to try once again to take Cemetery Ridge. General Longstreet and General Lee sent about twelve thousand troops into battle that afternoon amid ninety-degree heat and stifling humidity.

Around one o'clock that afternoon, the Rebels opened cannon fire on the Union position on Cemetery Ridge to pave the way for the Rebel charge. Cannon fire blasted the Union position, but most of the shells fell harmlessly behind the Federal troops. Longstreet would not give up. He sent thousands of Confederate soldiers to follow up the attack and they all spread out below Cemetery Ridge.

The Confederate line of soldiers stretched for at least a mile as it slowly advanced up the ridge. The Union Army watched in amazement before finally the Union Army opened fire. Given their considerable array of cannon artillery, they plowed into the Confederate Army. The volleys ripped into the Confederate infantry, quickly dismembering bodies as the horrible cries of thousands of men dying and wounded filled the air.

The remaining Confederate Army pushed on. A fierce battle raged on the ridge, with brutal hand-to-hand fighting, shooting at close range, and stabbing with bayonets. The Rebels seemed to be advancing, but then the additional forces Meade had ordered regrouped and also opened fire on the Rebel ranks.

The great human tide of the Confederate infantry was pushed down and away, leaving as many as 7,500 Confederate troops lying on the field of battle. General Lee's gambit had failed. The Union held both Culp's Hill and Cemetery Ridge, at the cost of heavy casualties on both sides.

By its end, the battle at Gettysburg would turn the tide of the Civil War against General Lee's army, pushing him back over the Potomac into Virginia.

<hr />

Miriam, Toby, and Trevor had survived the vicious battle of July 3rd. Although the Rebels had retreated for now, they were expected to make one last ditch effort the next day. The Fourth of July.

Exhausted, the Union soldiers tended to the dying and wounded, both blue and grey, compassionately trying to ease their pain. It was the bloodiest day of fighting in the young country's history. Neither side wanted to see another day like it.

Miriam and Major Trevor Tompkins sat together by the huge fire. Most of the soldiers were congregated on the other side; everyone was exhausted after the bloody battle and most spoke very quietly. Commiserating, comforting, and leaning on a friendly shoulder after the vicious fighting.

Grey soldiers were strewn all over the ridge and the countryside below, some Union as well. The constant moaning of dying soldiers was a sound everyone tried to tune out. Those that could be saved had been brought to the hospital or field-dressed on the battleground. Many more corpses joined the ones already stacked around the hospital. They had hastily erected a second tent. Luckily, General Meade had brought more nurses in with him, about ten. They could have used one hundred, but it eased some of the burden off of Miriam and her small contingent of nurses.

Trevor looked over at her tired face as he sipped muddy coffee. Miriam clutched her tin mug tightly, her gaze locked on the flames. She had worked tirelessly today and saved many lives. She was probably reflecting on the ones she could not save.

"You were very brave today, Miriam," he said quietly.

She smiled slightly, then grimaced, meeting his eyes across the flickering flames. "Didn't save as many as I wanted to."

"You will live to save many more. Look at it that way," he pointed out.

Miriam studied Trevor's face. He too looked weary and sad. He had been fighting enemy forces all through the day and late evening. It was now about two a.m. and many could not sleep. The battle was expected to begin again very soon. July Fourth. Independence Day. At that thought, her heart ached. Some independence. The country torn apart from state to state, brother to brother, cousin to cousin. For what? To end slavery, to keep the Union intact? That was what President Lincoln believed. All Miriam knew was that it was heartbreaking seeing men and boys die in the most horrible of ways right in front of her eyes. She felt so helpless. At least Toby was safe - for another day.

The Major was a man of few words. She wondered about him. Who was he really? Where did he come from? His answers had been vague when questioned. She was grateful for his help; his medical skills far surpassed her own. He was able to save men that she simply could not. His skill set seemed almost- superhuman. Like he could look into the minds and bodies of those injured and do or say just the right thing. He was such a mystery.

Trevor noticed her scrutiny and smiled slightly. "What? Do I look that terrible?" He wiped his sleeve across his face to try to remove the grime and blood. Neither had had a chance to freshen up at all. They were simply too exhausted.

Her full lips blossomed into a smile. "No. You don't look terrible at all. I was just thinking about how helpful you were today. You helped save many lives also."

"That's what I'm trained to do."

Another ambiguous answer.

She smiled slowly again. "A man with all of the skills; but none of the answers."

He arched a brow. "Meaning?"

"You're such a mystery, Major." She slowly sipped her coffee as her dark eyes probed his.

Trevor contemplated his answer. He wanted her to trust him, but he could not give away the reason for his presence here or his purpose. After a few moments, he spoke. "I'm not really all that mysterious. Like you, I just want to help others. War is hell, and believe me, I'd rather be anywhere but here - having to kill or be killed. But at least I can use my training to help the injured or dying." He shrugged. "That's something, right?"

"Yes, that is certainly something." She continued to study him questioningly, but his gaze went back to the fire.

She knew Toby was with a bunch of his regiment on the far side of the tent sleeping. Most of the soldiers had gone to bed, except for the few on the other side of the fire. She was so grateful her brother was safe, and she had a sneaking suspicion it was because of the man beside her... he was watching Toby's back for her.

"Thank you," she said.

"For what?"

"Lots of things. Looking after my little brother. Keeping him safe. Fighting a battle I know you don't really believe in, but doing so anyway. For helping the sick and dying. And for being here for me, at this moment. Without someone to talk to… I think I would go insane, after what I have witnessed. The other nurses don't really want to talk about the war, and I don't blame them. I wonder how they deal with it." She sighed, clutching her mug.

Trevor's blue eyes met hers in the shadows. "You don't have to thank me. I'm human. I hurt and I bleed just like everyone else."

She looked at the slight tear from a bayonet on his uniform sleeve. He had field-dressed it himself. The blood didn't seep through the bandage. It looked more like a scratch than anything else, although she was well aware it was not. Such skill was unusual, but she knew he claimed to be a doctor wherever he came from.

"What is the name of the town you come from?" she asked.

Okay, what's my answer? He asked the computer chip in his head.

"Mentor. Ohio. On the Great Lakes. Far from here," he shrugged.

Again, she could tell he was reluctant to talk about his past. She knew about the Ohio Valley past the Pennsylvania border, but not much. She had heard about the Great Lakes, but had never seen them. She and Toby had always resided in Pennsylvania, so Ohio was as foreign to her as Florida.

"Aren't there a lot of Indian tribes out that way?"

"Yep. Mostly peaceful ones. Most have moved out further west. The white man has pushed them further out," he replied.

She cocked her head. "The White Man?" she asked.

This phrase is not used in this century yet. "I mean, ya know, us. The non-natives." He was hoping this answer would suffice.

Apparently it did. She shook her head positively. "Yes. We push people away and then fight when they invade. Why can't people just get along? Never mind, that was a rhetorical question. War has been around since the beginning of time." She took another sip of coffee, gazing into the fire.

"Tell me about your home, where you and Toby live. What is it like?"

"Chambersburg?" At his slow nod, she continued. "It's a small farming community. Very rural and not much around. We have a small working farm to tend to our needs. Occasionally I will do some nursing, and people pay in whatever form they can. We manage to survive."

"Toby told me he had a special girl and he lost her."

Miriam's brows arched. "He told you about that? I'm surprised." She

23

paused. "Yes, Dorothy. She died from pleurisy. It was very sudden and quick, which was a blessing. But he was heartbroken. Then the war came along and - here we are."

He noticed she always talked quite a bit about her brother, but never herself.

"What about you, Miriam? No man in your life?" He knew he was getting personal, but it could be information that would eventually help him save her life.

She blushed a bit, pink staining her high cheekbones. "There was once a doctor I was involved with. We were friends, nothing serious." She shrugged. "When the Union called, we were both sent to different regiments. I haven't seen him in two years. He has a medical practice in Chambersburg. There were times I would help him out there."

"Does this Doctor have a name?"

She was silent. "Why do you ask?"

"Because in this war, it is possible we could come across his battalion... having his help would be a great boon."

Miriam was startled, never having thought of that. "His name is Dr. David Irvin."

File for future reference - Dr. David Irvin.

He smiled slowly. "So - just friends, huh?"

Her smile widened. "Yes. I mean - he has a thing for me. I liked him, but really just as a friend and fellow medical assistant. Much like you and I, although I've known him longer."

Trevor ruminated over the conversation, then sighed.

"We should try to get a couple of hours sleep. Lee will probably be here at the crack of dawn." He rose, dumping out the muddy coffee.

Miriam rose too as the soldiers on the other side turned to stare. A good-looking woman was quite a rarity nowadays, and Miriam was quite popular with the soldiers. She said goodnight to them and they nodded back.

She turned to Trevor as he leaned down for his rucksack.

"I'm gonna go over and bunk with Toby. The hospital is a bit overcrowded."

"A bit." She smiled at him. "I'll see you in the morning, Major."

"You bet," he said as he collected his stuff and turned to leave.

Miriam parted the flaps of the tent and sought out her cot.

At dawn on July 4th, 1863 General Lee sent his Confederate troops back to the slaughter site of the previous day. The Union troops watched warily, but as the Rebels approached in their creaking wagons, they merely began to load up as many dead and wounded Confederate soldiers as they could. General Lee had given orders to abandon the battle; the grey troops were in full retreat.

Seeing this, General Meade ordered his tired troops to stand down, allowing the Rebels to collect their dead. They were forced to leave many of their fellow soldiers behind, not able to accommodate the thousands that lay dead and dying.

Slowly, the wagons descended the ridge and the Confederate Army disappeared into the horizon with hot sun beating down on them, turning their backs on the Federal troops and dragging their compatriots home across the state borders, back to Virginia.

The bloody battle at Gettysburg was finally coming to a close.

General Meade ordered his remaining troops to care for the dead and wounded. Major Tompkins was tasked with overseeing the slow removal of wounded soldiers to be housed and cared for in the town below.

This was a major undertaking. Trevor knew it would be a long, drawn-out task to house, feed, and care for thousands of wounded men, many without limbs. But they were the lucky ones. At least they were not among the many dead that still littered the bloody battlefield at Cemetery Ridge.

How appropriately named, he thought in disgust.

The little town of Gettysburg was located downhill from the battle sites. Nestled into surrounding trees with occasional farms, Trevor counted maybe two hundred and fifty tiny dwellings. Typically in small American towns, the biggest building was the church located in the center of town, white spire pointing up into the blue cloudless sky. Other larger buildings appeared to be a jailhouse and a saloon. The sign read *The Black Horse Tavern*. That might be a good place to start tending to the wounded.

He was returning with five hundred wounded. Judging by the tiny homes, he might be able to fit two or three soldiers in each, but looking around, he thought even that was doubtful.

As though she had read his thoughts, Miriam said, "The homes aren't as tiny as they appear. Usually the family has an upper loft sleeping area accessed by stairs, with the living quarters and kitchen areas downstairs."

She was seated next to him on the creaking wagon that carried some of the badly wounded, others following by the dozens. Of the fifty nurses that Meade had sent out, Trevor ensured Miriam was assigned under him. He was mightily relieved that the General had ordered them both into town to help care for the wounded. At least now she was off of the battlefield, and he could breathe a little easier. Toby, however, had been ordered to stay behind with his regiment to bury the dead on the battlefields with help from local volunteers. Trevor could swear he still smelled the stench of death on him and near him. He knew he would never forget the horrible sights he had witnessed over the past several days. It would haunt him forever.

He felt uneasy that Toby was still with the regiment – additional battle was always a possibility - but burying the dead should take some time, possibly weeks or even up to a month. Why was he concerned all of a sudden about Toby Klark's fate? Maybe because if anything happened to him, it would devastate Miriam. He did have her welfare at stake, after all.

Shaking off his thoughts, he turned to answer her comment. "They hardly look big enough to house a family, let alone several visitors."

"The town has prepared for the arrival of the wounded. All homes during wartime are commandeered for the purpose of caring for the wounded. Clean pallets, food, supplies... everything we need should be available in all homes," she replied quietly.

"It looks like that tavern there," he gestured, "would be a good place to set up as a central planning area. We can assign our fifty nurses to certain homes and families." He paused, then glanced over at her profile, partially hidden by the white bonnet she wore to tuck in her abundant blonde hair. "You know you are assigned to be my assistant, so we must bunk in the same home."

She glanced at him archly. "Yes, Major, I am aware of that. Is there a certain reason you chose me over the others?" Her brown eyes studied his.

His face was shadowed by his Union hat, his eyes inscrutable. "I thought it made the most sense since you and I have been working together steadily throughout the battle."

She was silent as the creaking wagon slowly pulled up to the tavern.

Trevor dropped the reins and came around the side of the wagon to help her down.

"I'll go in and speak to the owner to make arrangements. Please make sure the other nurses know the plan for now."

She watched the tall form in navy blue, the gold braid riding wide shoulders as he strode purposefully toward the entrance of *The Black Horse Tavern*. Finally she turned to the other wagons of wounded as they lined up behind the first one.

<hr />

Trevor and Miriam worked tirelessly with other medical personnel throughout the day to make sure all of the wounded were fed and cared for. Unfortunately, the short ride into town alone had been too much for fifty or so soldiers who had been so badly wounded that they bled out before reaching the town. They were respectfully placed in the church and wrapped in blankets or tarps to be interred in the cemetery after identification.

Trevor put five nurses in charge of making sure each soldier, Union or Confederate, was identified by his tag number each soldier on either side had been assigned. Family members would be desperate to hear news of the fate of their loved ones. Some would get good news, many others would get only sad verification that their husband, brother, uncle, cousin or close friend had died in the battle of Gettysburg.

Trevor and Miriam were finally able to find shelter at the end of the long day with the Bell family. They had a homestead very close to *The Black Horse Tavern*, which made things more convenient. Trevor was able to get about fifty soldiers bedded down and cared for at the tavern. The other four hundred remaining were scattered throughout town, with nurses and the limited doctors assigned shifts to care for them. Dr. David Irvin was not among the doctors assigned by General Meade. Hmmm… Trevor wondered if Dr. Irvin was still on the battlefield somewhere else, or if he would eventually show. Something to keep in mind.

The Bell family had a fairly big home with a loft upstairs big enough to fit the entire family: husband, wife, and three children. The two older boys slept on pallets on the floor. The husband, wife and youngest girl sleeping in the bed.

The house was able to accommodate four soldiers lying in pallets in the living quarters. Trevor and Miriam were able to set up makeshift beds for themselves - he gave Miriam the couch and made himself as comfortable as he could with several overstuffed chairs. For once, he was not going to sleep in a tent, or on the ground permeated with the smell of blood and dying men.

He dropped off immediately, exhausted from battle and from trying to save lives that day.

⁂

Trevor woke to the smell of bacon frying in the kitchen area just off the main living room and to the moans of wounded men.

He shook his head as he wiped sleep from his eyes. He had fallen asleep fully dressed, boots included. Wearily he looked around and saw Miriam was already up, dressed for the day and attending the wounded.

She smiled over at him as he stumbled to his feet.

"There is a small area off the side of the kitchen if you would like to wash up a bit. Mary will show you. She's cooking breakfast for everyone. You'll find some coffee there." She bent back to her task of giving a soldier a cool drink of water from a tin mug.

Murmuring thanks, Trevor walked carefully around the wounded. After cleaning up a bit and grabbing a bite, he would have to inspect the wounded across the roughly twenty homes he had assigned to both himself and Miriam.

Mary and Tom Bell were the family graciously sharing their home, food, and supplies with them. Trevor walked into the kitchen area. Mary glanced up from her coal-fired stove. She was a very petite woman, not tall like Miriam. She had reddish brown hair, freckles, brown eyes, and a sweet smile. She directed him to a small outside shed featuring a tub with water, soap, and towels.

Thanking her, Trevor moved outside and shed his uniform. He found the water lukewarm but fairly clean. He used the soap generously, trying to remove the stench of battle as he soaped up his hair and body lavishly. He would have to see that the soap was replaced. The Union Army would compensate the Bell family at some point in the future for the Union Army's needs.

After drying off and cleaning his jacket and undershirt as best as he could, he rejoined Mary in the kitchen to grab some grub and coffee. After that, he would help Miriam out with her tasks. He knew Tom and his three children were working at *The Black Horse Tavern* helping out there.

Quickly, he ate his breakfast and joined his charge.

<hr />

About midday, Trevor dragged Miriam from the tenth house and pulled her toward *The Black Horse Tavern*.

He took her arm as he guided her gently, ignoring her protests. "Come. You've had enough for now. You need a break and some food, or you'll be no good to anybody."

Miriam eventually gave up protesting and followed the tall Major into the darkened interior of the tavern. Here, as in all the residences, the wounded moaned continuously. Miriam tried to block that out for now. About ten nurses moved amongst the wounded along with one doctor. A long wooden polished bar ran the length of the far wall with shelves behind it holding casks of ale and various bottles of what looked like whiskey or scotch. She knew there was a kitchen in the back, serving up hardy portions. Since the war, the portions were smaller but still filling.

Trevor steered her to one of the empty round tables before heading to the bar to speak to the owner to order some food and drinks. He could badly use a whiskey, but that would have to wait until later when his various tasks were completed. He ordered two large bowls of oatmeal, a basket of bread, and two strong coffees.

He waited several minutes at the bar as the keeper went into the back to fill his order. His gaze moved around. At this hour, there were nurses and a few doctors taking a much needed break; he counted about twenty or so. Miriam was at a smaller table that was empty at the moment, which he was happy about. He wanted to speak with her alone. They barely had a free moment to say anything to each other as they had worked side by side that day.

The barkeep returned with two bowls of steaming oatmeal, a small basket of muffins, and ceramic mugs holding steaming coffee that actually *smelled* like coffee and not mud.

Trevor laid a few gold coins on the bar, to the keeper's surprise. He smiled and hastily scooped up the coins as Trevor balanced meals and carried them over to the table.

"Whatever you have, it smells *wonderful*!" Miriam commented.

Smiling, Trevor placed a serving in front of her and sat beside her with his own. She had removed her white bonnet and her beautiful blonde hair, although matted with sweat, swept across her back and shoulders. As usual, when he could see her face the thought that always swept through his mind was how beautiful she was. Working alongside her for hours, he was able to put it out of his mind. When they were face to face, conversing, it always smacked him. Shaking off this thought, he smiled and answered. "Steaming filling oatmeal, muffins, and coffee, m'lady," he replied, digging into his food.

She did the same, blissfully closing her eyes as she ate some of the hot oatmeal. "A hot meal twice in one day. I don't know if I can stand it after cold grits and muddy coffee." She opened her chocolate eyes and slowly smiled at her companion.

Trevor smiled between bites. "Yep. I agree. We need good food for the tasks at hand."

"How long do you think it will take us to finish up today?"

"By my judgment, with ten more houses on the agenda, probably sundown," he replied. Since it was July, sundown came around nine thirty in the evening. They had been up since dawn.

She was silent for a moment. "And then? How long before we can get the more seriously injured to hospitals? I know there are several nearby within a day's travel."

"General Meade has made those arrangements. We are to try to get them stable enough to travel. At the end of this day, I will meet with the other doctors to determine which cases are the most serious and to check whether everyone survived today." He paused. "If there are further deaths, they will have to be placed in the church along with the others. They will be buried in the church cemetery."

She was silent, a sad look on her face. "And Toby?" she inquired.

"Toby has orders to stay with his regiment for now, on and near Cemetery Ridge to help bury the dead on the battlefield. They must be buried quickly, as the ones in the church, to prevent diseases from spreading."

"Yes, typhoid fever is a danger. I already encountered fifteen cases of it today… it will spread like wildfire."

"Which is why we need to work ceaselessly to keep everyone as well as humanly possible. But remember, Miriam," his sapphire eyes met hers, "we are only human. We can only do so much."

She ate her lunch in silence, occasionally drinking her coffee. He waited for a response, but she simply continued to eat, glancing around the tavern at the wounded and the men at the other tables that were scattered on the pub's perimeter. The wounded all lay on pallets on the center of the large floor, as many as could be accommodated.

She glanced back at the Major and found him studying her. She placed her mug down and answered him. "Yes, I am all too aware that we cannot save all souls. We do what we can do to save the ones we can. I just pity the ones we cannot." She looked back down at her almost empty bowl.

"Pray for them," he said softly. "That's all you can do."

She met his eyes. "Is that what you do? Pray for them?"

He was silent for a while, then answered her. "I do… in my own way."

Miriam found this a curious answer. "And which way is that?"

He stirred the remains of his oatmeal, which was now getting cold and congealed, spooning it around. Looking down at his meal, he said quietly, "Do you believe there is a God?"

"Of course! Doesn't everybody?"

"Would a God let all of this happen?" he gestured around them. Her gaze followed his sweeping arm.

She turned back to him. "It is not our place to question Him. Our place is to do His will."

"That is what you believe. That is fine; you have faith. I understand."

"And you do not?" she questioned.

He met her eyes directly. "At this point in time, I don't know what I believe." He paused. "If you have finished with your meal, we have another ten houses of wounded to tend to. Then I must meet with medical staff afterwards."

She sat up ramrod straight, being reminded of her duties. "I am through here, Major," she addressed him formally, putting her coffee mug down. She re-tied her bonnet, stuffing her hair back into it as she rearranged her blood-stained apron over her sturdy brown dress. She rose to full height, reaching for the dishes and cups.

He stopped her. "Leave them. I tipped the barkeep generously."

She looked up into his shadowed face. He had donned his braided hat once again. "Of course, Major."

Miriam followed him out of the cooler exterior of the tavern into the blinding heat as they headed out to finish the task of helping save the wounded.

<hr/>

Trevor met with the medical staff in the tavern after the grueling day ended. Miriam returned to the Bell household to help Mary and the other nurse assigned with the wounded. There were four wounded; when Trevor returned, the other nurse would be relieved.

After meeting with the other ten or so doctors, he learned twenty of the wounded had died, seventeen Confederate and three Union. They had been placed in the church along with the others, bringing the total to seventy dead. Trevor gave orders to have a memorial service immediately in the morning so as to stave off disease. The dead had already been lying in the hot church for one day and it was imperative that they were buried. He ignored the protests of the others saying people needed to mourn. "The dead are dead. We must tend to the living. Bury them all immediately. Identify them so families can be notified, but this is a priority."

Everyone in the room knew the Major outranked them all, so his word was law. Reluctantly they agreed to post a notice on the church doors so those in town could attend the services.

"As for us, we continue with our work. No mourning for us. We must tend to the living," he repeated. "Thank you all for your hard work and dedication. I will see you all at dawn." The Major picked up his hat and exited the tavern, moving out into the dark hot night.

When he returned to the Bell house, it was close to eleven in the evening. He thought everybody would be asleep, and everyone was, except for Miriam. Almost as if she was waiting for him. She sipped a cup of coffee.

Trevor walked over to where she was seated, grabbing a bottle of whiskey he took from the bar at the saloon. He poured a shot into her coffee. "Here. You need this after a hard day," he said as he took a short glass and poured a shot neat for himself. He drank it quickly and immediately poured a second, setting the bottle on the floor and taking the seat opposite her.

She was curled up in the overstuffed chair, her bonnet, apron, and shoes off. Her honey-colored hair tumbled around her shoulders. He could see she had brushed it out; it looked lustrous and full. The kind of hair a man would love to bury his face in. He shook off this thought as he sipped at his second shot.

"That really wasn't necessary, Major. I can handle my duties. I would not be a nurse if I could not."

"Drink anyway. You've lived through hell and back. It will relax you and help chase the demons away." He sipped.

She took a slow sip and wrinkled her nose before taking another. She could feel it warming her belly nicely, something even the coffee had failed to do. "I already told you, Major. I do not fear demons. I fear God." She sipped again, her eyes meeting his in the lantern light.

"Fear God? I thought you worshipped him."

"I do worship him. We are taught at an early age to fear him, worship him, and keep his tenets."

He arched a dark brow. "Which are? Which tenets?"

"You are not a religious man, are you, Major?" she replied, sipping slowly.

"No, I suppose I'm not. And you did not answer my question."

"You have never read the Holy Bible?"

"Yes. As an educated man, I have read the Bible."

"Then you must know about the Ten Commandments."

"Know of them. Doesn't mean I believe in them."

"Why not?" She arched a brow, staring at his face in the dim light.

He shrugged. "I believe in my own tenets."

"So, what are they, exactly?" she murmured so as to not wake anyone.

He was silent for a while, wondering how to answer this question. He needed to always remember he was Trevor Tompkins, not Jeremiah Whyte in a different century, time, and place. After a moment, he spoke. "I have always lived by the tenet of treating others the way I would like to be treated."

"Well, that is in the New Testament. Christ's teachings."

He arched a brow. "So it is."

She crooked her head to one side. "Then which is it? Do you believe or not believe?"

"I already answered that, Miriam. I have my own belief systems. They may or may not coincide with yours. Doesn't mean I can't do my job."

"Of course not. I did not mean to imply that. I have seen how compassionate you are with the fallen, from both sides. You heal. You are a healer. That makes you a compassionate person. Why else would you be a medical doctor?"

He poured a smaller shot into her half empty cup. "Drink up, then sleep. We have a long day tomorrow."

He stood, pouring a third shot from the bottle for himself. He corked it and took the bottle over to the chairs he had occupied last night.

Miriam watched him as she finished up the drink. Then she grabbed a thin cover and cuddled back into the chair and closed her eyes.

T he next morning, as Trevor and Miriam were working at a home
tending to wounded, the Major was informed that five more men
had perished the night before. That brought the total to seventy-
five souls that would be interred today. All had been identified the day
before and last evening. The memorial service was scheduled for mid-
morning, so that most of those in town could attend.

Trevor accepted the news silently, glancing over at Miriam.

She had paused in her task and was staring at him, her dark eyes
seeming to pierce him.

After a moment, she leaned down and said something quietly to the
soldier she was attending to before making her way over to the Major.

"I could not help but overhear. Five more are gone?"

He looked down at her. They were only two hours in, and already both
of them were blood-spattered and grimy. "Yes," he answered her quietly.

She looked away a moment, and then her eyes met his. "With your
permission, I would like to attend the memorial service. I know it will take
me away from my duties for a bit, but-"

He interrupted her. "I understand how you feel, Miriam. You deserve
a break anyway. You have my permission to attend the memorial and the
interment also, if you would like."

"Thank you, Major. I appreciate that," she murmured, turning back
to the soldiers.

They could probably get about three more homes in before she went
to the memorial. He would find another nurse to replace her while she
was gone.

He turned back to his tasks, trying to block out his reasons for not wanting to attend the memorial service. As he said the previous evening, the living needed him. There was nothing he could do for the dead.

While Miriam was at the service, Trevor had another nurse, Nancy, accompany him to five more homes. Then it was time to grab some food. He had no idea how long the memorial service would take. He knew the interment would take quite a while with seventy-five bodies to bury.

As he did yesterday, he bade Nancy to follow him to the tavern. They got food and coffee and spoke quietly about the wounded. She informed him of the several additional serious cases he had not yet visited. Mulling over this information, he informed her he would visit these homes and assign another nurse to help her until Miriam returned. Nancy agreed readily. They finished up and went back to their respective duties.

Nancy had been correct. The homes he visited had several soldiers missing limbs, and gangrene had set in in some cases. With his superior knowledge, he quickly drained the fluid from the limbs and bound them tightly after applying a topical anti-septic from their limited supply. He saw the pain-easing effects immediately as the soldiers promptly fell into much-needed sleep. The nurse assisting him looked at him in amazement, surprised at such advanced knowledge. She had heard rumors that the Major was quite skilled in medical treatment, but seeing it firsthand was wondrous. She could learn a lot from this man. Unfortunately, he had assigned Miriam Klark to work with him.

Major Tompkins glanced over at the nurse. "Can you take over from here? I still have about ten homes to check on for the rest of the day."

"Of course, Major. There are only these three, and they are sleeping comfortably now… thanks to you."

The Major merely nodded before exiting the small dwelling.

Not only was Miriam Klark fortunate to be working with such a talented doctor - her luck was two-fold. The Major was majorly handsome. She smiled at her own quip and went to make sure there was cool water.

When Trevor arrived at his next home, he found Miriam helping out the nurse assigned. He was surprised to see her. By his calculations, she had only been gone about two hours. He knew they were still burying the dead. The mournful bugle was still wailing sadly in the churchyard.

He dismissed the other nurse and turned to Miriam. "Decided not to stay for the interment?"

She glanced at him from under her bonnet. "No. It would take too long and I'm needed here." She bent down to wrap a tourniquet around a soldier's arm. She was gentle as she wrapped the gauze on the man's arm, and he looked up at her adoringly. Finishing her task, she looked over at the Major as he inspected the other nurse's work.

"I visited some other homes while you were gone. Serious cases; missing limbs. I did not get to our usual quota yet," he remarked over his shoulder.

"That is fine, Major. I am back now and can help out. How many homes are left?"

He straightened from his task, meeting her gaze. "About six or so. Should take us maybe five more hours." Which would bring them close to dusk.

"Fine." She turned back to her duties as he did the same.

<hr />

Evening set in, and Trevor and Miriam had done all they could for the remaining wounded. They returned exhausted, disheveled, and dirty to the Bell household. The Bells had finished supper and were in the process of getting the children bedded down. Mary had already seen to the four soldiers and fed them; they were resting now.

She looked up at the two weary people who entered her home. "There is beef stew left simmering on the stove for the two of you. I also made sure that there is hot water for you both to wash up. Please help yourselves. If you don't need me further, I was going to join my family upstairs."

The Major smiled tiredly. "Thank you very much, Mrs. Bell. We'll be fine."

"Please, Major. Call me Mary." She gave them her sweet smile and then climbed the sturdy wooden stairs to the upstairs loft.

Trevor turned to Miriam. "Do you want to clean up first or eat first?" He knew they would need to take turns with the outside tub area.

She pulled off her bonnet, letting blonde tresses escape. "If you don't mind, Major, I feel so filthy that eating can definitely wait."

He looked down at her and grinned slightly. "Okay. I'll eat for now, and when you are through I'll clean up."

"Thank you." She moved slowly outside to the enclosed tub area to bathe and shampoo.

Trevor turned to the stove. The stew smelled delicious. He scooped up a hardy portion then helped himself to some fresh bread. He poured a cup of coffee and took his food into the living quarters to eat.

Tonight the men were silent, no longer moaning as they had been the previous evening. With medical care, they were no longer in pain. They were able to rest more comfortably thanks to Miriam and himself, with Mary's help.

Trying to blank his duties out of his mind for now, he dug into the stew, which was as delicious as it smelled. Mary was a good cook, particularly given the meager supplies she had on hand due to war. The stew was thick and hot with some vegetables added to a few beefy chunks. He ate silently, wondering how long it would take Miriam to clean up and change.

He was finishing up the last of his coffee when she appeared in the room, looking fresh and clean. She had even changed into a fresh dress, another sturdy one in black. Her bright hair was even more luminous against the dark color. She made up her own dinner and sat across from him.

"I left enough hot water and soap for you, Major," she smiled over at him as she set her coffee down on a table.

He smiled and rose. "Thanks. I appreciate that."

He left her, taking his dishes into the kitchen area. He quickly washed them up for Mary and set them to drain, making sure the stove was turned off. Then he headed outside to clean up.

<hr />

Within twenty minutes he had rejoined Miriam in the living quarters. She had finished up her meal and was sipping coffee.

Trevor had put on his Union pants, long-sleeved undershirt, and some fresh socks. His hair was still crisp and wet; it emphasized his very blue eyes. Grinning, he sipped from a second cup of coffee of his own, deciding to leave the whiskey out for tonight. His stomach was nice and full with the hot supper.

Miriam smiled back slowly at him as she sipped her coffee. He looked fresh, clean and very handsome, the long sleeved shirt showing off lean powerful muscles.

Trevor cleared his throat slightly, feeling conversation was in order. "How did the service go today?"

She set her mug aside on a table, her dark eyes meeting his. "It was about two hours. There was a regular mass, then a memorial where each name was read aloud by the chaplain. It was solemn and very sad. Heartbreaking, actually. I feel so bad for all of the families who lost loved ones." She shrugged a bit. "I wanted to get back to my duties. When I work, I don't think about the war. I think about what needs to be done. At church, I had time for more... introspection."

"And where did your introspection take you?" he asked quietly.

She blinked back tears a bit. She sighed heavily. "I was... thinking about Toby, and hoping he makes it safely through this war. I know the Union has won the battle of Gettysburg, but there are many more to come. Many more will die," she murmured, glancing away.

Trevor was silent for a moment, ruminating over her words. Yes, many more would die, but it was his job to make sure Miriam survived and by proxy, if he could make it happen, Toby Klark. His number one priority needed to be Miriam's safety. He hoped that General Meade did not order them both back to battle stations when their work here was complete, but it was certainly a possibility.

Miriam's brown eyes studied his and he knew she was waiting for him to say something.

He sipped his coffee, giving himself time to find the right words. When he found them, he spoke softly. "Yes, Miriam. I cannot deny that many more will die. This is war, and war is hell, as you know." He knew from his memory chip that the war would end in roughly two more years. He also recalled The Civil War was the bloodiest one in American history, except for another he was not yet privy to. Sighing, he spoke further. "You and I can only do what we are trained to do... help the living and the wounded to ensure they will live to see their families again."

"Or fight another day," she added cynically.

He nodded. "Yes, there's that." He knew any soldier who recovered after medical treatment was immediately sent back to his regiment. They needed every soldier that was healthy enough to shoot and fight. He said nothing further, sipping at his coffee.

She picked up hers too, sipping slowly. "How about you, Major? When this conflict ends, whenever that is, will you be returning to your practice in Ohio?"

Okay, what is my answer to this question? After a moment, he spoke. "Probably." He left it at that.

She only nodded slowly.

"And you and Toby? Will you go home? Where was it you mentioned - Chambersburg?"

"Yes. I want to leave this war and suffering far behind. I hope Dr. Irvin survives also so that I can continue helping him in his practice."

Ah yes, the good Dr. Irvin. He had been on Trevor's mind too. He had a hunch that they would see this particular doctor during his time here.

He smiled at her. "And you will be happy to be reunited with him, won't you?"

She blushed, her high cheekbones turning pink. "We do not have a romantic relationship, Major. I already explained that. We work together."

He eyed her knowingly. "Yep, but he would like it to be more than just business. Am I right?"

She rose slowly, glancing down at him, picking up her dishes.

"That, Major, is none of your business," she said as she swept from the room.

Trevor Tompkins watched her go thoughtfully.

The days passed and eventually they got some badly-needed rain. Water, especially clean water, was a scarce commodity. All manner of containers were put outdoors to catch the fresh rainfall. The metal containers would be distributed throughout the town on Major Tompkins' orders. Typhoid fever was already prevalent throughout the little community – it wasn't only soldiers dying from it, but also the locals. The Major worked tirelessly to educate medical personnel on the value of cleanliness. He knew that in this century, certain bacteria had not even been discovered yet. Many residents did not know the dangers of drinking or cooking with infected water, which caused disease to quickly spread.

Miriam and the other nurses and doctors had tried as hard as they could to save as many lives as possible, but unfortunately there had been many more deaths. The bell tolled daily at the church. Services to bury the dead became a background noise that many were learning to ignore. The Major insisted the dead be buried quickly. If not, more could die. Many shook their heads at this, but did as instructed. The little burial site in the small churchyard was now becoming quite large as more were interred.

The healthy people stoically tried to help the many who were still alive and had a chance of survival. It was all they could do - survive.

At General Meade's request, Major Tompkins sent back any soldiers who were battle ready. They were ordered back to the battlefield to help bury the remaining dead. The General also informed Major Tompkins that about mid-month the regiment would be pulling out to pursue Lee's troops. General Meade had heard of Major Tompkins' extraordinary ability to heal and had ordered him to travel with the regiment once they left. He would be allowed to bring about ten hand-picked nurses. Trevor was relieved by this news. That meant that Miriam could join him. She would be in danger again in the battle camps, but at least he could protect her. Toby was also in the same regiment, so Miriam would be happy to be reunited with him.

In the meantime, Trevor and his medical personnel worked hard to try to save those that they could. Sometimes their efforts failed, but in many cases they did not. For that, they were grateful.

As the month moved along, Trevor sent back to Meade about fifty fight-worthy men. Between battle wounds and disease, two hundred and fifty more had died, leaving out of the original five hundred that had returned a little less than two hundred soldiers. Many still had serious wounds that would leave them out of commission for a long time, possibly for the remainder of the war. If he returned to battle by mid-July, he would need to use all of his knowledge and skill set with his limited resources to save those that he could. It was exhausting, dirty work, but he put filthy conditions from his mind and did what he could.

<hr />

One evening, after a particularly long day of work, Trevor invited Miriam to sit out on the back porch of the Bell house. From there they could look up at the dark summer night and gaze at the bright stars. They sipped coffee in quiet companionship, enjoying the respite from the heat of the day and a fresh breeze that had sprung up.

The wind ruffled Miriam's hair slightly and she reached up to tuck the tresses behind her ear. Trevor studied her profile as she silently gazed at the silvery stars, wondering what she was thinking.

They had sent back two of the soldiers that had been in the Bell household. Now there were two left and both would survive to return home. They had each lost limbs - one an arm, the other a leg, but Major Tompkins had managed to save their lives. When they were ambulatory, they would be returning home to family and loved ones, out of this miserable war. Not in one piece, but alive. That was something, he supposed.

As he continued to study the woman next to him, he thought about how courageous she had been, steadily working by his side, doing whatever he ordered, never questioning, silently obeying. She had been a great help to him; without her, he knew he would have lost more soldiers. She never complained although he knew she was exhausted. Some of the tasks were quite physically taxing, but she handled them without a qualm. He admired her greatly. He couldn't deny it – he found her very attractive, but he tried to set that thought aside.

But it wasn't easy. Especially not tonight, with the moonlight kissing her lovely face and her honey hair tousled slightly by the breezes, full lips parted slightly to sip at her mug. Trevor moved restlessly, flicking his gaze away. Romantic intimacy - that was *not* part of his mission. He hesitated. Or maybe it was. He had no idea what the end result of his mission was meant to be... only that she must survive the conflict of the Civil War.

At the Major's silence, Miriam glanced at him. He appeared to be studying the woods that grew close to the back of the house. They were dark and shadowed, tree boughs swaying a bit in the heavenly breeze. They were finally getting some relief from the heat after the rain.

She wondered about her superior. The man was still as mysterious as ever. She studied his handsome profile. He had removed his hat, the breeze teasing his dark hair. It was jet-black and he wore it on the long side, although she had noted every morning that he shaved, choosing not to sport a beard as many men did. His raven hair blended with the night; she could not see his bright blue eyes at the moment.

Miriam knew the other nurses all had major crushes on the man who they called "her Major". Miriam chuckled a bit at that.

At this sound, Tompkins looked over at Miriam, surprised by her little chuckle. "Something amusing?" he questioned.

Her smile widened. "No, just something I found a bit funny."

"Which would be?"

Miriam hesitated, then decided to tell him the truth. "Oh, the other nurses all find you very handsome. They tell me I am lucky to be working with you. They call you 'my Major.'" Smiling, she sipped at her coffee.

Trevor leaned forward, elbows on his knees, cradling his own coffee in large hands. He arched a brow at this response, studying her. After a moment, he spoke. "And you, Miriam? Do you find me handsome too?" His intent gaze probed hers.

Smiling, she gave a little shrug. "Of course, Major. It is quite obvious. Have no other women told you such a thing?"

He grinned back. "On occasion. Never thought much of it."

She was silent for a bit. "So why no special woman in your life, Major?"

She knew she was getting personal, but at the moment, they were not on duty.

Trevor considered his answer. He needed to give an honest reply without giving away the reason why he was here. He lifted his gaze to hers. "There just wasn't ever anyone special. Only the work. I *have* had some intimate relationships like most men. Nothing serious though."

She blushed a bit. "I'm sorry. That is really none of my business."

"It's okay for you to be curious. We have been working together for weeks now, after all." He paused. "What about you and Dr. Irvin? Any plans there?"

Her lovely brown eyes met his. "No. No plans. As I've explained, we are very good friends. Like you, it was always the work for me… and taking care of Toby. No interest in romance."

"That's a shame. You're such a lovely woman. Compassionate, dedicated. You would make someone a good wife."

She smiled again. "I know at my age I am considered more a spinster." She shrugged. "I don't mind."

Trevor consulted the computer chip in his head for more information on what she had just told him. *In this century, women and girls marry very early, sometimes as young as twelve, thirteen. Miriam is in her mid-twenties. The word 'spinster' is meant to convey she is past normal marriageable age.*

Startled by this information, Trevor studied Miriam more closely. After the answer the chip had just given him, this greatly surprised him. Miriam was a beauty and should have been snatched up long ago. However, by her own words, she preferred her life just the way it was.

At his silence, she teased him. "Well, don't you agree, Major? In a few years, I'll see thirty. Way past my prime," she chuckled.

Trevor again stared at Miriam in complete surprise, flabbergasted. What was more disturbing was that they were in the middle of a war and she could be killed before she ever saw the ripe old age of thirty.

He answered her. "I'm thirty myself, Miriam. I hardly think I'm past my prime."

"It's different for men. Men are considered in their prime well into their forties sometimes."

Although Trevor/Jeremiah had studied all time periods and cultures, actually having this kind of conversation with a woman who had been dead many centuries before he was born was just bizarre.

The chip in his head flicked on. *It is part of your mission, Jeremiah. Let it go.*

He straightened and stood to full height. "I don't think you're past your prime at all, Miriam. It's late. Let's get some sleep." He held the back door open for her.

She rose and just before she passed him she paused and whispered. "I know you're not past your prime, Trevor. It's very obvious." Then she left him standing there, not looking back as she walked inside.

◆━━━━━●◯●━━━━━◆

Early the next morning, a contingent of Union soldiers from further up north joined the soldiers still at Gettysburg. They all reined their horses to the posts at the tavern as wagons carried badly-needed supplies around the back.

There were four or five officers and the rest were enlisted men, about one hundred in all.

The officers entered the tavern where Miriam and Trevor were still caring for about twenty men.

As the double doors opened and Union blue officers entered, Miriam looked up and gasped in surprise.

"David!?" she gasped. She rose from her task. "Is it really you?"

A Captain removed his hat, revealing salt and pepper hair and a black, well-trimmed beard. He was handsome in a rough sort of way. Clasping his hat, he smiled. "Hello, Miriam. It is so good to see you!"

He walked quickly to her and embraced her as Major Trevor Tompkins looked on.

Major Trevor Tompkins watched curiously as Miriam and her doctor animatedly conversed. The huge smile on Miriam's face conveyed how happy she was to see David again. He smiled down at her with affection, and it was easy for Trevor to see that the doctor was more than just a little fond of Miriam. If he were not mistaken, he would even assume the man was in love with her.

After a few moments, Miriam remembered his presence. The other officers had retreated to the bar for a drink to quench their thirst after the long hot journey.

Miriam grabbed David's hand and led him over to the Major, still smiling.

As the two men appraised each other, Trevor could see Dr. David Irvin was tall for men in this time, maybe six feet. He had silvery grey eyes and rough-hewn features. With the salt and pepper hair and the neat black beard, he exuded confidence and intelligence. This was a doctor many people would seek out and trust.

"Major, may I please present Dr. David Irvin, my old friend I spoke of," Miriam made the introductions and the two men shook hands firmly.

"Hello, Doctor. Miriam has mentioned you frequently, always in a very positive light."

"I am pleased to make your acquaintance, Major. From the rumors I have already heard about you, you are quite adept at medical practice." David's manner was friendly and calm as he released his superior's hand.

"She gives me too much credit sometimes."

"Oh no!" Miriam intervened. Her brown eyes swung to David. "I have literally seen him perform miracles! The Major is a very talented doctor." She looked back at Trevor as the two men continued to assess each other.

Trevor could understand why Miriam admired Dr. Irvin. He was a leader and also, he suspected, a healer. The kind of man Miriam would put her trust in. She claimed to have no romantic feelings for this particular man, but he could see the doctor certainly did for his nurse.

Dr. Irvin silently studied the taller man. The Major was very tall, taller even than himself. Dr. Irvin had not met many such men. He could see the Major was handsome with high cheekbones, symmetrical features and deep blue eyes that contrasted sharply with black hair. He would be the type of man every woman would look twice at. Did Miriam? He knew they had been working together for some time now.

Miriam brought them both back to the moment. "Wherever have you been, David? I have heard no news about your regiment."

"General Meade assigned us a bit south of here, the Maryland/ Pennsylvania border. There was a short skirmish with some Confederates and they retreated across the border. We then received orders to swing north of Chambersburg to make sure there weren't any Confederate scouts further north. After that, we were to return to Gettysburg to assist." He paused, frowning. "Unfortunately, we were too late to be of any assistance to you. So many deaths…" his words trailed off.

His gaze swung around the room. "Do you need my help here?" he offered.

Trevor spoke up. "Please join your men for now, Captain. I am sure you are thirsty and hungry. Replenish. We can handle things here for now."

Nodding, David gave Miriam one last smile before joining his other officers at the bar.

Miriam turned back to the Major. "I am sorry, Major. David's arrival distracted me from my duties. I'll return to them immediately."

Trevor glanced down at her. "Take a break and visit with David for a bit. Everyone has been fed, and most of the men have been attended to. I'll finish up here. Then we will move onto our next home."

Her smile brightened. "Thank you, Major. Please let me know when you are ready. I'll grab a cup of coffee. Can I get you anything?" she offered him, glancing up into his blue eyes.

He shook his head. "No; I'm good for now, Miriam." He turned to his tasks as she made her way over to David at the bar.

Surprised to see her back at the bar, David turned to grin at her, putting down the mug of ale he had been sipping. "Miriam! The Major gave you a break for a bit?"

She took a wooden stool next to him, removing her bonnet and tossing out her blonde locks. "He did indeed."

The bartender approached and she ordered a coffee. Since typhoid fever had broken out, the Major had ordered all water-based drinks to be made with filtered water. He had hand-made a filter in the back of the building himself. She still did not know where he came up with such acute knowledge.

Smiling at David, Miriam accepted her hot mug of coffee. "How have you been, David?" she asked quietly.

"I am in one piece, thank the Good Lord," he responded. "I lost over seventy five of my original regiment." He paused. "How about you, Miriam? I heard you were in the thick of the battlefields of Gettysburg. I am so glad to see you seem to be doing well."

"Yes. The fighting was very intense and terrifying, but I did not think about that. I only thought of my duties. There were so many dead, dying, and maimed… I was busy from dawn to late evening for three days straight." She grimaced a bit. "Needless to say, I was dead on my feet, but I persevered."

"I heard you got some help from the Major there," he gestured behind him to where the tall Union officer was tending to the wounded soldiers.

Miriam's gaze followed his gesture before glancing back at David. "Yes, he was a great help to both myself and Toby." She paused for a bit, looking down into her coffee, not meeting his eyes. "Almost as though he was protecting us."

She was silent again and he waited her out, knowing she had more to say.

She looked up again and continued. "I don't know where he came from, what regiment. He appeared on the evening after the first battle. His knowledge and skill set far surpass my own."

He arched a brow. "Oh really? Since I taught you myself, your skill set just about equals my own."

Miriam placed her coffee cup on the bar very carefully and met his eyes directly. "I don't know much about him, David. The Major is very private. I get bits and pieces of information. He claims he has a medical practice in northern Ohio, near the Great Lakes. Wilderness, as he refers to it." She shrugged. "The Union Army called and here he is. He has saved many, many lives," she ended quietly.

Dr. Irvin turned to assess the Major again. The man was bending down listening to a soldier's hoarse words. Trevor nodded, removing a quill and parchment from his rucksack and starting to write out a letter as the soldier spoke. The man clearly was compassionate, kind, and from looking around at the other well-tended wounded, skilled indeed.

He turned back to Miriam. "Yes. He seems to be very good at what he does." He paused for a moment, trying to find the words for the questions he wanted to ask her. Did she have personal feelings for the handsome Major? Was their relationship purely business-like, as his and Miriam's had been? He loved Miriam, but had never told her. The timing had never been right, and then the war intervened. They had been separated and he had despaired, knowing nurses got very close to battles and other conflicts. He was greatly relieved to see her healthy and well.

"The Major - you have been working with him - how long now? Two, three weeks?"

"Yes, about three weeks. We do have orders to join General Meade's troops in a week to pursue General Lee's troops into Maryland. The Major has informed me that Toby and I are assigned to that particular regiment."

Dr. Irvin was alarmed to hear this news. That meant she would almost immediately be flung back into danger again. Unfortunately, Meade had given Irvin orders to stay in Gettysburg and relieve the Major, essentially taking his place.

David sighed deeply. "I am unhappy to hear that news, Miriam. You will be in danger again," he said solemnly.

She placed one hand gently on his arm. "Don't worry about me, David. The Major has protected us in the past. We probably will not see any major conflicts until we get closer to Lee's troops, and that is an unknown factor."

"There are many unknown factors in a war, Miriam. Not only could you get killed in battle or friendly fire, you could catch one of the many infectious diseases that are prevalent right now. I hear Gettysburg is infested with typhoid fever."

"The cases have gone down dramatically in the past two weeks," her gaze flitted to Major Tompkins then returned to David.

David also glanced at the Major and back. "You speak of him like he is some kind of god or superhero, Miriam. We have neither the knowledge nor supplies to fight such widespread disease."

"The Major does," she answered quietly.

David threw up one hand. "That's impossible, Miriam!" he insisted.

"No, David." She met his eyes steadily. "I have seen this with my own eyes, as you will. The Major insists infected water carries the disease. He has ordered ALL water be filtered and has shown us how to build such filters." She raised her coffee cup. "This coffee is made with just such filtered water. The Major built the first one in the back. Since we have done so, the cases have dropped immensely and we are not seeing any new ones arise."

David stared at her, clearly amazed. "In the water itself, you say?"

"Yes. He calls it 'bacteria', whatever that is."

"Miriam, we only know of a very few infectious bacteria. We have never discovered any treatment for typhoid fever. *Never!*" he insisted.

"Well, now you have." Her brown eyes met his directly.

He eyed her coffee before picking it up and taking a sip, rolling it on his tongue. It did taste - *different*. Not as bitter as the coffee he was accustomed to drinking. He placed it back in front of her.

"I have been drinking so-called 'infected' coffee for some time and I have not contracted typhoid fever... nor have any of my men."

"It could just be related to this area. After such a major battle, there are many dead and wounded. Fecal matter abounds in the water supplies, which contributes to the disease. According to the Major" she added quietly.

Again, David was flabbergasted, at a loss for words.

At that moment, the Major himself approached.

"Excuse me, please," he interrupted. He glanced at his nurse. "Miriam, if you are done, we need to get back to our duties, if Dr. Irvin does not mind." His eyes moved to the doctor.

Dr. Irvin rose quickly, as did Miriam reaching for her bonnet. "Of course not, Major. I've taken up quite enough of Miriam's time." He smiled at them both, returning his gaze to Miriam. "I'll see you later," he promised.

"Yes," she murmured before silently following the Major out of the tavern. Dr. Irvin watched the two of them leave.

He turned back to the bar, seeing the bartender had finally placed some food and more ale down for him. He contemplated his very strange conversation with Miriam as he slowly ate his food.

Trevor and Miriam returned to their medical tasks. The next home hosted two badly wounded soldiers and one woman from town recovering from typhoid fever.

They went about their tasks silently as usual, the Major tending to the two soldiers as Miriam attended to the woman. The Major glanced warily at Miriam now and then, wondering what she may have discussed with Dr. Irwin. Of course, it was none of his business, and yet he had a sneaking suspicion their conversation had been about him.

Trying to dismiss his thoughts, Trevor got on with his work. He and Miriam completed their duties in the town by early evening, an hour or so after suppertime.

They returned to the Bell household for supper and coffee and, as always, to clean and refresh. The Major wondered if Miriam would be joining the good doctor for drinks. However, after she finished her dinner, she went to check on the two remaining soldiers, making sure they were bedded down and fed.

He continued to eat his meal, watching her, ruminating about the day. She never mentioned Dr. Irvin to him for the remainder of the day. As usual, their conversations had centered around their duties. She was as efficient as ever. If her mind were somewhere else, it did not show. She had always assured him that David Irvin was just a good friend who she had worked with, but somehow, he knew there was more to it than that. Gut instinct, or perhaps information gleaned from his computer chip. Maybe both. Silently he consulted the chip. *Is there anything important I need to know about Dr. David Irvin?* He waited a beat and the chip clicked on. *Yes. But you will not be given this information yet. It is not the time.* This answer did not satisfy Jeremiah, so he persisted. *Is he a danger to Miriam Klark?* After a beat, *No. He is not.*

Okay, that was the only information he was going to get for now. Unless he could get more out of his charge, which so far did not seem promising.

He sighed, finishing his dinner and standing as he headed outside to clean up.

Miriam watched the Major as he left the room, frowning a bit.

Miriam did not arrive to the tavern until well into the evening, about nine or so. David was waiting for her at the bar. There were several townspeople at the other end, yet many empty stools around David.

She took an empty seat next to her friend and smiled.

"Would you like a drink? I'm having a bit of whiskey," he gestured to his glass.

"I'll just have a cup of coffee. You can ask the barkeep to put one shot in it," she replied.

"How did your day go?" He smiled and placed the order before glancing back at her.

She had replaced her usual bonnet and apron with a fresh dress. Her hair was clean and shiny, tumbling around her shoulders. Now that she was not dirty and bloodstained, she looked as lovely as he remembered. He tried not to stare as the barkeep brought over Miriam's drink, then went to the other side to attend to other patrons.

Sighing, she straightened as she reached for her mug. "Tiring, as always. But it's not so bad now. There are less wounded to tend to and fewer sickened. Many soldiers have even been sent back to rejoin General Meade's forces."

At this, David's brow arched. "Oh, really? That many have made a full recovery?"

"Yes, David." Miriam paused. "I know you do not believe me about the Major's skills, but I spoke the truth. He can heal wounds that I could only dream of saving. Without his help, many more soldiers would be buried in that small churchyard." She slowly sipped her coffee.

David picked up his drink and took a healthy slug. Turning back to her, he replied. "Miriam, quite frankly, I find that hard to believe."

She shrugged. "Seeing is believing. Accompany us tomorrow and you will see."

"Those are my exact orders - to shadow the Major for a week to learn from him. Meade sent me here to replace Major Tompkins. As I understand it, you will be leaving with said Major."

"Yes, that is correct."

He sighed heavily. "Don't you see how much that worries me, Miriam? To have you go back into this bloody war, maybe to lose your own life. Maybe I can get Meade to change his mind and keep you here assisting me where it's safer."

She placed a gentle hand on his arm. "David, I don't want you to do that. I *must* accompany the Major. Between the two of us, we have been able to save many lives. More lives than I ever thought possible. I *want* to go with the Major," she ended.

David was silent for a moment, contemplating her words as he stared at his drink. "Are you sure that is the reason, Miriam? Could there be other reasons you may want to accompany the Major?" He did not meet her eyes as he questioned.

"David. Look at me," she demanded.

Slowly his grey eyes met dark chocolate brown.

"I want to accompany the Major to save lives, David! I am a nurse; that is what I do. That is my sole purpose. Also, Toby is assigned to the regiment. I can do my job AND make sure my brother is safe. That is something, is it not?"

"Yes, that is certainly something," he sighed. "Alright, let's talk about something else for now. Do you miss home?" he asked her.

She smiled slowly as they quietly chatted.

As ordered, the next day Dr. David Irvin reported to the Bell household to shadow both Major Tompkins and Miriam Klark. He had bunked up at rooms at *The Black Horse Tavern*, along with several of his fellow officers. The rest of his men had slept outdoors in their sleeping sacks and made the best of it.

The doctor arrived right after stuffing down a quick breakfast so he could be on time by dawn.

He knocked briefly on the wooden door in front of him, glancing around at the porch area. It was one of the nicer, bigger homes close by the tavern, so the Bell family were obviously doing well for themselves.

His knock was answered promptly by a petite, red-headed woman with freckles scattered across her smiling face. This must be Mrs. Bell.

"Hello. I'm-"

Before he could say anything further, she swung the door open wide, motioning him inside. "Hello! You must be Dr. Irvin. We've been expecting you."

She brought him further into the spacious main living quarters. There were two wounded soldiers lying in the middle of the living space, with comfortable pallets (that were very clean, he noticed) beneath them. Looking further, he could see there was a door leading off to what he assumed was the cooking area and there was a spacious loft for sleeping quarters.

At the moment, Miriam was bending down and feeding one soldier breakfast while the Major tended to the other soldier's wounds. When Dr. Irvin entered, they both looked up.

Miriam continued her chore as she smiled sweetly at him. The Major rose, gesturing him over as Mrs. Bell made her way into the cooking area.

David approached the Major and looked down at the soldier, who was quite young, he guessed maybe twenty. He had lost his left leg; gangrene should have set in and killed him weeks ago. But here he was, on the mend, and even looked like he would be ready to try crutches soon.

The Doctor looked back up at the Major, waiting for his diagnosis of this particular soldier.

As if reading his mind, Major Tompkins started speaking. "He has been here since we returned from the battlefields, close to four weeks now. In a couple of days, if his strength keeps improving, we will try to get him to use a pair of crutches." He pointed to a crude wooden pair setting in one corner of the room. David's eyes followed the gesture before returning to the Major.

"This other soldier lost his right arm. He also was in rather bad shape, but within days I expect him to make a full recovery. I plan to sign his papers releasing him from the Union Army, so that he can return home."

The Major fell silent, his gaze probing Dr. Irvin who, he noticed, was in full dress uniform, complete with hat. Big mistake. By the end of the day, his fancy dress uniform would be ruined. Should he say something to the man or let him find out on his own?

At the next moment, the Captain answered his unspoken question. He removed his jacket and hat, rolled up the sleeves of his shirt, tossing the items onto a nearby chair.

"What do you need me to do, Major?"

Trevor was impressed. For now. He would reserve full judgment until the end of the day.

"Right now, I would just like you to observe as Miriam and I tend to the wounded. We have about ten houses we are assigned to every day. I've split up the rest of the medical personnel between about thirty other homes, but the wounded and sick have gone down considerably." He paused. "Of course, as the day goes on, if you have any questions, please feel free to ask."

Dr. Irvin nodded. "Very good, sir."

The doctor folded his hands behind his back as the Major bent to finish his task, the doctor watching intently.

<hr />

As Trevor and Miriam tended to the wounded in town, Dr. Irvin helped supply various medical tools or medicines as needed. Dr. Irvin was well-versed with all items and usually had them ready before they were even requested, which helped to speed up the process of caring for soldiers in various homes.

At mid-day, Miriam and the Major went to the tavern for food and a break, and the doctor joined them.

They sat at a small table on the perimeter of the room as they quietly chatted about the morning and the wounded they had attended to. Dr. Irvin had many questions for the Major related to the various cases. They were intelligent, insightful questions, and the Major answered in detail.

Dr. Irvin was quite impressed with the Major's knowledge and skill so far. He'd noticed too how the Major was gentle and compassionate with his patients, a fine quality in a doctor. He wondered again about this particular Major's medical practice. David tried to draw him out a bit about that, but the Major's answers remained vague.

After finishing their food, they returned to their duties which again passed relatively quickly with the three of them attending to the soldiers. They finished up around five that afternoon, the sun still quite high in the sky and the day blazingly hot.

They returned to the Bell household, all three hot, dirty and tired.

<hr />

The Bell family ate dinner quickly and retired upstairs to the family quarters, leaving the living areas downstairs to the three medical personnel. They spoke quietly among themselves as they went through their evening routine.

Miriam checked both soldiers and made sure they had dinner. Satisfied to learn that Mrs. Bell had already seen to that, Miriam joined the Major and David to eat her own dinner. Tonight's fare was venison stew and it was tasty and filling, just as Mary's cooking always was.

The three ate quietly in the living area and when through, Miriam collected all dishes and washed them up quickly and efficiently. The men had assured her they would wait to clean up after she did, so she left them both to go outside to the enclosed tub area.

The Major and Doctor both cradled cups of coffee. It was strong and good. Major Tompkins rose and went to his rucksack, producing a bottle of whiskey.

He poured a generous shot into the doctor's mug and then some into his own. Grinning, he placed the bottle on the floor.

He toasted the doctor casually. "Miriam does not really prefer the shot of whiskey. However, on your first evening, I felt it could not hurt." He took a healthy sip as the doctor did the same.

David settled back in his chair, crossing his booted legs at the ankles. "Ahh... that tastes so good after such a long day." The chair was comfortable.

The Major snorted briefly. "Today was hardly a long day. Miriam and I are usually still at it at this hour, sometimes until sunset. Your presence helped the day move along much quicker. This is the earliest we have ever been done." He gestured upstairs where the Bell family were still awake and moving around their quarters. "The family is usually bedded down and sleeping when we return. Mary leaves dinner on the stove heating for us," he explained.

David was surprised by this, his eyebrows raising. He took another sip of his spiked coffee. "Well, glad I could help move things along." He paused. "Miriam has learned much from you. She was always a very good nurse, but now she has some skills that exceed my own."

"Miriam has been a great help to me. She is a fine nurse."

David sighed. "Yes, I know. She left my practice to join the war, amongst my protests, but then she has always had a mind of her own."

The Major grinned at this, sipping coffee.

"I hope to talk her into returning to help me after this bloody war ends. I am hoping she will accept."

The Major shrugged. "I don't see why not. I assume she would want to continue nursing. It is what she does."

"Well, there is the matter of her brother, Toby. They live together, in a small place in Chambersburg. They have a small farm that Toby would maintain while Miriam helped me out. It gives them income for their upkeep and the farm also helps support them." He fell silent.

Trevor Tompkins studied this doctor who knew Miriam so well. He was a talented doctor for this particular century, but his knowledge only extended as far as the medical field had advanced in the nineteenth century.

Soon Miriam joined them and both men looked up. She was clean and her freshly washed hair fell around her shoulders and down her back, the lovely blonde locks framing her pretty face.

She held a mug of coffee. The Major rose as she sat opposite David.

"I'll freshen up first, Doctor, if you don't mind. That way you can spend some time with Miriam." He grabbed his jacket and hat as he left them to go to the cooking area.

After the Major had left, there was silence for a bit as they sipped their coffee.

David spoke first. "Your Major is quite the doctor for sure," he mentioned, propping his feet up on a nearby ottoman. He was just about finished with his spiked coffee, but decided to wait until freshening up before a refill. Besides, it was the Major's whiskey, not his.

She smiled at his remark. "I told you so," she said teasingly.

"The Major told me we finished up quite early today."

"We did. Several hours earlier than normal. With your help, David, we went pretty quickly. The fact that the wounded are less in number also makes the tasks go more quickly."

He smiled at her comment.

"So, how do you think the first day went, David?" Miriam asked, curious to get his feedback on the Major.

He was silent for a moment, then he spoke. "Yesterday, I was a bit skeptical. Today," he paused, looking over at her, "I learned some medical terms even I am not familiar with, and that in and of itself is very unusual, Miriam." His grey eyes studied hers.

"Yes. I've mentioned he has a rather superior medical skill set. Now you know."

He hesitated, then replied. "Miriam, what I am trying to say, in a round-about way, is his skill set is not taught in medical universities." He sipped at his coffee, waiting for her reaction.

Miriam looked at him quizzically. "David, I know that such skill *is* unusual, but I would not say impossible."

"Yes, I would use the word 'impossible'".

"How so?" She cocked her head to the side, brows raised.

"The things I witnessed today, the way he treated the wounded and his advanced knowledge of what different medicines can do - it is just astounding. He has knowledge and skills that far surpass what is known."

"David, what are you saying exactly?"

He shrugged his shoulders. "I don't really know exactly. Just that such skill is -" he tried to find the right words - "not natural. Did he mention which medical hospital he received his medical degree from?"

"No. He just told me he had a practice in Mentor, Ohio. Northern Ohio on the Great Lakes. That is all I know about him, David."

"Not a lot. Just what he tells you."

"David, you and I have witnessed his skill firsthand. I don't care where the man got his medical license. I just know hundreds more would be dead without the Major's medical knowledge and help," she insisted, her dark eyes earnest as they met his.

David decided to let it go for now. He still had a week to observe Major Trevor Tompkins. Maybe he could find out a bit more about him from General Meade. He smiled and changed the subject. "After cleaning up, you look as lovely as ever, Miriam." He knew he was still grimy and dirty himself.

She smiled slowly. "Thank you, David."

At that moment, the Major appeared, wearing his white undershirt and Union pants, rubbing his wet black hair with a towel. "The cleaning area is all yours, Dr. Irvin."

David rose at this remark, placing his mug on a table.

"Please. Call me David, Major Tompkins."

The Major arched a brow. "You earned the title and thus deserve it." He glanced over at Miriam. "I'll have another coffee for you when you are through." He winked at the doctor, who chuckled as he left to clean up.

<hr />

Major Tompkins settled into the seat that David had vacated, seating himself across from Miriam with a second cup of coffee, leaving the whiskey out for now.

"Your Dr. Irvin is quite a talented doctor, Miriam," he remarked.

She smiled. "He said the same about you, Major."

"Oh?" He waited for her to elaborate.

She was silent a moment, deciding what to say and what to leave out. "He told me your skill set is very... unusual." She waited for his reaction.

The Major raised one brow, his demeanor calm and unruffled. "Really? How so?"

"He claims your knowledge of medicines and how to use them far surpasses his own, and he claims that should not be." She sipped at her coffee, glancing up to meet those deep blue eyes over her coffee mug.

Jeremiah consulted the chip. *Okay, the doctor has figured some things out. What is my answer?* After a beat, *You know you must not reveal you are from the future.*

Yes, I know, he answered the chip. *I need some guidance here. These two are very intelligent for this century.*

Several seconds went by, Miriam staring at him all the while. *Tell her you attended an advanced university in Europe before immigrating into the United States. That should be sufficient.* The chip clicked off.

Trevor leaned forward a bit, cradling his coffee. "Okay. To satisfy yours and the good doctor's curiosity - I attended an advanced medical university in Europe. I decided I wanted to immigrate to the United States and I eventually ended up in Ohio."

"You are European? From where? You don't have an accent," she remarked.

He snorted. "That's probably because I've been here for ten years or so. You don't have one either. Aren't your ancestors from Europe?" He gestured to her blonde hair.

"Yes, of course. My ancestors were Dutch."

"There you go," he replied, as though that settled the entire matter.

She still had a puzzled quirk to her brow, but she did not ask any further questions, to Trevor's relief.

10

Dr. David Irvin shadowed both Major Tompkins and Miriam Klark for the week. He paid careful attention to the Major's methods of treatment, as well as which tools and medicines he seemed to prefer. The man certainly had a way with medical practice. The soldiers they visited had been very severely injured when they first reached the town several weeks back, and yet most of them were well on their way to full or partial recovery. Men who - in his medical opinion- should have been past the point of saving. Cleanliness seemed to be the most important order that the Major had given his staff. The doctor took note that all bandages were freshly washed, all water was run through a small distiller device. The Major had even fashioned some kind of strip device that caught flies and all manner of bugs that could not only annoy any soldiers recovering, but keep diseases from spreading. All in all, the Major introduced improvements that Dr. Irvin found astounding.

He tried to observe as keenly as possible so that he could try to replicate the Major's methods, since he would be replacing him within days. All of the soldiers always greeted both the Major and especially Miriam with admiration and gratefulness. Their spirits seemed high. Additionally, the Major insisted each household had enough food and supplies from the Union Army supply so that everyone was well-fed. This was a difficult task, as supplies both for the Army and for the locals were running low at this stage in the war. However, the Major had coaxed more supplies out of Meade than any other officer. Just one month out, Gettysburg was well on the way to recuperating after such a horrific battle, and to Dr. Irvin that was simply an amazing feat.

The doctor also took careful note - nonchalantly, of course - of the Major and Miriam's relationship. It seemed to be strictly business, with the Major giving orders or having his needs anticipated. They worked well together, calmly and efficiently dealing with their various tasks. Dr. Irvin was now helping out, administering to the wounded and sick, being careful to follow the Major's rule of cleanliness first.

The trio worked together through the days and mid-day they would have a meal at the tavern. Although David was staying at the tavern, he usually returned to the Bell household in the evening to chat with both the Major and Miriam after they finished their duties, had dinner, and cleaned up.

The last week before the Major and Miriam's scheduled deployment thus passed uneventfully.

◆━━━━━●◆◆━━━━●◆

One evening, Major Tompkins was working particularly late with a soldier who had lost his leg. Gangrene was setting in for the second time. The Major did not need his two companions for his task, so he sent them back to the Bell household.

After dinner and freshening up, Miriam and David took coffee out to the back porch to enjoy the summer evening.

Miriam sipped her coffee silently, listening to the bugs chirping and whirring in the summer night. The heat had lessened and it was quite pleasant out. Miriam had pinned her abundant hair up, with tendrils touching her cheeks and neck, the breeze gently teasing them.

David watched her as she contemplated the sky and the dark trees. She seemed pensive. He knew that both she and the Major would be leaving to join Meade within four or five days, depending on when the Major thought he could leave all medical duties in his care. He knew he had caught on quickly, as he had noticed both Miriam and Major Tompkins approved of his work. It was a hot, filthy job, but he had expected no less. He was vastly surprised at the amount of soldiers battle-ready and sent back to Meade. Additionally, he was touched by those who were returning home to family and friends, thanks to the heroic efforts of all the medical staff in town.

"What's on your mind, Miriam?" he finally spoke.

She sighed a bit, sipping her coffee, still gazing out into the night. "Nothing. Just... tired, I guess."

"We're all tired. Something is bothering you. What is it?" he persisted.

Miriam finally met his gaze in the faint light. "It is just - returning

62

to the battles and camps - I don't know." She shrugged a bit. "In one way, it will be a relief from gaping wounds and such. In another way, I will be happy to be reunited with Toby. But... going back into war..." her words drifted off.

He understood her dilemma. She was a nurse and wanted to tend to the sick and wounded, but Gettysburg had been so tragic, and so many had died. Luckily, many had survived also. His task, which he took very seriously, would be to ensure that more survived. This was exactly what he had been worried about - her safety going back into the battles.

David moved a bit closer to Miriam and spoke quietly. "Miriam, I understand your ambivalence. Believe me, I do."

Her dark eyes met his as he continued.

"War is something no one wants a part of, or anyone sane anyway. We all have a duty to do. I have orders to follow, and so do you. Having said that," he paused for a moment before continuing, "I worry about you going back to Meade's troops. Even with the Major to help back you up and such. I know you miss Toby but - *I* will miss *you*. A great deal... and I will worry about you."

"David, there will be danger. I know that. There has been all along, and I've managed to survive. Hopefully I will live to see this war end. I pray we both do. Nothing is a given. You know that as well as I."

He sipped at his coffee before answering. "Yes, nothing is a given. Either one of us could perish." He took a deep breath, fearing her reaction to his next words but knowing they had to be said. "I want you to know something important before you leave to go to General Meade's forces."

He paused again and Miriam met his eyes; they were serious and sad.

"Miriam, I have wanted to tell you this for years, but the timing was never right." He gently placed a hand over hers. "I am in love with you. I have been since shortly after I met you. I know you do not feel the same. At least not yet, but I needed you to know. I needed you to know," he repeated quietly.

Miriam's dark eyes studied David intensely and she was silent, contemplating his words.

After a moment, she spoke. "Yes, I kind of knew deep down somewhere how you felt about me, but I pushed it away. Nursing is my passion, and Toby is my family. Funny thing, I never wanted a family of my own," she gave a brief laugh and waved one hand. "You know, children, a spouse, all of the things most women want at an early age. I always just wanted to nurture the sick and needy, so I really did not feel the need for my own family." She looked at him. "I'm probably saying this all wrong, but the only thing I can offer to you is my friendship, David. Nothing more. I hope that will suffice for now. I don't know what the future holds, with the war… Afterwards," she paused and was silent a moment, "after the war, perhaps if I survive, I will feel differently."

She looked into his rugged features, her brown eyes moist with tears. "I hope my answer has not hurt you, David. That is all I can give for now. Just my friendship."

David sighed and looked away. "That is pretty much what I expected to hear, but I wanted you to know how I feel before we are separated again by the war." He finished his coffee in a long gulp, setting the mug aside.

Leaning towards her, he gently kissed her lips. "I must go back to the tavern and get some shut-eye. We will be busy again tomorrow. Good night, Miriam."

He rose, scooping up his cap and striding out into the black velvet evening.

Miriam watched until she could no longer see his tall figure, contemplating everything he had told her. She finished her own coffee and slowly made her way into the back entrance.

◦••••••••••••••◦●◦••••••••••••••◦

Major Tompkins noticed over the next several days that Miriam and David were more subdued than before as they worked together. Before, the two had been happy to see one another and work side by side doing what they both did best - healing. Their work itself remained exemplary as always, but their demeanor had certainly changed. They now worked silently and efficiently. During mid-day breaks they were not as chatty as in the past. They tried to talk together as though everything were the same, but the mood had shifted. Dr. Irvin was more silent and Miriam did not smile as much as she normally did. Perhaps they were both sad they would be parting in several days? That was quite possible and understandable. He knew Dr. Irvin was in love with Miriam and he suspected Miriam knew it too; she was not a fool. So, that left the two of them in quite a dilemma. However, it was none of Trevor's business, so he carefully refrained from saying anything. Dr. Irvin would be an excellent replacement for him; he was glad he was leaving his soldiers and patients in competent hands.

Nancy would replace Miriam as the head nurse and she would be an excellent companion for Dr. Irvin.

These thoughts slipped through Trevor's mind as he worked alongside the doctor and Miriam. He would be able to take back about twenty soldiers when he returned to Meade's unit next Monday. Today was Friday, which left only three more days for Miriam and David to work together...

Tamping down his thoughts, he bent to re-dress a soldier's broken arm.

⸺●●⸺

That Friday evening, Major Tompkins invited both Dr. Irvin and Miriam to be his guests for dinner at *The Black Horse Tavern*. He informed Mrs. Bell they would not be needing dinner that evening, so there would be larger portions for the family.

Trevor found a table that seated four on a far wall where they could talk in privacy. He went to the bar and ordered dinner and drinks. He was assured they would be right out and served at the table.

The Major joined the doctor and Miriam, removing his braided hat as David did the same. Miriam had removed her apron and bonnet already. The three had freshened up a bit at the Bell's before heading out. Miriam's hair fell about her shoulders and she wore a clean dress, dark green in color. Both men noted how her blonde hair glinted under the iron candelabras.

Trevor sat across from David and Miriam so that the two of them could sit beside each other. Shortly, they were served mugs of ale for the men and tea for Miriam, which Trevor knew she preferred. There were venison steaks along with homegrown vegetables and a huge basket of crispy bread. They all dug into the meal before speaking, as they were all famished.

After satisfying their hunger and thirst a bit, David spoke. "So, only two more days in town for you two," he said between bites.

"Yep," the Major answered between chewing his venison, which was delicious. He never thought he would develop a fondness for deer meat. He washed it down with a bit of ale. It was a bit on the bitter side, but it did have a bite to it that he found refreshing.

Miriam was silent, chewing her food, glancing between the two men.

David turned to her, clearly expecting some type of response.

She smiled, answering after a moment. "Yes. Two more days and then you take over. Are you ready?" Her brown eyes were amused.

65

So, she wanted to talk business, David thought. Okay. "Yes. I have carefully observed everything the Major and the nursing staff have been doing. I am confident I can continue your good work," he nodded at the two of them.

Trevor chuckled as Miriam sipped at her tea.

She knew it was not the answer he expected, but she did not want to talk about personal things in front of the Major. Her gaze returned to her steak and she picked at her food pensively, not as hungry as the two men seemed to be.

The Doctor and the Major both noticed her brooding mood, and both knew the reason for it.

Trevor changed the topic to their medical cases and the three chatted as they enjoyed their dinner, keeping their conversation neutral for now.

After dinner, Miriam and the Major walked back to the Bell household as the doctor retired upstairs.

⊷━━━━━●●━━━━━⊶

The stars shone brightly in the summer sky, a full moon lighting up the short pathway to the Bell's. Miriam and Trevor walked slowly and he waited her out, knowing she had something to say to him.

She stopped by the little picket fence that enclosed the small front yard at the Bell's house. Miriam glanced up into Trevor's face, which was shaded by the brim of his hat. She could not see his blue eyes clearly, but the moon brightened the rest of his chiseled features.

"You know that I will miss my duties here, even though I will be happy to be reunited with Toby," she began.

Trevor removed his hat, running a hand through his thick black hair, meeting her gaze. "Yes... I know that, Miriam," he answered quietly.

She was silent for several moments. Again, he waited her out.

Miriam leaned against a post in the fence, crossing her arms over her chest, her bonnet and apron dangling from her hand. Her gaze moved up to the splendid summer sky before returning to the Major.

"Trevor," she rarely called him by his first name, but now it seemed appropriate, "how do you feel about going back into battle?"

He sighed, measuring his own words. Hands on his hips, he gazed down at her, thoughtful and silent, meeting her lovely brown eyes. "Miriam, I am just as conflicted as you are. Maybe more so."

"Why?"

Trevor glanced away, trying to decide how to answer. He was here to protect Miriam, so he had to go wherever she went. Fortunately, Meade had assigned them both to the same regiment. But he hated the thought of going back into more bloody battles. The horror at Gettysburg was certainly enough madness and terror, the sort he hoped to never see again, nor in the future. If there was to be a future. The Master had not guaranteed whether he would live through this assignment or not. Of course, the woman he was sent to protect could never know his true identity and thus could never really know him. Who he *really* was, what kind of a man Jeremiah Whyte was. But then... weren't Jeremiah Whyte/Trevor Tompkins one and the same man?

The chip clicked on unbidden. *Yes, they are.*

His surprise must have shown in his expression.

"What?" Miriam asked anxiously.

Trevor faced her. "It's nothing. It's just that I want to see this bloody war end. The sooner, the better. I want you safe and sound, and Toby too. Those are my priorities, Miriam. Nothing more, nothing less."

She straightened up at that, studying his eyes. "I see. "Well. I am very glad to hear that, Major. Shall we retire?"

Miriam moved toward the entrance of the small gate, opening it and approaching the porch.

Sighing, Trevor followed her.

11

The weekend passed quickly - too quickly for Dr. David Irvin. As usual, they saw to the needs of the sick and wounded during their rounds in homes. Dr. Irvin could see that taking over Major Tompkins' duties would be much easier than he had thought after such a savage battle as Gettysburg. For that, he was indeed grateful. He had to admit it, however - he was a bit jealous that the Major and Miriam would be spending time together while he was left behind here in Gettysburg. But he had orders to follow, and so did the Major and Miriam. He would have to make the most of his time with her over the weekend.

Sunday evening arrived all too soon. After having dinner and cleaning up, Major Tompkins informed Miriam and David that he needed to make sure the regiment and soldiers were prepared to move out with General Meade in the morning. He mounted his horse and was gone.

David was greatly relieved. This would give him some alone time with Miriam. He suggested a walk after they finished supper. It was a fine summer evening with a slight breeze. The sun was just starting to sink behind the trees.

They walked side by side in companionable silence, listening to the crickets and insects humming and chirping, slowly walking down the main thoroughfare of town. David could see Miriam was once again in a distant mood tonight, and he knew she was probably thinking about leaving in the morning and rejoining the Union Army.

He spoke softly. "You are very pensive this evening."

She glanced up at him briefly, then looked away. She gave a brief sigh. "Yes. Back into the battles with General Meade's forces."

He was silent for several moments, thinking about her being sent back into danger. It greatly worried him that she would be close to the fighting again, but there was nothing either of them could do about it. All he could do was hope and pray she remained safe.

"I do hope you are safe for the remainder of the war, Miriam. I am very worried about your safety. I want to see you return to Chambersburg."

She smiled a bit at his comment. "I plan to try, David. But nothing is certain in war time, as you know." She glanced up. "I want you to be safe, too."

David shrugged. "I will be here tending to wounded. I will not be at the battlefront."

"For now… That could change at any moment; you may receive orders to join a battalion. So my words stand. I am worried for your safety too, my friend."

David guided her off the main road onto a little side path that cut through some trees in the neighborhood. At a different time one would smell the sweet aroma of roses and other flowers, but during wartime, there was only the slight scent of grass and hay. There were not sufficient water supplies for anything as mundane as flowers in a war zone. One more pity the war had brought to this little town, he thought.

The coverage of the tree tops and surrounding woods gave them some privacy and they walked slowly down the little path, occasionally swatting at mosquitos and flies, both of which could carry diseases.

"I- I want you to know-" he paused, hesitating. He stopped on the path and faced her directly. "I want you to know I'll be waiting for you after the war, Miriam. I - I hope that you will want to return to my practice with me."

Her dark eyes met his. "I have every intention of returning home if I survive this war, David. I do wish to continue nursing. Hopefully, Toby will survive also." She sighed. "I am so worried about him. He will see more battle than I will…" her words drifted off.

"The Major-" Again, he hesitated. "He seems like a fine man. I think he will help look after the two of you."

Miriam's smile widened a bit. "Yes. He is a fine man. And a wonderful doctor. I am pleased he requested I return to the regiment with him."

This surprised David. He had no idea the Major had personally requested Miriam to return to the front. A foolish decision, he thought, considering she would be in constant danger.

"He asked for you personally?" David tried to get more information.

"The Major requested myself and nine other nurses return to the regiment with Meade's forces. Nurses will be needed on the front lines... just as here in Gettysburg."

"Yes, that is why I am so worried about you."

"David, all I can do is reassure you that I will be as cautious about my safety as I have always been." She shrugged a bit. "I have survived a little over a year of the war. I just hope the conflict ends soon. Now that Lee's forces have retreated, there is a stronger possibility that could happen."

"Yet you have orders to pursue General Lee."

"The General and the Major have those orders. I take orders from them. I must do what I can in this war, to help whoever I can. You know that, David." The breeze blew her honey hair around her face and she gently pushed it back as she gazed up at him.

David sighed, facing away. "I know you have orders, Miriam. We all do until this hell is over. It's just that," he looked down, rolling a stone with his boot, "I want you to come back to me safely. Just come back to me." He turned to look at her.

She placed a gentle hand on his cheek. "I will try my best, David."

David put a hand behind her neck and leaned down to draw her close, capturing her lips in a deep kiss. He had never kissed her before and she tasted sweet, like fresh honey. He kissed her gently, noticing she was not returning the kiss.

He straightened and slowly moved his hand away, clasping his hands behind his back. He could see she was very surprised as she softly touched her lips, her eyes widened.

"I'm sorry, Miriam. I should not have -"

"Don't. Don't apologize, David. After tomorrow, I do not know if we will see each other again." Her eyes teared up a bit.

David gently lifted her chin to gaze directly into her brown eyes. "Miriam, we *will* see each other again. I just know it."

"How can you be so sure?"

He shrugged. "It is just a feeling I have." He paused and gestured back down the path. "Shall we return to the Bells? I have a bit of wine we can share on this last evening together, if you would like."

She smiled sweetly. "I would love to. I have not had wine since - I cannot remember! Sounds marvelous."

David took her hand, squeezing briefly and they turned to retrace their steps back into town.

By the time they returned, they could see the Bell family was settled in their beds and sleeping. The Major had not returned yet, and the two soldiers on pallets were also sleeping.

David went to his pack and produced a bottle of dark red wine. He moved into the kitchen area and returned with two glasses. He poured out the wine and clinked his glass against hers.

"To you. May you come back safely," he toasted.

She sipped the wine slowly then sighed in bliss. "It is delicious. However did you get it?"

"Oh, the barkeep let me take a bottle at the tavern. He said it was thanks for all I have done there." He shrugged. "Just doing my duties, but I did not turn down the offer." He smiled slowly.

"Well, however you came by it, this is a very nice way to end our final evening." She paused. "I am surprised the Major is not back yet."

David shrugged as he sipped. "There is probably quite a lot to do to prepare for Meade first thing in the morning."

Miriam took several sips of wine, then answered. "Yes, you're probably right."

"About the Major–" he hesitated.

"Yes?" she prompted.

He settled back into his chair as he studied her. "How close are you two?" He decided to be blunt.

Her brows arched in surprise at this question. "I told you, David. We work together. We are friends, but I would not say we are close. The Major is very private. We usually only discuss our work." She gave a slight shrug, meeting his eyes while sipping her wine.

David glanced down into his glass, swirling the dark red liquid, contemplating her words. He had observed them for a week together, and her words seemed true. However, he had caught the Major covertly glancing at Miriam here and there when he thought he was not being watched. It did not go unobserved by David. He had caught those looks and wondered what the Major was thinking. Every now and then, when the Major was mentioned between the two of them, Miriam's face would light up slightly, and he knew she was more than just a little fond of the man. He decided to let it go. He really did not care to discuss the Major on their last night together.

He started talking to her about people they both knew back home, and he could see her relax slightly as they chatted together. He refilled their wine once more before he headed back to the tavern for the evening.

He did kiss her gently again before leaving her at the door, touching her cheek and softly caressing it. "Be safe, Miriam."

The Captain clapped his hat on and briskly moved down the steps and away from her.

Miriam's eyes misted as she watched her good friend blend into the evening shadows. She remained still for a long moment, then finally entered the house, quietly closing the door.

Geneal Meade and his regiments of men arrived in Gettysburg an hour after dawn. He met with his officers immediately at *The Black Horse Tavern* and they plotted their strategy to pursue General Lee's forces. Lee's Confederates had had a two to three week jump on Meade because the Union Army had been at the battlefield burying their dead comrades. Also Meade's forces were tired and war weary after the bloody battle in Gettysburg. While the battle had turned the tide of the war in the Union's favor, no one knew this yet, least of all Meade and President Lincoln. Now, Meade was rallying his forces, and the pursuit of Lee's Rebel troops would begin immediately.

The Army of the Potomac (as Meade's regiments were called) left Gettysburg to enter Maryland and cross the Potomac. July was waning but the hot weather continued. Meade was steadily losing men either through wounded soldiers or men whose enlistment had ended. Still, Meade was determined to push Lee's forces further into Virginia and kept his regiment on the roads. It certainly wouldn't be easy - General Meade's soldiers would have to travel over longer roads and tougher terrain than his opponent; Lee.

The Army of the Potomac crossed the Potomac River at Harper's Ferry and advanced across the east side of the Blue Ridge Mountains in pursuit of General Lee's troops.

Meade lost about a thousand men during the pursuit, but he persevered, pushing his Union blue troops further into Virginia.

⋖⟝┄┄┄┄┄┄┄●◍●┄┄┄┄┄┄┄⟞⟝

Miriam was so glad to be reunited with Toby. Even though Toby seemed physically healthy, she could see that burying the dead at Gettysburg had taken a toll on her brother. His eyes were haunted and he was much quieter. She tried to lift her brother's spirits but they both had duties to attend to; she had nursing to do and there were minor skirmishes with outlying Rebel troops that Toby and the Major had to participate in. It was nothing compared to the battle of Gettysburg, but they were still in the middle of a war zone.

The parting with David had also been bittersweet. Miriam was sad to leave him behind, but she wanted to be with Toby – and, even if she would not admit it to herself, the Major also.

Conditions on the roads were tough on everyone. The wagons were overloaded with supplies and some wounded. The camps were very crude and rough. Water was in short supply. Meade had requested more supplies for his army but they were slow in arriving, if they did at all.

The weary Army carried on towards Manassas Pass, Virginia. General Meade decided his tired men needed to camp and rest for several days. He ordered tents be erected and all wounded cared for.

The Army of the Potomac had reached their objective of crossing over into Virginia, but Lee's Army remained elusive.

<hr />

The campfire was huge, erected in the middle of the large encampment. At this point, Meade's forces had dwindled to about five thousand men. Miriam's nursing force was at about fifty nurses, and many more were needed.

Tents and crude hovels were erected to house the various men. Three tents were allotted to the nurses and the wounded. Many built tiny campfires near their tents or sleeping rucks. Others scattered about, quietly talking, mostly about home and their families.

Miriam and Major Tompkins were at the center campfire along with many others, taking comfort from the huge flames. General Meade had erected a large tent for his officers, but Major Tompkins preferred to be with the wounded and nurses and bunked there.

Tonight they were silent as they contemplated the flames, sipping muddy coffee once again. The two-week journey to reach Manassas Pass had taken its toll on everyone. Tired, dirty, and exhausted, everyone tried to forget the war for a few days until Meade would order them further into Virginia in pursuit of their Confederate foe.

Trevor glanced over at Miriam's face in the orange glow from the flames. She had removed her bonnet and apron and her glorious hair cascaded around her shoulders. He knew the past several weeks had been hard on her, as they had been for everyone. The nurses had it extra hard trying to keep the remaining troops healthy and ready to fight. There had been minor skirmishes, but Trevor knew there would be more to come. However, he was pretty sure from what he knew of history they would not be fighting another Gettysburg. He could not mention that. The subject was off limits.

He reached over and rubbed her shoulder a bit. "How are you holding up?" he asked quietly.

Miriam glanced up into his flame-lit blue eyes. Such beautiful eyes, she thought. Why am I having such thoughts *now* in the middle of a war? She smiled wanly. "I am trying my best. Toby is asleep, thank God."

"Maybe that is where you should be."

She shrugged a bit, her gaze returning to the huge fire. "I would rather be outside, enjoying the fresh air."

He could understand that. The tent containing the wounded was stifling, hot, and, as usual, smelled of blood. He had been putting his rucksack outside the tent, but Miriam had been sleeping inside.

Trevor glanced up at the sky. The silver stars shone brightly in the black night. The forest surrounding the encampment was alive with summer sounds. The chirping of insects, animals rustling in the trees, the murmur of the soldiers quietly talking in the background.

"Yes, I can understand why." He paused. "I want you to know that you have been very brave, Miriam. Both you and Toby. I am proud of you both."

She grimaced a bit at this. "We are simply doing our duties, just as everyone else is."

Trevor was silent a moment but his eyes remained steady on her profile as she gazed at the fire once again. "There are many who are brave, yet many more who just don't have the heart to be here anymore. As soon as their enlistment is up, they leave. And I can't say that I blame them."

"Did you enlist as we did, Major?"

"No. I'm here for the duration, however long that is."

She nodded, glancing away.

"How about you and Toby? I know you both enlisted. When does your enlistment expire?"

She sighed deeply. "This fall. November or so, I believe." She took a deep sip of her coffee, still watching the flames.

This autumn she would be out of this hellhole. Would that mean that his mission would be completed? He knew the war had a little under two years to go before Lee's forces surrendered. The Master had told him the chip would let him know when his task was complete. He had a feeling he was nowhere near that point yet.

Trevor eventually spoke. "So then this fall you get to go home, to Chambersburg, correct?"

She nodded her head in assent.

"Will you be rejoining Dr. Irvin's practice there?"

Her dark eyes met his. "I don't know. It depends on when David is released. As an officer, I am unsure about that. I do know he enlisted as Toby and I did." She shrugged. "Other than that, I don't know. But it will be so good to go home. Get away from war and death."

He contemplated her words. If she returned home, was he meant to follow? Again, he knew any answers would come from the chip. So far, the only instructions he had been given were to protect her during this war and make sure she survived.

"How about you, Major? You mentioned you are staying for the duration. That could be years. Are you willing to give years of your life to this war?"

Trevor glanced at the flames and thought about his answer. "I'll know when my mission is complete." He left it at that.

Another very enigmatic answer, Miriam thought. Major Trevor Tompkins was still a mystery she had yet to figure out.

Major Trevor Tompkins approached Toby Klark where he sat near his small tent, apparently cleaning and oiling some rifles. He was intent on his task, ignoring those close by as he worked diligently. He sat on a rock, a pile of rifles stacked next to him. As he finished up with one, he carefully placed it aside before picking up another.

Trevor paused, standing above the younger man. "Can I speak to you a moment, Private Klark?"

Toby glanced up to see Major Tompkins standing nearby. He rose and saluted sharply.

The Major returned the salute. "At ease, Mr. Klark. I'd like to speak with you. Take a break from your duties for a bit."

Toby looked up into the Major's eyes, although they were shadowed by his hat. "I'd like to sir, but I am pretty busy here," he gestured down at the armament.

Trevor glanced at a soldier nearby that was sitting and staring intently into his coffee tin as though it held the secrets of life. "Private Sullivan!"

The soldier looked up as his name was called. He rose slowly. "Major?" he questioned.

Major Tompkins motioned him over. Sullivan approached them, dumping his coffee.

"Take over for Private Klark here for a moment," the Major ordered.

"Sure, sir." He hesitated.

The Major arched a brow. "I assume you know how to clean and maintain weaponry?"

The Private blushed red. "Yes, yes sir!"

"Then I'll leave you to it. Come with me please, Mr. Klark,"

Trevor motioned Toby away and they walked toward a strand of trees that were deserted at the moment. Trevor wanted to talk to Toby privately.

He gestured for Toby to join him under a large oak on the grass and fished out his water satchel from his ruck. "Here. Have a cool drink. Looks like you could use it." He offered the leather pouch to Toby.

Toby met his eyes a moment then reached for the satchel, taking a long, slow sip. He wiped his mouth off with his hand, giving the satchel back to the Major who also took a sip.

"Ah...that tastes so good on a hot day," the Major remarked.

Toby was silent, glancing around, wondering why the Major had called him away from his duties. He did not speak, waiting for the Major to say his piece.

Trevor studied Toby in silence for several moments before he spoke.

"How are you doing, son?" he asked quietly.

Toby's eyes met the Major's, puzzled. "Sir?"

"Look," Trevor settled back against the tree a bit, one booted leg stretched out, the other bent as he leaned an arm on his knee. He removed his hat, tossing it to the side, running his fingers through his sweaty dark hair. "I know burying the dead after the battle had to be a helluva chore. I think you need to talk to someone about it. That someone may as well be me."

Toby met intense eyes with indifference. "Nothing to talk about, sir. We did our duties. Nothin' more, nothin' less."

The Major sighed and studied the younger man. He knew Miriam was concerned about her brother, and so was he. When he left this time period, the man in Miriam's life would be her brother. It was important to Trevor that the man survived the war not only physically, but mentally as well. He knew that right now, Toby was not dealing well with the brutality of this war. Who could blame him? He was young and had seen more death and suffering than many people would be able to stand.

"Toby, you need to level with me. You're carrying around too much grief. You need to let it out. Otherwise it will slowly kill you from the inside, make you a husk of a man."

Toby's hazel eyes were angry now. "You're my superior, Major. Not my mother, nor my sister. How I feel and what I am going through is my business."

Trevor tried another tact. "Remember when you told me about Dorothy? How much you loved her?"

Toby slowly nodded.

"That was a man who had intense *feelings*. That was a man who was *alive* even though death shadowed all of us on that damned ridge. Now, look at you," he gestured to the other man. "You barely speak to your sister, you keep to yourself, don't pal around with the friends you've made. Toby, you got a lot going for you, kid. I know you've been to hell but now it's time to come back," he said earnestly.

"Okay! Okay! You want to hear the gory details?! Well, here they are! We were burying *body parts* most of the time because the soldiers were blown to pieces! There were so many dead... so many." Toby's eyes were tearing up. "Under the pile of bodies, we even found some still *alive*. But not for long. Not for long." He paused, remembering the devastating scene. "They didn't last and had to be buried too. We ran out of space. Hell, we started burying one on top of another and I kept thinking - this is someone's husband or father, someone somewhere loves this person and he's just being buried with the rest like he's- he's-"

He could not go on, burying his face in his hands and cried.

The Major looked away, giving the kid the privacy he needed for the moment.

After a couple of minutes, Toby's sobs died away and he raised his head, meeting the Major's eyes. "I'm sorry I lost it like that, sir. I just-"

"Don't apologize, Toby. Like I said, you've been to hell and back. A lot has been asked of you, and a lot more will be asked in the future. You have to be able to handle that. Think you can do that?"

Toby swallowed and wiped at his eyes. He straightened and met the Major's gaze. "Yes. I can do that," he said solemnly.

Trevor hesitated. "Toby, this war is hell on everybody. We all deal with it in our own way. I want you to know this war *will* end someday. It might not seem like it now, but it will. You have a future ahead of you. You can have a life, meet a nice girl again, settle down, start a family. Those things are important to you, are they not?"

This time Toby snorted in disgust. "Yeah, I don't know. Who knows if I'll survive this war?"

"You must try. We all must, but you especially need to keep safe for Miriam's sake too. She needs you. And you might not want to hear it now, but I bet you will meet a girl just as special as your Dorothy was to you. You have the capacity to love, and you're an attractive guy." He paused. "There will be life after this war. Trust me."

"How can you be so sure I'll survive? That *you* will? How can you be so sure I'll meet someone to replace my Dorothy? No one can replace her."

Trevor sighed, crossing his arms. "Guess you'll just have to trust me."

Toby glanced away, silent, contemplating the Major's words. "Once you're in love and you lose it, it's very hard to regain that feeling," he said softly.

"Maybe you feel that way now, Toby, but that won't always be the case."

Toby met the Major's eyes, wondering about the man and his past. Miriam claimed the Major had almost miraculous healing knowledge. He knew the Major had been watching his back during battle. But this particular Major would not always be around. Toby needed to learn to protect himself. That was part of being a man, wasn't it? He was no longer a boy. No, he was no longer a boy.

The Major reached into his rucksack and pulled out a pair of black leather boots. "These appear to be about your size," he said as he handed the boots to Toby. "Your shoes are tattered beyond repair. It's mid-August and soon fall and winter will be upon us. You need proper foot gear."

"Where did you get these?" Toby was astonished.

A wry grin curled around Major Tompkins' lips. "An officer donated them. He had a second pair and offered them. Now they're yours, kid."

"Why would a Major give me new boots? And what do I say to the other soldiers who have tattered or no shoes? How do I explain my shiny new boots?"

The Major rose, clapping Toby on the back. "I'm sure you'll come up with some explanation. You're clever enough." Glancing down, he picked up his hat and placed it on his head. "Think about everything I've said, Toby."

The Major saluted quickly and walked away.

Toby saluted smartly and glanced down at his new footgear. Damn, he was glad he would not be walking over rough roads anymore in practically bare feet.

Maybe the Major wasn't so bad after all.

Shoving off his tattered shoes, he threw them away, putting on his new boots, standing. They fit perfectly. Amazing.

—————◦●◦—————

Miriam and Major Tompkins were sipping coffee by the fire as they usually did in the evenings after their duties were complete.

"You know, it has not gone unnoticed that Toby is sporting new boots.

Did you perhaps have something to do with that, Major?" Her dark eyes met his in the firelight.

Trevor smiled briefly, sipping his own coffee. "Yes. I managed to find a pair not being used and gave them to him."

Miriam considered this and concluded the Major was still looking after her little brother. "Thank you," she said quietly.

"No thanks required," he said. "Foot soldiers should have decent foot gear." His manner was nonchalant.

"There are many soldiers that need new foot gear. I am aware that you cannot supply them all. So, thank you again."

He met her eyes. "You're welcome."

"Did you talk with Toby?" Her glance went back to the fire as she waited for his answer.

"A bit."

She met his gaze directly. "About what?"

Trevor hesitated, wondering how much to tell her and what to leave out. "I wanted to talk to him because I believed he needed an ear. Perhaps he feels uncomfortable talking to you about the war because you have so much on your plate. I think he needed to talk to another man." He shrugged, hoping this would suffice.

Obviously, it did not. "What did he tell you exactly?" Her dark eyes probed his.

"Just some bits and pieces of what they dealt with up on the ridge, burying the dead. I think there were some things he needed to get off of his chest. Hopefully, he did."

"I see," she replied, still studying him intently.

He sipped at his coffee, meeting her gaze, silent.

She brushed back a strand of her long blonde hair. "You know Major, it seems to me that you have a certain - let us say... interest - in my brother and myself that seems... unusual," she finally concluded.

Trevor shrugged. "I'm just helping out as best I can."

"Yes, I know. You are a brilliant doctor, there is no doubt about that. But personally - on a personal note, I guess - you take an interest in us that I have not really seen you display for -" she waved one elegant hand around, "well, for anyone else."

Trevor was silent for many moments, trying to decide how to answer her. He was here to make sure she survived this conflict. If they were returning home in November, there was a good chance she would. He also knew a lot could happen between August and November.

Sighing, he turned, facing her. "Let's just say I am concerned for your safety. I want both you and Toby to be able to return home in the fall."

"Many of the enlisted men have been leaving, much to General Meade's consternation."

He sighed again. "Yes. I know. It does deplete our ranks. We pick up new recruits here and there, but not really enough." He shrugged. "We will have to fight with what we have. Thankfully, we have only seen minor skirmishes so far."

"So far," she pointed out.

He met her gaze. "You're right. We could see battle anytime Meade decides we leave this pass. We just need to do what we've done in the past. Look out for each other."

Miriam noticed that the flames in the fire made his blue eyes more intense, sapphire blue. She blushed, realizing she was staring at him and she looked quickly away.

She stood, pouring out her coffee, looking down at the man still seated.

"It's late. I'm going to get some rest. I just wanted to say thank you again." She turned to walk toward the nursing tent.

Trevor watched her go, a quirk in his brow.

T oby Klark gently parted the opening of the nursing tent, stepping inside. Glancing around he noticed about twenty wounded men crammed into the space. There were three nurses (one of whom was his sister) and Major Tompkins attending to the men.

As he entered, both his sister and the Major looked up from their tasks.

Toby smiled a bit hesitantly and approached Major Tompkins. He had been binding a soldier's arm, but he stood as Toby stopped near him.

Private Klark had his army-issued cap in his hands, his thick russet hair a bit unruly as he stood a little awkwardly.

"Major, is it okay if I talk with you for a moment?" he asked tentatively.

"Sure, Toby. What's on your mind?" the Major asked as he wiped his hands with a clean towel.

"Well, I just wanted to say thanks for the kind words yesterday. I been doin' a lot of thinkin' and everything…"

His words trailed off. Trevor waited him out. The younger man's eyes were less haunted than yesterday. He seemed more like the man Trevor knew during Gettysburg, friendly and outgoing.

"I know that - I know… well - I know I'll never forget all of the horrors of Gettysburg -" he waved his hand a bit, "but after thinking things through, I realized… you're right. I do have a life ahead of me. I plan to survive this war, come hell or high water, so I can live that life." He glanced over briefly at his sister attending a nearby soldier, then he met the Major's eyes again. He stuck out one hand and the Major clasped it firmly as they shook hands. "Thank ya again, Major. No matter what happens down the line, I know I won't forget ya." He blushed a bit.

He smiled at his sister, who returned his smile as she stood, watching the two men.

"Well, I best be letting you get back to your duties and I'll see to mine," he threw a thumb over his shoulder and then clapped his cap back on. "See ya." He waved to them both as he left the tent.

Miriam approached Major Tompkins and smiled up into his face.

"You're a good man, Major."

She left him to continue her duties and Trevor stared at her for a few moments, then returned to his tasks.

<hr>

After the third day at Manassas Pass, General Meade announced they would be packing up again to pursue General Lee's Confederate Army, penetrating further into Virginia.

Everyone tried their best to make the last day at the camp a way to renew their energy and spirits. Meade declared that all men would get extra rations at supper that evening to help prepare them for the long, grueling task ahead.

That evening many soldiers occupied the main campfire or gathered around smaller fires by their tents. Content from their extra rations, they talked quietly over their coffee or beef tacky.

Toby Klark, Miriam, and Major Tompkins all sat at the main campfire. Miriam sat between the two men. There were about thirty other soldiers scattered around the campfire. One man quietly strummed his banjo and some of the soldiers started humming along, singing songs from home. The tune was melancholy, bittersweet.

"What do you think we can expect tomorrow, Major? Do you think there are any Reb patrols nearby?" Toby asked his superior.

The Major looked down, kicking a pebble towards the fire. Then he glanced up at the fire flickering in the dark evening. "There are always Rebel patrols this far south. Whether we run into any or not is another story." He paused. "I know that doesn't exactly answer your question, but your guess is as good as mine." The Major shrugged broad shoulders.

Toby glanced back at the fire. "Sure wish this fightin' would end soon," he commented.

"It will for you in several months. Miriam here," he gestured to the woman between them, "has mentioned your enlistments are up in the fall."

"Yeah, but fall is still a long ways away," Toby pointed out.

"Yep. A lot can happen in the meantime. We just need to be prepared.

I am sure we will see some battles, but nothing that will compare to Gettysburg, if that is any consolation."

"Yeah, that's some. Don't want to be in the middle of something like *that* again." He shuddered a bit. His sister gently placed a hand on his knee.

"Toby, I believe the Major is correct. I think Gettysburg will be the biggest conflict we face, and that is behind us now."

The young man sighed. "I know it's behind us. I guess I'm just worried about what's ahead of us."

Miriam gestured at the three of them and then at the other soldiers nearby. "We all have each other. We have to see to it that we all survive, one way or another." She paused. "I know you saw many awful things, Toby, but try to look to the future. The past is past. I know it's hard, but try to leave it there."

Toby sighed. "I know you're right, sis." He leaned in and kissed her cheek, then sat back, finishing up his coffee. "Think I'm going to go join the soldiers yonder," he gestured to the soldiers gathered around the banjo player. "Could use some music and companionship this one last night here."

Miriam kissed him back. "You go. Forget the war. For now."

Toby smiled, stood, and moved over to the soldiers on the other side of the campfire, who greeted him with smiles and claps on the back. Toby settled among them and quietly began to sing along.

"He's a fine young man. You should be proud of him," Trevor remarked.

She smiled, her dark eyes meeting his as she clasped her mug. "I am proud of him," she said quietly. "I also want to add my thanks to Toby's. Thank you for speaking to him yesterday. It seems to have made a difference."

Trevor's blue eyes met hers. "I'm glad. I was hoping I could get through to him. It seems he listened to me. I wasn't sure if he was hearing me or not." He sipped at his coffee, his glance chasing to the other soldiers.

Miriam smiled slowly. "So. This may be our last quiet moment for a while. What shall we talk about?"

Trevor smiled back and settled more comfortably on the large rock he was seated on. "Whatever you prefer to talk about, Miriam."

She was silent for several moments as she studied the fire., finally glancing back at the man next to her. "Tell me more about yourself. Tell me more about your practice, about where you live. What's it like?"

Dangerous territory, Trevor. Hmmm...

"Oh... it's a lot like I described. Very rural, many forests, but the lake is huge. Goes on forever, almost looks like an ocean. It's a mighty pretty sight. Not many people there, it's not as settled as here in the east, both north and south. My practice is small." He grinned. "I don't even have a nurse."

This surprised Miriam greatly. "Really? Who assists you?"

He shrugged. "I don't really need any assistance. It's just me. I manage."

Her smile widened. "You remain very mysterious, Major. Bits and pieces. Tell me, was there ever anyone special in your life? A child, a woman? What about your parents?" She knew she was getting personal, but he always gave her such enigmatic answers.

Okay, she's getting personal. She wants more answers. Need a bit of help here.

"Well. You already know I studied medicine abroad, right?"

She nodded her head in assent.

"When I returned to the States, I wasn't sure where I would end up. My parents stayed in Europe, in France. I don't have siblings like you do," he gestured briefly to Toby. "I've pretty much been on my own since I finished my medical studies and immigrated here. As far as anyone special," he hesitated, meeting her eyes. "I never had anyone special in my life like you have in Dr. Irvin." He put up a hand as she started to speak. "I know you claim you are both just good friends. I get that. But I have never been close to anyone, really. Not a woman or a child as you mentioned. I see to my practice and that's about it." He shrugged. "I guess you could call me a loner."

"That's too bad, Major," she replied softly. "You are an excellent doctor and a good person. You have a lot to offer a," she put up her hands in quotes, "'special person.'"

He grinned at her. "You flatter me, Miriam."

"No. I am being sincere. Quite frankly, I am amazed that you are still single and unattached."

"Well, so are you," he pointed out.

She laughed a bit. "Yes, I am still the spinster I spoke of earlier."

"And *you* do not give yourself enough credit, Miriam. There are many men that would be pleased to be with you. I believe the good doctor is among them."

She looked away at this response, her gaze flicking to the fire. She answered quietly. "There has never been a man I wanted to share my life with. Not even David." Her gaze dropped to her coffee and she sipped slowly.

He leaned forward a bit, catching her eye. "And why is that, Miriam?" he asked softly.

Her dark eyes met his. "I have not met the right man yet."

Trevor had a sudden urge to lean closer and kiss her lips. He immediately squelched it. He leaned a little further back and answered her. "I think you will. Someday." He glanced away at the campfire.

Miriam continued to study him. She had received more information out of him tonight than she had for the past month and a half she had known him. So, he was a loner. That explained some things. Not *all* things, but some. He preferred to be alone and just help others. That part she could understand, but preferring to be alone with no one special in your life - that she could not fathom. If she did not have Toby in her life and special friends like David she would feel miserable. Other people who you cared for made life worth living. Being separated from the only family he had - his parents – something like that made you isolated, apart from others. Of course, as he had said, his medical practice kept him busy, but somehow Miriam suspected there was more to the man than he was willing to disclose. She knew they had several more months together. She also realized she was more attracted to Major Tompkins than any other man she had met in her life. This thought made her uneasy. After she and Toby left when their enlistments were up, she would probably never see this man again.

Trevor broke the long silence. "What are you thinking about?"

She smiled a bit. "About you, Major. You reveal and you don't reveal. But that is fine. You can keep your secrets. For now."

This startled Trevor a bit. He had to always remember that Miriam was an intelligent woman for this century, and perceptive too. Probably because she was a nurse and had more education than the average woman in this century.

He grinned at her. "We all have our secrets, Miriam. All of us."

<hr />

The next morning was a blur of activity as the regiments stocked up the last of the wagons. The officers were lucky to all have horses; the foot soldiers were not that lucky. The nurses were spared walking the rough trails as they rode in a creaky wagon with some of the wounded. Meade wanted the nurses in fairly good health so they would be able to attend to their duties, and did not want them getting weary by walking for miles.

Toby was grateful for the new boots the Major had given him. The difference between walking the trails in his new boots and his tattered, worn-out shoes was like night and day. It gave him more energy, more confidence in his ability to fight.

The long column of the Army of the Potomac left Manassas Pass to pursue General Lee's forces, heading further south into Virginia.

Meade's forces moved slowly south. For days, they did not encounter any enemy troops. The foot soldiers were tired. The wagons creaked with a rhythmic sway as they carried the nurses and wounded. All officers were mounted, including Major Tompkins. They headed the long column of the Army as the foot soldiers brought up the rear.

August was over, and early September was upon them. This helped a great deal; the cooler temperatures were a relief from the stifling heat of July and August. The trees were changing colors as summer crept into autumn.

The Union soldiers confronted a Confederate patrol at Monterey Pass led by General Gregg. The grey and blue armies clashed. Many Confederates were killed in the fight.

The fighting was fierce, but Meade's exhausted troops fought back with the tenacity that had helped them win in Gettysburg. They gave no quarter and expected none in return.

The nurses were kept quite busy as more and more wounded were sent to the tents, both grey and blue. Fortunately, they were not in the thick of the battle, as the men fought in the heavy woods. The medical personnel worked tirelessly to save those they could.

By the end of the battle at Monterey Pass, Gregg lost five thousand troops; one thousand were captured. He fled further into Virginia to escape Meade's forces.

General Meade called for a stop at the Pass to identify the enemies captured and give his troops a much-needed rest.

It was not to last long.

The next day, he gave orders to immediately move out to pursue the rebels, pushing on to Cunningham's Crossroads.

The weary Union Army was once again on the march.

◄•━━━━━━━━━◦ ● ◦━━━━━━━━━•►

Miriam clutched the side of the wagon she was riding in as it swayed and shook over the rough roads. She was seated next to several other nurses. They all looked as weary as she felt. She tucked a blonde tress inside her sweaty bonnet and then glanced behind her.

Many men in both grey and blue uniforms moaned and occasionally screamed from the pain of their wounds. In battle, sometimes there was no opportunity to attend to them until they stopped. Meade halted in the evening to give the Army a brief rest, then it was back on the road again.

She pitied those who were in such pain, and quickly looked away, knowing there was nothing she could do for them at this moment.

Susan was sitting next to her and noted Miriam's perusal of the men. As Miriam turned back, she grabbed Miriam's hand and squeezed, a quiet moment of commiseration.

Miriam smiled as she gave a gentle squeeze back, her gaze moving forward. The nurses and some of the wounded were riding directly behind the officers. Miriam's gaze easily found Major Tompkins riding a brown horse, his Union hat tucked over his dark hair. He was much taller than the other officers and rode ramrod straight, even though he had to be as weary as everyone else. The fighting at the Pass had been quick but savage.

The Major had helped her with the wounded after the battle, doing what he could to save many, but many more died.

As she continued to gaze at the Major, her thoughts drifted to their past discussions. He was always very kind to everyone... the other nurses, herself, and all of his patients - be they the enemy or not. She admired his medical skill. The man himself she still had not quite figured out. He had given her a bit more information about his background, but he remained as mysterious as ever to her. It bothered her that she was greatly attracted to the man... and, she had to admit, it was just not a physical connection she felt. He would be leaving with Meade's troops as they continued to fight, and she and Toby would be out of this war in several more months, thank the Good Lord. Would she ever see him again? So many questions... too little answers.

Sighing, she turned her gaze to the early autumn trees as they continued on the path.

⚬

The war-weary Army reached Cunningham's Crossroads and General Meade called a halt, ordering camp be set up. Union scouts had reported Rebel stragglers in the area and Meade intended to pursue them. For now, camp was ordered to be set up in a large field surrounded by some trees that allowed for some cover and protection. Meade sent his own scouts out to search for the enemy and report back to him.

Tents were erected and ruck sacks taken out. A food tent was erected, as well as several for the wounded and nurses. As usual, the officers had a tent of their own.

Food was quickly devoured. Small campfires were started with whatever wood and sticks were available. A larger campfire was erected in the center of the camp.

Miriam was so weary she decided eating could wait. She bathed and cleaned up a bit in the nurses' tent, changing into a fresh dress and brushing out her hair as best she could.

She headed to the food tent and took her meal over to the main campfire. She spotted Major Tompkins sitting alone, already eating his dinner. Miriam smiled as she sat next to him, spooning up what looked like gruel. At least it was food - the strong coffee helped.

Trevor returned her smile. They hadn't had a chance to talk in weeks and it was good to see her pretty face fresh and clean. He had yet to clean up himself and felt quite grimy next to her. He had removed his hat and ran his fingers back through his thick hair, clearing his throat.

"How you doing?" he asked her.

She shrugged, focused on her food. "All right, I guess. As well as can be expected."

Trevor was done eating and set his bowl aside, crossing his long legs at the ankles as he leaned back, sipping coffee. He eyed her profile as she ate. Her long lashes swept her high cheekbones and the firelight softly caressed her features, lighting up her hair. He was silent as he studied her.

She glanced over at him. "Finished already?"

"I got a head start on you, I guess. Looks like you freshened up a bit."

"Yes. I felt so filthy that dinner could certainly wait."

He sipped at his coffee, contemplating the flames.

"What can we expect tomorrow?" she asked quietly.

He took a moment to answer her before turning to her, catching her eye. "Meade has sent out scouts. I think they will locate the stragglers and we may see some skirmishes. Hopefully nothing like Monterey Pass."

Miriam contemplated his words as she gazed at the campfire. She worried about Toby, who would be in the thick of the fighting. She also worried about the Major, although it seemed he could handle himself well in a fight. Rumors always came back to the camps about the battles. He was known as a fierce and ruthless fighter. She was thankful to have him on their side, and very grateful that he seemed to still be looking after Toby in battle. Still, war was war, and anything could happen.

"Yes, that was very intense," she answered. "Luckily, it was over within a day. So many dead and wounded though…" her words trailed off.

"There will be many more to come I'm sure. We just do the best we can to stay alive."

"To live to fight another day," she added bitterly.

"There's that," he conceded. "But there is also the fact that one day, somehow, somewhere, the fighting will end."

She sighed as she set her empty bowl aside, picking up her mug and taking a sip of her coffee before answering. "Yes, but when will that be? Months, years, a decade? I hope all of these men are not dying for nothing."

"We are fighting to keep the Union intact, to keep the country intact."

"Really?" Miriam arched a brow. "Do you really believe that?"

"Yes. That is the purpose of this war. I think the secondary purpose is to free the slaves, so they may be free men and women. As you have noticed," he waved around the campfire at several other soldiers, "there are black soldiers fighting alongside us for that very purpose. So, is freedom not worth dying for?"

Her dark eyes met his. "I don't know anymore. I guess I don't care anymore. I've seen too much suffering to ever-" Her eyes teared up and she looked away.

He moved closer to her. "Miriam, the war *will* end. Trust me on this. And it *will* be worth it."

She met his blue eyes. "How can you be so sure?"

Trevor hesitated a moment, wondering how to address that. "Because I have to. I *have* to believe that, to keep me going, to keep me motivated, to keep me steady." He paused. "You believe in your God. I believe in my mission."

"Do you think God believes in your mission? Or not?"

He shook his dark head. "I don't know. I don't know what God can do. I only know what *I* can do."

Her eyes searched his. "And that is?"

Trevor looked away, kicking a pebble with his boot. "That is… to survive, to make sure as many as possible survive." He sipped from his mug, his gaze moving to the fire.

Miriam thought about his words and she sipped her coffee. He seemed so certain, so sure of upcoming events and things, while she felt lost and vulnerable. She constantly worried about her brother's safety in this bloody war. However, there was nothing she could do but what she was already doing, saving those she could, healing. That was something, she supposed.

"Yes. We must survive and maybe, just maybe, we can have a life after this war."

He grinned at her. "Now you're thinking positive. I know it is hard to do with all of the bloodshed and death you have witnessed, but you are helping a great deal. Keep that in mind, Miriam."

She stood. "I shall try, Major. I am exhausted. I will see you in the morning."

He stood too, glancing down at her. "Good night, Miriam."

He watched as she turned away and walked towards the nursing tent.

General Meade's scouts returned in the middle of the night and reported back that there were a couple hundred rebel troops spread out in the area. The closest encampment was ten miles south of the Crossroads.

The General met with his officers. They planned a strategy to pursue the various rebel forces. He split up several regiments to pursue different factions of the Confederates. Fortunately, Meade assigned both Toby Klark and Miriam Klark to Tompkins' division.

He gave orders that after everyone ate a filling breakfast, camp was to unfold and the various regiments would pursue the rebel stragglers.

Major Trevor Tompkins rode at the front of his assigned regiment. The other officers were split up by Meade to pursue General Gregg and the various Confederate patrols.

The Major was disappointed that his regiment only contained about three hundred infantry and roughly one hundred cavalrymen. He could have used twice or thrice that number, but you took what you could get when it came to war.

The Army of the Potomac slowly made their way south towards Falling Waters. The September weather turned wet and they slogged through muddy roads and torrents of rain. This slowed the wagons and foot soldiers but they stoically plodded on, only stopping at night for camp. Days went by and they did not see any Confederate patrols.

Major Tompkins knew it was only a matter of time. They would encounter some of Gregg's troops somewhere towards Falling Waters. He also knew the inclement weather wasn't helping the spirits of his regiment.

When the sun came out, the heat returned, turning the muddy roads dusty. Still, it was a relief from the rain, although they had put out all containers they could to fill up with the clean water as it was so scarce. Many enjoyed fresh water from their satchels, helping to stave off their thirst.

After a week of travel, Major Tompkins' forces finally spotted a cavalry from Gregg's forces. Down a hilltop, Tompkins could see an array of grey spread below him, about a thousand men in all. He was greatly outnumbered, so he would have to be cunning and break up his regiment into two flanks and attack from the outer edges. Charging up the middle would be suicide.

The Major called for a complete halt so that he could consult with several of his cavalrymen to lay out the plan.

◄——————●●——————►

Major Tompkins ordered the nurses to erect a large tent about a mile or so away from where he planned to attack. Two large regiments of men would be attacking the flanks of the Rebels at dusk.

When the Major felt it was dark enough, he ordered his forces to charge the Rebels. He led his soldiers into battle atop his horse but quickly was knocked down. He fought fiercely, clashing with the grey soldiers. Even though Tompkins was outnumbered, his forces eventually made a dent in the Confederate patrol. He prayed the other half of his regiment was making progress. It was imperative to stop the grey Army from moving further south and escaping.

Trevor always kept his eye out for Toby, whom he had ordered to fight close by him. The fighting was so fierce that he could not always see the kid as he fought to save his own life.

The bloody battle was a whirl of steel. The smell of musket and cannon smoke was strong in the air and sometimes prevented soldiers from seeing their opponents.

Both blue and grey soldiers fell, dead or dying. The survivors fought over them, slipping in the blood that covered the ground everywhere. The scene was as gruesome as Gettysburg, there were just fewer soldiers fighting.

Trevor slashed with his bayonet, ducking for cover behind a rock as he saw a Confederate mounted soldier aiming a musket at him. Trevor shot the soldier from behind the rock and the horse whinnied wildly as the soldier toppled off, trampling on the rider and those close about. The horse quickly trotted away as the carnage surrounded both men and animals.

Leaving the cover of the rock, Trevor saw Toby trying to fight another Rebel foot soldier. Before Trevor could reach Toby, the grey soldier shot Toby in the leg and the kid went down. Screaming, Trevor attacked the soldier, stabbing him in the chest and kicking him away. Looking around, he could see the Rebels were retreating. A second regiment had now joined Trevor's, and between the two they squeezed the remaining Rebel troops with a pincer movement, killing many. Some threw their weapons down and surrendered.

Most of the fighting was now over. They had been fighting for hours; Trevor estimated it was about midnight from the location of the moon.

Sheathing his sword, he quickly went to check on Toby. He was bleeding badly from his upper thigh and Trevor knew he had to put pressure on it immediately or the boy would bleed out. Taking the yellow sash from his uniform, he quickly fashioned a quick tourniquet, tying it tightly around the wound and knotting it.

Toby screamed in pain and glanced down at his left leg. All he could see was blood everywhere and Major Tompkins leaning over him. Toby screamed once more and passed out from the pain.

Both Armies withdrew into their separate camps after the fighting. All wounded were taken to the nursing tent, including Toby Klark. Tompkins' regiment had captured about two hundred Rebel soldiers and the news from other Meade regiments reported capturing a total of three hundred. The fighting would continue for many days at Falling Waters. For now, there were many wounded to care for.

※

Major Tompkins brought Toby Klark to the nursing tent, cradled on his horse. He carried the unconscious boy into the nursing tent. It was already crowded. The place was packed and quite busy as the nurses bustled about attending to wounded men.

Trevor found a clean pallet and laid Toby down gently. Thank God Miriam wasn't close by yet because right now, she would be more of a hindrance than help. He quickly waved another nurse over to him to help out. Toby's wound was very serious, and if he didn't move quickly, that leg would be lost, or the boy himself, neither of which were an option for Trevor.

A brunette nurse joined him, crouching next to him. Trevor tersely gave her instructions about the instruments and medications he would need. She quickly went off to fetch the required items as Trevor gently unwound the bloody sash. He was thankful that Toby remained unconscious - if the kid woke up and saw the condition of his leg... well, he did not want to contemplate that.

The nurse returned and Trevor quickly went to work with her assistance. The wound was bad, it was deep and had shattered the femur bone. He was capable of staunching the wound and might be able to save

Toby's life, but with the limited amount of medical instruments he had, he was doubtful he could save Toby's leg. He worked quickly, trying not to think about that, doing what he could to save the young man's life.

He quickly sewed the ragged wound shut after applying an anesthetic to keep infection and gangrene from the wound. If that happened, there was a good chance Toby could lose his leg. Trevor prayed that would not happen.

Leaning up, he glanced at the nurse. She looked back at him, her brow furrowed with worry. She too was aware of how severe the wound was.

Trevor rose to full height, wiping Toby's blood off of his hands. "Please give him some morphine for pain right away. It will help him sleep. He needs rest more than anything right now," he quietly instructed the nurse.

"Yes, sir," she replied, taking out a needle to give the required dose.

Trevor moved slightly away from Toby's pallet, glancing down at the boy as he breathed shallowly. He waited several minutes for the morphine to take effect. In several moments Toby's breathing became more even and rhythmic. He was now sleeping quietly.

Turning, he saw Miriam approaching quickly. The news must have reached her that her brother was down.

Her gaze met Trevor's as she quickly walked to the pallet, seeing Toby lying pale and sleeping in the cot. A clean sheet had been pulled up to his chest.

She swung around to confront Major Tompkins.

"What happened?" she demanded. The other nurse quietly moved away to the next cot.

Trevor took off his bloodstained uniform coat then removed his undershirt, taking a clean cloth to clean blood off of his bare chest. His lean muscles moved as he cleaned himself off as good as he could manage.

Finally Trevor's blue eyes met Miriam's.

"He was wounded in battle. Shot in the upper thigh, femur bone." He paused. "I bound the wound and put antiseptic in to prevent infection, then sewed him back up. It's a bad wound, Miriam," he warned. "I hope I was able to save his leg."

She gasped, quickly moving the sheet down. Toby only wore his underwear. She could see his left thigh was thickly bandaged. Tears appeared in her eyes. Gently she covered her brother back up. He was sleeping quietly.

Miriam turned to Trevor. She swiped at tears running down her face. "Tell me the truth, Trevor. How bad?"

She removed her bonnet, wiping blood and tears off of her face with her apron. Her dark eyes met his.

Trevor sighed. "It's bad. The femur bone was shattered. I removed some bone shards, but the bone itself is mainly intact. If he does not develop a fever, I think he will keep the leg. If infection *does* set in, well..." he shrugged, "I don't know. We'll have to wait to see."

Crying, she crouched by her brother's side, softly stroking his hand lying outside the sheet. She bowed her head.

Major Tompkins turned away. He had done all he could do for now.

The dawn sunshine shone into the tent. The nurses, three doctors, and the Major tended to the wounded. The captured Rebel soldiers were housed in a very large tent with Union soldiers guarding them. Major Tompkins gave orders that they were to attend to all wounded before pursuing the Confederate patrol. For now, they set up camp.

As usual, the few officers had a tent, another nursing tent was erected, and the foot soldiers made due as they could. The weary soldiers were glad for the respite, having been on the road for a week and then fighting another savage battle. They congregated around campfires, eating what few provisions they had, talking quietly to each other about their families, missing home.

Miriam insisted on helping Major Tompkins attend to her brother. At first he instructed her to tend to other wounded, but she stubbornly refused to obey his order and the Major allowed it because the patient was her brother.

Toby slept until well into the morning, ten or so. He woke groggily to see his sister's face above him.

"Miriam?" he said faintly.

"Yes, it's me, Toby. Here," she held out a tin cup to him. "Drink. It's cold water." She gently lifted his head so he could drink from the cup.

The water felt delicious; his throat was so parched.

She lowered his head back to the pillow. Toby glanced around blearily, blinking, trying to clear his vision.

"Where am I?" he asked his sister.

"You are in the nursing tent, Toby. You were wounded in battle," she said quietly.

He lowered his head, groaning softly.

"Are you in pain?" she quickly asked.

"Yeah, it seems to be my left-"

"Here." She quickly applied an alcohol swab to his arm and injected a needle.

"Ow! What the hell?"

"For your pain." She paused a moment. "It's your left leg, Toby. You are badly wounded." Her brown eyes teared up.

"What? How bad?" He tried to rise to look and quickly fell back to the pallet, groaning. "How bad?" he asked her again quietly.

She bit her lip before replying. "The Major brought you in. You were shot in the upper thigh. The Major attended to you himself. He did all he could to save your leg, Toby." She paused. "We have to wait and see. You need to get much rest and take in as much nourishment as you can to heal."

Toby could see tears in his big sister's eyes. It was bad, real bad. The morphine was starting to take effect; his lids were getting heavy.

"Here," she demanded, helping him up a bit, placing a bowl of oatmeal in his lap. "I want you to eat before you sleep. You *must* eat something before sleeping."

"I don't know... I'm so tired-"

"Eat." She insisted, spooning the oatmeal into his mouth, little bites at a time, giving him trickles of water also. She only managed to get him to eat half a bowl before he fell asleep. Standing, she put a hand to her back, glancing down at her brother as he slept. At least she had gotten some food into him. She placed the bowl down and turned to see the Major behind her.

"How is he doing?"

Miriam straightened, meeting his gaze. "He's in pain. I gave him a bit of morphine. I was also able to get him to eat a bit," she gestured to the bowl.

Trevor glanced over at the man sleeping in the pallet. "Okay. That is good. I want to check the bandage."

She moved away slightly as the Major took her place, removing the sheet. Toby's leg had swelled during the night... not a good sign.

He gave directions over his shoulder. "I have to unwrap the bandage and relieve the swelling. Bring over the bowl."

As the Major unwrapped the wound (thank God the kid was asleep), Miriam went to fetch the bowl. When she returned Toby's wound was visible. Even sewn up, it looked horrible. She had seen many such wounds and usually the soldier ended up losing the limb. She could not help gasping as she readied the bowl for the Major, holding it steady so he could open and drain the wound.

"Are you up for this or shall I call another nurse? I totally understand if-"

"No, Major. I can do my job," she said steadily, holding the bowl beneath the wound.

"Okay, then. Here we go."

The Major tenderly removed the incisions he had put in last evening and peeled the flesh away from the wound, exposing a deep gaping wound that immediately started to bleed. Quickly he staunched the bleeding and noticed all of the fluid surrounding the wound. Way too much fluid; it had to be drained immediately.

He drained and the fluid dripped and washed into the bowl Miriam held. After removing all fluid, he quickly applied more of the antiseptic, coating it liberally everywhere. He pulled the flaps of flesh together and quickly sewed the wound up again. Taking clean bandages, he wrapped the incision tightly and bound it heavily. Once through, he leaned back up.

He turned to Miriam, who had been watching him work. Her gaze now rested on Toby's face. He grimaced slightly in his sleep before finally settling into a quiet sleep.

"Give him another dose of morphine in five hours, please."

"Yes, Major," she said shakily.

The Major wiped his bloodstained hands off and then used water to clean them. "You all right?" he asked, glancing down at his nurse.

Placing the bowl aside, she nodded.

"I know there are other wounded to attend to, but could I please sit with him for a while? At least until I finish up my lunch?" she asked.

"You have an hour." He paused. "And Miriam, I am sorry. I promise I'll do everything in my power to heal him." His eyes met hers.

Her eyes were moist but she met his gaze directly and nodded.

Miriam and the Major checked on Toby periodically throughout the day and into the evening. The morphine shots helped him to sleep peacefully. Miriam was able to feed him some dinner and then he quickly went back to sleep.

Toby's leg did not swell up again and he slept all day and into the evening when he was not eating.

Miriam placed her cot next to Toby's pallet so that she could keep vigil throughout the night.

Trevor observed Miriam moving her cot at the end of shift. He watched her remove her bloody apron, along with her bonnet and shoes, reaching for her blanket. She laid down facing Toby, her eyes wide open. He knew she would not sleep for a while.

Shaking his head, he left for the officer's tent.

17

The first task on Major Trevor Tompkins' agenda at dawn was to check on his protégé. After quickly cleaning up and donning a fresh uniform, he grabbed food and coffee, consuming both as he made his way over to the nursing tent nearby.

He parted the sheeted entry and set his cup and bowl down, immediately going to Toby's pallet. He was sleeping. Glancing next to the boy, Trevor could see Miriam was also still asleep at this early hour. She must have been up half the night watching over her brother and was probably exhausted, emotionally and physically. Deciding to let her sleep for now, he bent down to attend to Toby. One of the nurses approached and offered assistance, but he waved her away, taking on the task himself.

Carefully he unwrapped Toby's bandage, very disappointed to see his leg had swelled to twice its size overnight. Trevor was very worried by this and removed the bindings and bandage, inspecting the wound. Not only was it swollen, it was tinged with a slight greenish tone. Not good at all; gangrene had set in, and with the limited amount of medical antiseptics in this century, he would be hard-pressed to save the leg. Still, he must try.

He heard a gasp by his side. Looking over his shoulder, he saw that Miriam had woken and was also studying the wound. She had her hands clasped to her mouth as though to hold back a scream and her brows were furrowed with worry.

"Oh, my God!" she gasped.

"Miriam, I need you to leave. I will attend to Toby myself. *Now!*" he insisted.

"I can't! I must stay to do what I can-"

He interrupted her. "I want you to find me another nurse and go clean up and eat. That is an order!" he said sternly.

Her dark eyes met his and she swallowed slowly, nodding. She quickly found a nurse and moved to the back end of the tent to clean up.

A nurse joined him and seeing the condition of the leg, she questioned the Major. "Gangrene has set in, has it not, sir?"

Trevor remembered she was a very competent nurse. He nodded and instructed what medications he wanted her to get as he went to work on the leg.

She returned shortly to assist. Trevor peeled the flesh apart. Gangrene had indeed set in, deeply infecting the wound and the flesh around it. A foul smell arose from the wound and Trevor despaired. With the medical items at his disposal it would not be enough even with his skill to save Toby's leg.

My God, what am I to do? he thought.

The chip in his head clicked on. *Use your medical knowledge to clean the wound. You will then find a medicine in your left pocket. It is a powerful antibiotic that was introduced in mid twenty-first century. It will save his leg and his life. Do NOT let the nurse see you using it.*

Trevor turned to the nurse. "Please assist me in cleaning out the wound. Then I want you to take all of the foul tissue and blood and dispose of it properly. I'll take over from there."

"Yes, sir," she answered, crouching by his side with sponges and clean cloths and a basin.

The Major quickly went to work, cleaning and draining the wound. He worked thoroughly, making sure all gangrene tissue was removed as much as possible. Finally satisfied, he turned to the nurse.

"All right. Please dispose of the basin and its contents. I'll take over."

"But sir, won't you need my help to-"

"*Now*, please, Nurse Baskin."

"Of course, sir." She rose and moved away to the back of the tent.

Trevor could see Miriam was still in the back, but also that she was glancing this way. He knew it would only be a matter of time before she returned.

Reaching into his left pocket, he found a syringe that appeared to be filled with a silvery fluid. Not hesitating, he injected the syringe and its contents into the wound directly and watched as the fluid spread throughout the wound and the surrounding tissue. Toby gasped in pain even though he still slept. He quieted and Trevor made sure the antibiotic covered the entire area completely. Satisfied that it had, he started to sew the wound back up.

He noticed a presence by his side and looked up to see Miriam watching him with a puzzled expression.

As he sewed up the wound, he addressed her. "Nurse Baskin helped me with the wound. I was able to clean out all gangrene and cleanse the wound. I am pretty sure he will keep the leg."

He finished with his task, binding the wound and bandaging the leg tightly. He rose to full height, again washing his hands thoroughly. He had already deposited the empty syringe in his pocket before she approached.

Miriam looked down at Toby resting peacefully, his leg almost down to normal size. It was impossible. When she had left Toby she had been positive her brother was going to lose his leg. She had been trying to grapple with that, and had failed miserably.

She looked up at the tall Major who was still cleaning up. He removed his coat and put a fresh jacket on. Miriam gripped her coffee mug tightly.

"Major, please explain what you did. I felt sure that Toby would lose his leg when the gangrene set in. It has happened time after time and even *you* could not save such soldiers." She waited for an explanation.

Trevor was looking down at gold buttons as he closed up his jacket. "Sometimes you get lucky, Miriam."

As he looked up, she faced him directly. "Major," she caught his eyes, "I *know* for a fact that this wound was bad enough for my brother to lose his leg. Now tell me again," she insisted, "what did you do? I think I have a right to know."

Ah hell, what was he going to tell her now? He sighed heavily and then met her eyes. "Toby is special to me, as you know. With the limited medicines available," he waved at the tray nearby covered with bloody cloths and some medicines and devices, "you know it is hard to save such cases. I made damn sure I removed ALL gangrene with Nurse Baskin's help. Together we were able to save him."

"Not good enough." She crossed her arms over her chest. "Try again. My skill set surpasses Baskins' and you know it." Her brown eyes were steady on his.

Okay, help me out here, he demanded of the chip.

Just insist that you used some superior knowledge she does not know and that no, you will not share such knowledge right now. It is part of the truth. Simply say you will not tell her anything further. You HAVE just saved her brother's life and his leg.

He bowed his head for a moment, then his sapphire eyes met hers. "Miriam, I do have superior medical knowledge, you know this." She started to interrupt, but he held up his hand to stop her. "I know you think such medical skill is not possible but for me, it is. I won't tell you how or why it is, just accept it. I have saved Toby's life, and his left leg. When he is well enough to walk again, I will be signing his papers releasing him early from the Union Army so that he can return home to Chambersburg and get the hell out of this bloody war. That is all I am prepared to tell you. Please attend to your brother. He'll be waking soon, and will need breakfast."

He turned abruptly and walked away, attending to other wounded men.

Miriam watched him leave with a curious quirk in her brow. She turned to Toby, who was still sleeping peacefully. She went to perform the task assigned to her, getting hot food for her brother.

◄ ▬▬▬▬▬●●▬▬▬▬▬ ►

Throughout the day, Miriam checked on her brother. He woke occasionally to eat, but mostly slept. He was sleeping peacefully and did not even need morphine for pain. The Major had indeed performed another miracle it seemed. Surreptitiously, Miriam watched him throughout the day as he cared for the wounded. She noticed that he tended to them in the same manner he always had; nothing was different. There was a soldier who screamed because he *did* lose a leg and the Major attended to him, unable to save the leg. He did bind it up thoroughly after draining it, but the man would have bled out and it was necessary to remove it. Trevor had cleaned and bound up the stump just as the two of them had done many times before. Sure, there were some the Major could save, but not *all*. Why was Toby the exception? Well, he would not tell her, but she should be extremely grateful to him. It was because of Major Trevor Tompkins that her brother would survive this war and be able to walk. He would be able to go home to his farm and make a living after returning from this hell-hole. She herself still had several months to serve, but she would now not have to worry about Toby's safety thanks to Trevor Tompkins.

As she helped care for the wounded and worked side by side with the Major, her mind was preoccupied all day by the miracle that he had wrought, because indeed, that was what it was. A miracle.

Finally, she took a much-needed break and took her coffee to Toby's bedside. He had been fed dinner and was sleeping quietly. She studied her brother as his chest rose and fell softly. Tenderly, she kept vigil over her little brother.

Eventually Major Tompkins joined her with his own dinner, taking a seat next to her.

"How is he doing?" he asked between bites, setting his mug on the floor. He had removed his bloodstained jacket and wore his Union shirt.

Miriam glanced sideways at the Major. "He is resting calmly. He did have dinner."

"That is good. How about you? Did you have dinner?"

"Not yet." She took a sip of her coffee.

He rose, setting his plate aside. "Well, I'm going to get you some. You need to eat too."

"Major, I can-" She closed her mouth as she saw him stride away, ignoring her words, going to the back of the tent where food and coffee were laid out.

He soon returned with a plate of food and a fresh hot cup of coffee, handing them both over to her. She placed her mug on the floor, accepting the new mug and plate. The steaming food looked delicious. She dug in as she watched the Major once again seat himself next to her.

They ate in silence, both occasionally glancing at Toby who continued to sleep. They managed to get a full underwear set on him now that his leg was back to normal size. He looked comfortable and pain-free. A very good sign, Trevor thought.

He finished up his food and picked up his coffee mug, glancing at Miriam. She was finishing up her dinner and caught his gaze. She smiled slowly.

"I don't think I have thanked you yet for saving Toby." Her brown eyes met his, and they were solemn. "Thank you, Major. I am forever in your debt," she murmured.

Trevor met her gaze, smiling back. "You're very welcome, Miriam. And," he paused for a moment, "since I have saved your brother I do have one request."

She arched a brow. She had removed her bonnet and her lovely blonde hair cascaded around her shoulders.

"From now on, I want you to call me Trevor when we're alone. If you feel uncomfortable doing so when others are around you can still use Major. Otherwise, I'd like for it to be Trevor."

Her whole face lit up with her smile. "I can certainly do that. Trevor," she answered.

He sipped at his coffee. "Good. I have a few more to check on, then I'm done for the evening. I think we will be here another two or three days until the wounded can travel. I still intend to pursue the Rebel patrols, as ordered."

A worried expression crossed her face. "And Toby?"

"Toby will be able to travel in about three days I believe. As I said, he will be released from duty. I will provide him a horse and an escort home. He needs to heal up for a month before he does any work on his farm. I will inform him of such."

Her expression lightened. "Thank you, Trevor. Again, I am very grateful for all you have done for my brother."

He tipped a finger to his forehead, mussing his dark locks, grinning down at her. "My pleasure, Miriam."

Trevor then turned away with his dishes and Miriam went back to her dinner, once again wondering about her mysterious Major.

18

Several days passed and the wounded improved with the help of the medical staff. Toby made an amazing recovery - much better in just two days. He was even able to walk with crutches with his sister's help. By the third day, he could walk unsteadily on his own, but he was very grateful to walk at all. He knew he had Major Tompkins to thank for that.

Out of the four hundred troops in the Major's regiment, fifty had died in battle or succumbed to wounds. They were all identified so their families could be notified and the dead were respectfully buried with markers. The Confederate soldiers captured were sent with Union escort to General Meade to be sent to a Union prison until hostilities ceased.

Major Tompkins supervised the medical personnel, making sure that the wounded were ready to travel. Those wounded too severely to fight anymore, including Toby, were released from duty, about twenty-five in all.

Major Tompkins wanted to leave camp on the fourth day, which would be tomorrow, to pursue the Rebel patrols.

Major Tompkins was attending to the wounded soldiers when Toby approached him, walking slowly and stiffly, but upright. Trevor turned as he noticed Toby's presence. Trevor arched a dark brow, wiping his hands off.

"Do ya got a moment, sir?" Toby inquired.

The Major nodded at a nurse nearby. "Can you take over for a bit?"

"Certainly, sir." She moved over to the pallet as Toby and the Major stepped aside.

The taller man looked down at the younger man. Toby had much more color in his face and Trevor could see that he was well on the way to being healthy. It would take him awhile to regain full strength and the Major had already warned Toby about that.

"I just wanted to tell ya how grateful I am that you saved my life and my leg." He paused uncertainly. "I just want you to know- well-" he shrugged, at a loss. "I just want you to know I'll never forget ya, Major. I have my life back because of you." His hazel eyes met dark blue.

The Major gently pressed Toby's shoulder, meeting his gaze. "You are important to me, Toby. I wanted you to keep your leg. If was iffy there for a while, but we pulled through. We both did. You did your part too."

Toby snorted. "My part? I was stupid enough to get my leg all shot up!"

"It's war, Toby. Men get wounded or killed. You know that."

"I know that very well, sir. It's just very different when it happens to you." He paused. "I know my sis has to stay for several more months. I know I am not in a position to ask a favor since I already owe you, but I'm gonna ask anyway. Can you keep an eye on my sister, protect her for the time she has remaining? It would mean a lot to me. I'll be worried about her."

"Of course, Toby. As you know, you're both special to me. I'll protect her, just as I have been doing. You don't need to worry," Trevor assured the other man.

Toby grinned at the Major. "Thank you very much, sir. And thanks for signing my papers for release. Mighty obliged." He reached out to shake the Major's hand firmly.

The two men shook hands and the Major nodded.

Toby nodded back and walked away, returning to his pallet to rest up some more. Trevor returned to his duties.

Unseen by both men, Miriam watched the two part, smiling as she continued her own duties.

◀ ━━━━━●●●━━━━━ ▶

After Toby had dinner, Miriam made him comfortable and informed him she would return after having dinner with the Major. She wanted to spend her last night in camp with her brother as much as possible.

Toby grinned, pulling up his sheet, sipping from a mug of tea.

Miriam joined Major Tompkins as he ate his dinner out at the main campfire.

Trevor looked up briefly, smiling at her as she sat next to him, continuing to eat his dinner.

"It was a good day, wasn't it? Most of the men are healthy enough to travel tomorrow," she remarked as she began to eat her own dinner.

"Yep. We'll load up early, about eight or so. Make sure all the men released have proper escorts home too." He continued to eat, sneaking glances at her lovely profile. The flames kissed her features with a soft glow. He glanced away, eating his dinner, occasionally sipping his coffee.

Miriam was also studying Trevor in between bites. He was silent as he ate and Miriam's thoughts again tried to analyze this strange man. Who was he really? Why was he here at this time with her? Was there a reason? In her heart, she felt that there was. How to articulate what she was thinking and feeling?

"Major-"

"Hmmmm?" he glanced over at her, chewing his food and swallowing. His eyes met hers in the firelight.

"I want you to tell me something Trevor, and please be honest with me. Why are you really here? I don't recall you being active until the second day of Gettysburg." Her dark eyes questioned his.

"I already told you, Miriam. I was sent to replace a Major who died in battle. I was not privy to his name or his regiment. I received my orders, and here I am."

He continued to eat dinner as she reflected on his words. Again, he was being extremely vague.

"I guess that's not what I meant. I guess what I am asking you is if-" she hesitated, trying to find the right words.

"If what?" he prompted.

She met his gaze directly, resting her plate in her lap. "If there is another reason why you are here."

Trevor was startled by her words and quickly tried to hide his surprise. He shrugged casually. "Meaning what?"

"Trevor, you are being disingenuous. Can't you answer my question?"

"Another reason that I am here? Is that the question?"

"Yes."

He was silent a moment, looking down. "I guess I'm here to help save as many lives as I can. Including yours." There, he had told her the truth at last. His blue eyes met hers steadily. "Does that answer your question?"

Miriam ruminated on his answer. He had saved hundreds of lives, including her brother's. Was he meant to save hers too? Was that why he was here? She did not know. She figured this would be the most she would get out of him for now.

"Yes, I suppose it does. So, thank you Trevor. Thank you for everything."

Trevor looked down at his meal, pushing the food around with the tin fork. "No need for thanks. I'm just doing my job and following orders."

"Oh, you are doing much more than that... and you know it. But keep your secrets for now, Trevor." She rose, taking her plate and mug. "I'm going to join Toby. I'd like to spend as much time as I can with him tonight. Good night, Trevor."

She turned to him as he answered her. "Good night, Miriam."

Miriam washed her dishes then freshened up, putting on a clean dress after washing and brushing out her hair. Her duties were done for the evening and she planned to spend some time with Toby before turning in. She needed to get a lot of rest since they would be back on the road again tomorrow.

She made her way to Toby's pallet with two mugs. She smiled as she sat next to him, handing him a cup of steaming coffee.

Toby accepted it gratefully, smiling back at his sister. He sipped from the mug and laid his head back on the pillow, settling back comfortably. "Ahhh, that tastes good," he remarked.

Miriam smiled slowly at her brother as she sipped her brew. "Yes, it certainly does after a hard day's work."

"And tomorrow you will be back on the road again with the Major, back into the war again." He looked down at his coffee. "I'm gonna worry about you, sis," he added quietly.

"Don't worry, Toby. The Major has been looking after me and has assured me he will continue to." Her dark eyes met his.

Toby sighed deeply. "That might be so, and I do trust him, but it'll be hard. I'll be holed up at the farm and won't be able to do anything except see the doc occasionally and worry about you."

"Toby, you have friends in town. They will be eager to see you and will be so glad you have survived the war. They will also help you out at the farm. You know this."

He shook his head. "Not the same without my big sis," he insisted.

Miriam smiled. "Well, you know I will be leaving in a couple months and will be returning home."

Toby set aside his coffee, crossing his arms, his hazel eyes studying her. "That's if you survive the war."

She put one hand under her chin, leaning forward a bit. She smiled. "Don't be so pessimistic, little bro."

He shrugged. "Can't help it. You are my sister, my family."

Miriam looked down and swirled her coffee a bit. "As you are mine." She glanced back up. "I am so glad the Major was able to save you, Toby. Your wound was very bad. You could have died," she said in a subdued voice.

He grinned, nudging her. "But I didn't. Thanks to the Major and to you."

"I only helped, Toby. The Major is the one who saved your life."

"I know. I told him I am indebted to him, along with my thanks." He paused, glancing at his sister's face. "He is quite a man, the Major..." he trailed off.

She sat back a bit, sipping her coffee. She answered him, keeping her expression neutral. "Yes, he certainly is." Sensing that Toby was waiting for a further comment, she eventually added, "He is quite the talented doctor."

"Yeah, and so is David Irvin," Toby said.

Miriam was startled by this remark.

"Don't ya think? David is talented too." Toby noticed the blush now on his sister's cheekbones. "So," Toby crossed his arms, "if David should survive the war, are you planning to return to his practice?"

"Probably. It helps supplement our income."

Toby waited a beat. "What about the Major?"

He startled his sister a second time. She looked up in surprise, her lips parted slightly. After a moment, she spoke. "What about him?"

"Oh come, Miriam. I'm not blind. I've seen the way you look at him. It's not the way you look at David," he said firmly, watching her closely.

Miriam's blush deepened, turning her gaze away from her brother, shocked and at a loss for words. She considered her brother's words. Was it *that* obvious that she thought Trevor was special? She turned back to her brother. "What do you mean?"

"Oh, just when you work together... sometimes I catch this look in your eyes. It's a special look that I've never seen before. You don't even look at me like that and I know how much you love me."

"What are you saying, Toby?"

"I guess I'm asking if you're in love with the Major."

Miriam's jaw dropped and she quickly closed it, her brown eyes wide and astonished. "In love with him?! No, of course not! What makes you think that? He is my supervisor and I respect him. That is all."

"Miriam, you're my sister. I *know* you. It is more than just mutual respect. And the Major-" he paused here for effect- "I've seen the same look in *his* eyes when he looks at you. Oh, he tries to hide it, and he is very good at it. Even *you* haven't noticed, but over the past several days, I have. Didn't see it so much before, always being in battle and not around you two as much." Toby fell silent, his eyes probing hers.

"Toby, I don't know where any of this is coming from," she insisted.

"Yes, you do, Miriam. You can fool yourself if you want to, but you're not fooling me," he answered as he once again picked up his coffee mug, sipping slowly.

Miriam was again at a complete loss for words. Yes, the Major was special to her. Yes, she liked and admired him greatly, but *love*? No, that word was not in her vocabulary. She wasn't in love with any man.

She sipped at her own coffee. "Think what you like, Toby," she said nonchalantly, "but I am not in love with anybody."

He grinned back at her. "Sure, sis."

"Can we please change the subject? This is our last night together."

"Sure. What would you like to talk about?"

"Let's talk about home. I know we both miss it."

Toby and Miriam began to reminisce for the rest of the evening.

As Miriam prepared for bed, she thought about her conversations with both Trevor and her brother. The conversation with Toby was especially troublesome. He thought she was in love with Trevor. She scoffed to herself.

As she lay down, she pulled the cover up and turned the idea over in her mind. She was physically attracted to the Major; he was very handsome. The other nurses thought so too. She respected his medical expertise, had learned much from him, and thus admired him, but *love*? She wasn't sure about the concept. There had never been anyone special in her life. David was just a good friend. She knew he was in love with her, but she did not feel the same. What were her feelings for Trevor?

Well, she always liked being in his presence. She felt safe, secure, protected. She frowned a bit. She had never been in love, but Toby had been. He knew the signs. Was he right? Was she falling for Trevor without realizing it?

She dismissed her thoughts. She needed rest. Tomorrow would be a busy and tiring day. It was to be the last day she would get to see Toby for months. She closed her eyes, trying to summon sleep.

19

The next morning was a bustle of activity. Supplies were packed up and stored, tents folded up and horses readied. The cavalrymen, the Major, and several of his doctors rode horses. As usual, the nurses would ride in a wagon and the foot soldiers would bring up the rear.

Major Tompkins had a horse and an escort readied for Toby Klark and several other soldiers returning home.

Toby stood near his mount to say his goodbyes. After shaking hands with several friends, he turned to his sister and Major Tompkins. He clapped his union cap on his head and smiled at them both. The Major stepped away a moment so that Toby could say goodbye to his sister privately.

Toby grinned down at his big sister, scooping her up in his arms to hug her tightly. "This isn't goodbye," he whispered, "it's so long for now."

Leaning back, Miriam gazed up into her brother's hazel eyes. He was wearing his Union uniform and was still walking a bit stiffly. The Major had chosen a very capable Corporal to escort Toby to Chambersburg and for this she was grateful.

She smiled up at him after hugging him back. "Be safe, little bro. I love you. *You* are the man in my life."

Toby's gaze flicked to the Major and back. "For now," he grinned.

"For always," she said seriously, her chocolate brown eyes tender and soft.

He leaned down and gently kissed her cheek, giving her one last hug.

"Be safe," she said quietly.

"You too, sis. Always be safe."

He turned toward the Major and Trevor approached them.

Trevor reached out a hand to shake Toby's hand firmly. "You will be safe in Corporal Grey's hands. I made sure you both have enough supplies for the entire journey home."

"Thank you, Major. Mighty obliged. As always." Toby clasped the Major's hand firmly, squeezing hard, then releasing the man's hand.

"You're welcome. Be safe on your journey home. The Rebels have been routed throughout the territory you'll be passing through, so you should be safe."

Toby nodded at the Major and smiled at his sister, blowing her a kiss. He mounted his horse and looked down at them both, smiling. "Farewell. Take good care of my sister, Major Tompkins. And that's an order!" Toby joked.

Trevor cracked a smile as he saluted. Toby kicked his horse into action, turning north as Corporal Grey did the same. A cloud of dust was kicked up in the warm October day as the two men rode off in the hazy morning.

"Go with God," Miriam whispered, wiping tears from her eyes.

Trevor turned away to supervise departure, giving Miriam a quiet moment.

⊱───────●●───────⊰

The Army of the Potomac headed further south into Virginia. Since they were well into October the foliage was changing into many hues and the scenery was breathtaking. The first week was uneventful. They rode through roads that were little more than footpaths at some points, which slowed the Army down. The soldiers marched stoically. The autumn weather was milder than the previous months and it was more pleasant to march. Evenings were spent in camp, only to be back on the road the next morning. Everyone was healthy and well, there were no wounded and the nurses enjoyed the respite. For now. There was no telling when they would meet up with a stray Rebel patrol - this far south, it was bound to happen sooner or later. Everyone was hoping for the latter. This early in the march, they still had enough provisions for everyone to eat and drink without paring down portions. Spirits were high and the men tended to sing as they marched.

As the month waned, it started to get cooler, especially in the evenings. A campfire was built each evening and the soldiers huddled around it with their rucks and quilts, trying to stay warm. Camp broke each morning, and with every passing day the Army headed further into enemy territory.

⊲ ⊶───────•●•───────⊷ ⊳

The Army finally found a Rebel patrol about two weeks out. The Rebels were outnumbered two to one, so the fighting was brief and only the soldiers in grey were wounded. They were quickly taken into custody. After their wounds were treated, they were sent with a Union escort to join Meade's forces for incarceration. The Army of the Potomac pushed on as the weather continued to get colder.

⊲ ⊶───────•●•───────⊷ ⊳

November arrived, snow flurries flying here and there. The roads turned muddier and it was harder for the wagons to move the provisions and nurses. The soldiers often had to push the wagons out of the muddy roadways. This slowed progress and also tired the soldiers. Major Tompkins called for a halt and for an encampment to be set up for several days to give his weary men a much-needed break.

Everyone broke out of formation to build several large tents for officers and nurses, a food tent, and smaller tents for the soldiers themselves. Meals were provided in the food tent. The weary soldiers grabbed some grub, some gathering at the main fire and others splitting off to build their own small fires. It was very chilly and once again the ruck sacks and quilts came out as everyone huddled to eat and rest, quietly talking.

After seeing everything was organized in the encampment, Major Tompkins took his plate of food and joined Miriam at the main fire. He was wearing his heavier Union uniform but the air still felt frigid; the fire would help. He spotted Miriam towards the middle of the group with a quilt firmly wrapped around her as she gazed into the fire and ate.

Trevor sat next to her and she glanced up briefly. Recognizing the Major, she smiled as she pulled her quilt a bit closer. She still wore her bonnet, probably for warmth.

"Chilly night, isn't it?" he said. They had had only moments to snatch conversations here and there on the road. This was their first opportunity in some time to really speak to each other.

"Yes. Yes, it is," she answered him as her gaze went back to her food.

They both ate in silence for several moments. Trevor spoke again.

"Do you miss Toby?" he asked quietly.

Miriam sighed, turning to meet his eyes. "Yes, I do. A great deal. But I knew I would." She glanced back down at her food, pushing it around on the plate.

Trevor ate a few more bites, silently studying her, wondering what to say. He never had siblings so he really did not know what she was going through, how much it must hurt to be in a war and away from your only family.

"It must be tough, being so far away from him in the middle of this," he waved his arm to encompass the camp.

His blue eyes met hers in the flames. He could see her brown eyes were a bit moist and he glanced away, waiting for her answer.

She sighed again, putting her plate on the ground and pulling the quilt tighter around her body. Gazing into the flames, she answered him. "It is hard. Harder than I thought it would be, but I have a job to do and I'm staying to finish it. Toby knows me and he realizes this. I miss him; I'm sure he misses me."

Trevor studied her profile, wondering what words of comfort he could offer and coming up short. "I'm sorry," he tried.

She turned to him. "For what?"

He shrugged. "I don't know what to say to you. I don't have a sibling. I guess I can't find the words to..." his voice drifted off.

Miriam smiled at him slowly. "Those words work just fine. Thank you, Trevor."

He looked back down as he continued to eat. "I know you were not only a sister to Toby, but you also raised him. I know how close you two are. I've never been close to anyone like that in my life."

"Not even your parents?"

Oh yeah. His parents in Europe. How was he supposed to answer a question about people that did not exist? The chip clicked on. *Just be honest with her.*

"I was never that close with my parents. I was always separated from them."

"How so?"

"Well," he said, placing his own plate down, glancing up at the fire, "I was always away from them. First at boarding school, then I was at medical school in France, then I immigrated. I don't really have contact with them. Mail service just doesn't cut it." He hoped this explanation was sufficient.

Her brown eyes turned sad. "That is- lonely, I guess. There was never *anyone* special in your life?"

"Nope. Just my studies and then my medical practice. Of course, I am friends with some of my patients, but they are just that- my patients."

She arched a brow. "No woman?"

Trevor sighed. "There were women here and there. Nobody special, nobody I wanted to spend my life with. Ya know," he shrugged, "physical partners."

"You mean as in sex?" She decided to be blunt.

Trevor was a bit startled and it showed, then he nodded slowly. "Yeah, you could say that." His eyes met hers, but she looked away, blushing a bit.

She was quiet and Trevor decided to let the silence hang. He drank coffee as he gazed into the flames, wondering what she was thinking.

Finally she turned to him. "Well, it is cold and getting late. I think I'll head to my cot and get some rest, Trevor. I am exhausted."

As she rose to go, he rose also. "Have a good night, Miriam."

She smiled. "Sweet dreams, Major."

She turned to leave him and he watched her until she disappeared into the nursing tent.

20

The second day of encampment Major Tompkins had the soldiers ensure all weapons were cleaned and all ammunition accounted for. The nurses and doctors inventoried medical supplies and their locations so they would be readily available when needed.

A large campfire was again built at the end of the day. It had been slightly warmer than yesterday and the evening wasn't quite as cold.

As he had the previous evening, Trevor joined Miriam at the campfire as they ate supper. He could see she was more relaxed than yesterday, having had an opportunity to get more sleep. He figured they would stay another day, then he planned to pursue Lee.

He smiled at her as he sat next to her and she smiled back at him. She was done with her dinner, sipping coffee. Tonight she wore a heavy dark green dress with a dark cloak thrown over her shoulders as she clasped her mug. Her long blonde tresses swept over her chest and back, the firelight picking out honey glints in it.

"Good evening," Trevor greeted as he dug into his food.

"Hello, Trevor," she smiled.

"Done with dinner already?"

"Yes. I guess I got an earlier start," she chuckled.

He ate his dinner, then glanced up. "Didn't you mention your enlistment is up in November?"

Miriam smiled, slowly sipping coffee. "Yes. But it is not for several weeks. November 20th or so, I think."

"Hmm… about ten days away," he mused, "then you'll be able to return home to Toby."

"Yes," she murmured.

"That should make you happy. I believe David Irvin's enlistment is up at the same time."

This startled Miriam. She did not know when David's enlistment was up. Obviously the Major did. "How did you know that?"

He shrugged. "I get dispatches from Meade here and there. It was mentioned in one of them. There will be a new doctor sent to Gettysburg to relieve him." He continued to eat as she mulled over this information.

"What about you, Trevor? You said you're in for the duration. That could be years," she said quietly.

He was silent for a few moments, pushing his food around. He met her eyes. "I'll be in it until my mission is complete. Then I'll be out."

Miriam thought this was a rather strange explanation. "When your mission is complete? Don't you mean when the war ends?" She arched a brow, studying his features.

Trevor set aside his food and grabbed his coffee mug. "I'll know when my mission is complete. I don't think the war will take forever. A few more years, maybe." He shrugged, sipping coffee, staring at the fire.

Miriam's brows were still quirked as she looked at him, puzzled. "Still the mysterious answers, Trevor." Her dark eyes met his.

Trevor sighed. "When your enlistment is up, it will be time to say goodbye." *Will my mission then be completed?* He asked the chip in his head. *No, you will be informed when your mission is completed. You are nowhere near that moment yet.* This answer startled Trevor. He assumed once Miriam was safe and out of the war, his task would be done.

Miriam noticed his surprised expression, although he quickly tried to hide it. "What?"

Trevor stretched out his long legs closer to the fire, leaning against the rock as he sipped his brew. "Nothing. I just had a thought that startled me a bit."

"Care to share?" she asked as she studied the fire.

Trevor's blue eyes moved to her face. "It's just that— I've been fighting the war since its inception and at some point it will end. I don't know when or where," he lied through his teeth, "but it will end. At some point. Then life as we know it will go on."

"Once my enlistment is up, I will never see you again, will I, Trevor?" she murmured.

He grinned widely. "Never say never. You can't always predict the future." Well, I can but that is a secret I must keep from her. So many things I cannot tell her and I need her trust.

"Miriam, do you trust me?" he asked suddenly.

"Of course, Trevor. You have saved Toby's life and mine. Along with many fighting men and women. You have my complete trust," she looked at him as the fire crackled and popped in front of them.

He glanced down at his coffee. "That is important to me, that you trust me. I want you to know that I will always keep you safe," he said quietly.

She reached out and gently touched his shoulder briefly. "I know that, Trevor."

Trevor was silent, just gazing down.

Miriam waited a couple of beats, then she spoke, raising her eyes to gaze deeply into his. "I know there is something that you're not telling me...I'm astute enough to know that. You will tell me when you are ready. I know-" she hesitated a moment, "I know you have not told me the entire story of your past, but that is your business and not mine. I only care about the here and now, Trevor."

His eyes met hers. Again he was surprised at how wise she was. Fortunately she could not view the future as he could. He had no idea what Miriam's particular future held. He was not privy to that. All he knew was that he must protect her at all costs. Wherever she went, he was meant to follow. Was he meant to follow her back to Chambersburg? So many questions and no answers yet from the chip.

"I guess we all have our secrets, Miriam," he replied.

She leaned back, smiling. "I don't have any secrets, Trevor. I'm an open book." She sipped at her coffee as she studied him. "Ask me anything you want."

"Okay. Have you ever been in love?"

Miriam was startled but she answered him. "No. Not with any particular man. I love Toby, but there has never been a special man in my life. Not yet, anyways." She shrugged.

"What about David Irvin?" he questioned.

She met his eyes. "I have told you in the past, Trevor. We are only good friends. Occasionally he is my supervisor when I work for him."

"I saw the way he looks at you, Miriam. For him, it is much more. I believe he has very deep feelings for you."

At this remark, Miriam looked down. She sighed a bit, glancing up at the fire. "Yes, I know. He has even confessed that to me." She was silent a moment and he waited. "But I was honest and told him all I could offer was my friendship and my nursing skills for his practice. Nothing more." She paused. "It was hard to tell him that because I know how much he cares about me, but I had to be honest with him… maybe some other woman can make him happy."

"I doubt that, Miriam, when he is in love with you," he said quietly.

She met his gaze. "Why did you ask about David?"

Trevor shrugged a bit, straightening up, crossing his arms over his chest. "I wondered how you felt. Know it's none of my business, but you said to ask you anything." He grinned.

Miriam looked away, sipping at her coffee. "I still can't quite believe there has never been a special woman in your life. You have—" she waved her hand briefly- "so much to offer…" her words trailed off.

Smiling, he replied, "What do you mean by that?"

"Trevor, it is quite obvious. You are a very handsome man, a very dedicated and compassionate doctor and a protector. You would make some woman a fine husband," she blushed a bit, glancing away from him.

Trevor ruminated on her words for a few moments. The silence strung out.

"I'm not ready to settle down yet, I guess. Like you, I haven't met the right woman."

Miriam glanced quickly back to study his face. He met her gaze, smiling slowly.

After a moment, she glanced away. "Then we are both destined to either be alone or with someone else." She shrugged, "I don't know," she murmured.

"Well, you'll have your chance at a normal life in about ten days or so, I guess. I will get your dispatch notice from Meade when it arrives."

At this comment, Miriam felt somewhat depressed. She didn't know why. Was it because she would not see Trevor every day, probably not ever again? She did not know. She would be going home to Toby and friends. She would be safe, out of the fighting while the Major soldiered on.

Miriam rose, taking her plate and mug with her. "I've enjoyed our conversation tonight, Trevor. Now I think I'll get another cup of coffee and retire for the night. Good night."

"Good night, Miriam," he replied.

She turned to go and he watched her figure merge with the dark shadows. He knew his last comment had upset her a bit. He had no idea why. Wouldn't she be happy to go home again? Puzzled, he continued to drink his coffee, staring into the flames of the fire.

T he third day at camp went much the same as the past few days. Everyone tried their best to refresh themselves because they would be back on the road tomorrow, penetrating further south in the state.

The weather had again turned very cold and campfires were lit throughout the camp. Many stayed by the fires and enjoyed hot coffee to warm up. Others stayed inside their tents for the warmth and relative comfort.

The last evening everyone retired early to get lots of rest for the long march ahead. As the evening descended, the first swirls of snowflakes started to fall.

The next morning, amid light snow, everyone packed up supplies and tents were stored away. The Major made sure everyone had a filling breakfast and that the horses were well-fed and watered.

After everything was organized, the officers mounted their horses and led the way out of the camp, out ahead of the cavalry, nurses in the wagons, and foot soldiers marching in a column.

As they marched through the day, the snowfall grew heavier and heavier. It got to the point that it was hard to see more than a few feet in front of the rough road, slowing the Army down quite a bit.

They forged on; they had had their three days of rest and now it was time to pursue the enemy, snow or no snow. The wind picked up and the men had to use their chin straps so they would not lose their headgear. Putting their heads down and trying to protect their eyes, they marched on steadily, hoping for the storm to die down. It did not. It continued to get worse.

◆——————◦●◦——————◆

The Army had to stop several times to push the wagons out of the snow that was building up. Major Tompkins surmised they had about a foot already and it was only mid-day.

During one of the halts, one of his scouts approached him. The man was mounted for the rough conditions and he dismounted to speak with the Major.

Tompkins turned to the man as he reported.

The scout saluted and the Major returned it sharply. "Sir, I have discovered a Union soldier, badly hurt, in need of medical assistance. About two miles away to the west." The man's breath came out raggedly in the cold as snow continued to swirl.

The Major looked off to the west and could see the snow clouds were even blacker and denser than their current area, and it was bad here. The Major knew that the Army needed to keep on the move to get to Lee.

He glanced down at his scout. "Please report to Captain Harris and tell him to keep the Army on the move, only stopping in the evenings. I will take a nurse with medical supplies and food to the wounded man. Give me a detailed description on a note so I can find him."

"Yes, sir." The scout quickly jotted down a rough map of the soldier's whereabouts, handing it over to the Major who studied it intently.

"Very good. Give the Captain my orders. I'll be taking my horse and Nurse Klark with me to help this soldier." He glanced up at the man.

The scout saluted again. "Yes, Major. Right away, sir." The man went in search of Captain Harris to give him orders.

Major Tompkins went to the nursing wagon, gesturing to Miriam to come outside. The Major reached up and pulled her down beside him. "Make sure you have a very warm cloak and hat. I need you to gather up a case of all necessary medical supplies. I will gather up food and rations. I have a report of a wounded Union soldier a few miles west. You and I will take my horse and assist him. I have a rough map but it will be hard in this weather to locate him, but we must try. Captain Harris has orders to keep the Army on the march. After we rescue this soldier, we will rejoin them." The Major glanced down at his nurse and her dark eyes met his.

126

"Yes, Major. I can be ready in about twenty minutes," she replied, reaching for her heavier coat in the wagon.

"Good. I'll get supplies and meet you here with my horse when we are ready to head out. I must also speak with Captain Harris."

"Very good, sir," she replied, turning to her tasks.

The Major left her to gather supplies and give orders to the Captain, who would be in charge in his absence.

Major Tompkins and Miriam Klark set out on the Major's horse with a small wagon attached loaded with supplies. The storm continued to swirl all around them and Miriam leaned close to Trevor for body heat. The snow storm was worsening and they could barely see in front of them. They had left the Army behind two hours ago and were heading into late afternoon. Soon, it would be sundown.

The Major despaired. If they could not find the soldier before sundown, the man would not last the evening and it was his job to save Union lives. He pushed his horse on, braving the blowing snow, squinting, trying to stay in the middle of the lane. There was no roadway, they just plodded on in the middle of the forest, heading due west. The sunlight was weak and the gray storm clouds worsened the visual conditions, as well as the blowing snow. Ignoring the weather, he pushed his horse as hard as he could.

Within an hour, he finally spotted faint drag marks in the snow heading into the woods on his left. He turned his horse towards the shallow marks and followed the markings, squinting his eyes, trying to keep the drag marks in sight.

They spotted a flash of color among the trees, navy blue - a Union uniform. The Major kicked his horse and directed it in the woods toward the color and arriving in a small clearing, they found a Union soldier face down in the snow.

Right away the Major could see why the scout had not returned with him. If he tried to move the man, he probably would have bled out. He was badly wounded, lying in a pool of blood that was congealing around him in the snow.

Tompkins quickly dismounted, taking the medical kit from Miriam as she also dismounted, following him.

The Major turned the soldier over gently but it was too late. The man had bled out from his chest wound and he gazed sightlessly into the winter sky. The snow covered him and he was very stiff. Rigor mortis had already begun to set in.

The Major rose slowly, taking off his hat, bowing his head as Miriam did the same. He turned to her.

"There is nothing we can do for him except bury him here. I'll try to find his tags so he can be identified. I do have a shovel in the wagon. I will get it. Can you find some thick tarps for me?"

"Yes, of course, Major. I believe there are some tucked away with our tents." She moved to the wagon as the Major readied the corpse.

⊷━━━━━●━━━━━⊶

It took the Major a couple hours of digging in the snowy landscape. He finally was able to inter the soldier in the ground after wrapping tarps around the body. Miriam had his tags and the soldier's family would be told where the burial marker was located.

Trevor erected a crude cross at the site and hastily moved his horse and the wagon further into the woods so he and Miriam could erect tents and find shelter for the evening. Hopefully, the storm would end in the morning and they could rejoin the Army.

⊷━━━━━●━━━━━⊶

Within a half hour, Trevor had a tent erected and lanterns lit inside. They both huddled together in thick cloaks and blankets after eating and drinking hot coffee over a crude tin burner.

They both used rucksacks to sleep and slept close together for warmth. Trevor doused the lanterns and they lay close to each other as they drifted off to sleep.

The wind continued to howl throughout the evening, but the sturdy tent kept them warm and dry.

⊷━━━━━●━━━━━⊶

At dawn, when the dim daylight woke Trevor, he glanced over to Miriam who was still sleeping soundly. Her long eyelashes swept her cheeks; her long tresses were mussed in sleep.

128

Trevor pulled his heavy cloak over his uniform and went outside to check the weather conditions. It was heavily snowing but not as badly as yesterday. If they left now, they could possibly catch up with the Army today, but they would need to move out quickly.

He entered the tent and gently shook Miriam's shoulder until her eyes blinked open.

"Miriam, we need to eat some breakfast and move out. It is still snowing but not quite as bad. If we leave early, we can quite possibly hook back up with the division."

She sat up, pushing her rucksack and the covers away. "Can you give me a moment to dress, and, you know-" she waved her hand toward the toilet can.

"Of course, I'll be outside collecting some wood and sticks. We may need them if we have to set up camp again. Hopefully, we won't."

He left the tent and Miriam sighed. Quickly she dressed and groomed. Eventually, she parted the tent entrance and met Trevor outside bundled up in her heavy cloak with her scarf and hat, her hair stuffed inside the warm knit hat.

"We should eat quickly, Trevor. Then we can move out."

He moved toward her. "We'll do just that."

They both entered the tent and broke out food rations. Soon after, they broke camp and mounted Trevor's horse in the snowfall. Trevor had already put a feedbag on his mount's nose so they were all ready for travel. Squinting into the snow and wind, Trevor kicked his horse into motion.

22

As they continued to travel east toward the Army, the storm intensified. Trevor squinted into blizzard-like conditions, trying to find some semblance of a path between the trees. The trees were sheltering them from the worst of the storm but after two hours of travel, he was starting to get really worried. They would not be able to travel much further in these conditions; they would not make it to nightfall. He needed to find shelter for them both, as well as the horse.

He guided his horse further into the woods, off the beaten path. Maybe he could find an abandoned barn or something to take shelter in for a while, at least until this storm blew over.

He turned to Miriam and had to shout a bit so she could hear him over the howling winds. "We need to find some shelter. The storm is worse than I anticipated. I'm looking in the woods for something," he informed her.

Her head was down to avoid the spitting snow but she nodded and he continued to press the horse through the thick woods.

Trevor knew he had keen eyesight but it was hard even for him to make anything out in the blowing snow. After traveling another hour, he was really concerned. He knew Miriam could not be out in this weather much longer, nor could the horse. He squinted hard and in the corner of his eye he spotted something that looked like a structure further back in the woods. He gazed hard through the wind and thought he saw a brown dwelling of some sort.

He kicked his horse and turned him in the direction of the dwelling and as they drew closer, he was greatly relieved. It was a log structure that looked like perhaps a hunting lodge. It was not large but he could see there was a fireplace and someone had split wood and placed it nearby. There was also a small shed that he could house the horse in.

The horse trotted up to the log house and Trevor dismounted, reaching up to help Miriam down. She huddled close to him as they both looked up at the house. There were a few stairs, a small porch, and a sturdy wooden door.

"Okay. You take our rations and belongings from the wagon. I'm going to take care of the horse, then I'll be right in to build a fire," he informed her over the wind.

Nodding, she moved to the wagon, took several bags, and headed to the porch as Trevor unfastened the horse and led him into shelter.

Miriam tried the heavy door and to her relief the thing swung open with a loud creak. She entered and closed the door behind her tightly, keeping out the wind and snow.

She placed the bags down near the door and took several steps, inspecting the place. It was deserted; no one was here. Looking around, she could see a fairly large fireplace to the right with various stones surrounding it. The chimney was built of the same material. There was a comfortable couch placed in front of it and a large rug. Stepping further inside, Miriam glanced to the left and saw a table with two chairs, a small crude kitchen with a stove, and a large tub. There were shelves that held some cans and she quickly went to the wall to inspect them.

There were several cans of beef tacky and beans, some vegetables and stew and they looked carefully cared for. No dust, hardly any dirt. Looking further she could see some simple kitchen instruments also. To the far left, in the center of the wall was a window with heavy drapes to keep out the sun or in this case, weather. They were lucky to find such a place; it must be a hunting lodge for someone. There was a crude staircase and she carefully climbed it to find a bed that could accommodate maybe two people with colorful quilts piled on it. There was a table next to it with an oil lantern set on it. A small chest was nearby to hold clothing or supplies. There was a tiny window here, but there was nothing covering it.

Descending the stairs, she could hear Trevor entering. A swirl of snow followed him in as he closed the door against the elements. He rubbed his gloved hands together, blowing on them, trying to warm up a bit. The horse was fed and he had found a blanket large enough to place over his mount; there was some hay to keep the horse warm and would be a source of food for him. He had carried the rest of their supplies in and placed them by the others Miriam had brought inside.

Glancing around, he nodded and went directly to the fireplace. They needed heat and light immediately but he was so relieved they had found shelter. The blizzard had not let up and he suspected when evening came it could become worse.

There were about three dozen split logs sitting next to the fireplace and he was quick to throw some into the pit, setting them alight. They caught after a few minutes and he piled on more logs as Miriam came to join him.

He stood, looking down at her. She still had snow and ice on her clothes and hat, as he probably did himself. She went to the flames, stretching her gloved hands towards the fire.

Trevor glanced around the little house and noticed the stairs. "Did you check upstairs?"

"Yes, I did. There is a bed, a small table with a lantern, and a chest. A tiny window. It is not covered as the larger one is," she gestured to the center window.

Trevor continued to study the log house, noting the provisions and the kitchen. The food here would supplement the rations they already had. They would be able to stay here until the storm blew over. They were lucky to find this place. He had an eerie feeling, almost like it were fated.

Brushing the snow off of his uniform, he glanced at Miriam.

"I'll pack our stuff away and get organized a bit. The horse is all set for the rest of the day and evening. I'll keep the fire going and light some lanterns. I'll also put a heavy blanket on the window upstairs. Could you please fix us something to eat?"

"Of course, Trevor. Right away." She turned to move away from the fire and he approached her, gently stopping her by placing his hands on her shoulders.

He glanced down at her. "Warm up first, Miriam. I know you are freezing. Just let me know when the food is ready. I'll light lanterns then I'll check upstairs."

She blushed a bit. "Yeah, okay," she answered, slowly removing her gloves.

Trevor took two lanterns and lit them, placing two downstairs then heading upstairs. Miriam turned back to the fire for a bit longer, drinking in the heat so it chased away the chills.

<hr/>

Trevor could see that the bed was spacious enough for two people. He smiled at that. For now, he would let Miriam have the warm bed. He would cover up the window so that the cold could not penetrate the room.

Taking some tarps from the wagon, he quickly wrapped the entire window, using rope to tighten everything up so it was snug.

Satisfied, he stepped back and put his hands on his hips, glancing around. He had removed his heavy coat and just wore his uniform. The little cottage was now starting to warm up a bit with the roaring fire going below.

"Trevor?" Miriam called his name.

"Yes?" he answered.

"I have a meal prepared for us now," she informed him.

"All right. I'm coming down."

He glanced around one more time, then headed downstairs to join Miriam at the little table.

He sat across from her. There were two chairs and a square sturdy wooden table. She managed to find some tin plates and utensils. Glancing down, he saw she had heated some beans, fried up some beef tacky, and brewed some hot coffee.

"I thought this would do for now. For dinner, I'll make a bigger meal," she remarked.

"This is fine, Miriam," he said as he dug into the food, drinking the coffee as he glanced at her. She had removed her scarf and hat but she still wore her warm cloak, her hair tumbling around her shoulders. He smiled at that as he continued to eat, wondering idly how long the storm would last.

As if she had read his mind, she asked, "How long do you think this storm will last?" Her brown eyes studied his.

Trevor shrugged as he chewed his food, swallowing. "Hard to say. This is an unusual storm this far south and especially at the end of November. A day, maybe a couple… we should be comfortable and warm here for a while."

Her gaze returned to her food as she continued to eat.

After several moments, he spoke again. "Don't worry, Miriam. We will be safe here. The cabin is remote, but we have everything we need to survive for a while. Everything will be all right," he assured her.

Miriam knew with Trevor she would always be safe. She was so glad Toby was home and out of this war. Soon enough, she would be too - hopefully. Her enlistment was up, but the storm had other ideas for her. Strangely, she wasn't surprised.

⸻ ● ⸻

They passed the afternoon on the couch by the fire, reading. The wind continued to howl and when Trevor lifted the drape to glance outside, he could see about a foot of snow added to the landscape. It still was hurling down in sheets. The wind blew the snow around, shaking the windowpane a bit. Trevor covered the window back up and returned to the fire.

The storm continued throughout the day. Trevor went to check on the horse. He returned covered in frost from head to toe. He spent a good half hour in front of the fire as Miriam curled up with a quilt.

Evening arrived and they kept the lanterns lit. Miriam made dinner, frying more of the beef tacky and adding a mixture of beans and some vegetables... and, of course, more coffee. This time Trevor produced some whiskey and put a shot in both their cups. At this, she smiled.

"It will help warm us up," he said, taking a sip.

She did the same as she smiled at him, continuing to eat.

After a few moments, she glanced up at him. "So," she met his blue eyes, "there is only one bed. Who gets to use it?" She smiled slowly.

He answered immediately. "You do. I'll make do on the couch with some quilts and the fire. There are plenty of quilts up there for you to use and the heat from the fire will travel upstairs. I bound up the window tightly so the cold air cannot get in." He continued to eat as she smiled.

They talked briefly about the war and friends they both had known for a bit. They both retired early, exhausted from traveling in the blizzard and getting their retreat set up.

Miriam took her clothes and effects upstairs to the small bedroom as Trevor took some of their quilts, making up a comfy bed on the couch. He made sure he placed enough logs on the fire to last for hours.

He removed his shirt and decided to sleep in his undershirt with

134

pants. Wrapping quilts around him, he glanced into the flames as he heard Miriam moving about upstairs, preparing for bed.

Soon she doused the lantern and the firelight bounced off the walls of the log cabin. Trevor watched the flames for several moments, drifting off to sleep.

23

Trevor woke up to a very cold room. Blearily he glanced at the fire. There were a few orange coals still burning a bit, but the fire had died probably hours ago. Judging by the amount of sun coming through he surmised it was probably dawn. The wind still howled around the little cabin.

Pushing back quilts, he rubbed his face; he had a bit of rough whiskers this morning. Nothing he could do about that now. He grabbed up his shirt and socks, glancing around for his boots. Finding them, he pulled them on and went over to the logs. Placing several on the coals, he stirred them until they caught. He piled more on, then looked about.

He strode over to the drape to look outside. The windowpane was completely frosted over and he could not see much. He opened the front door and a blast of snow and wind smacked his face. He put up one hand to shield his face. The storm had not abated. It was as bad as yesterday.

From the silence upstairs, he supposed Miriam was still sleeping. He grabbed his heavy coat, hat, and gloves. He needed to attend to the horse, make sure it was fed and rub it down a bit.

Finding a pail in the shed, he filled it with snow and went into the cabin to melt it into water. Not only did the horse need water, they would too. He knew he had to look around the property more today, even in the awful weather, to see what else was around that they could utilize. It looked like they might be here several days. In fact, the snow was now so deep, there was no way the horse could travel until several feet of it melted, and he had no idea how long that would be.

Trevor finished up with the horse and shielded his face as he walked back toward the little cabin. Opening the door, he entered, shaking off the cold and snow.

Glancing to the left, he smelled coffee. He saw Miriam at the table.

That would taste like heaven right about now. Smiling at her, he removed his outer effects and joined her. She handed him a mug of hot coffee and he accepted it gratefully.

She wore a warm white robe and she looked lovely in the low morning light. He sipped as she watched him.

"You were outside?"

"Yep. Had to take care of the horse, water him and feed him. We're going to need a source of water. For now, I can bring in big pails of snow and we can melt it over the fire, but judging by the weather, we are going to be here a while. I'm going to go out again and see if there are any provisions I missed yesterday."

"I have some dough mix from our rations. Would you like me to make pancakes?"

His eyes met hers as he sipped. "That would be great, Miriam."

She finished up her coffee then moved over to a bottom shelf where she had stored some of their items. Removing a bag, she prepared to make food for them.

Trevor helped himself to a second cup of coffee.

Miriam brought over the tin plates and utensils she had cleaned up last evening. She glanced at the big tub nearby.

"It would be heaven to wash up a bit," she remarked.

"I can bring in several pails of snow for you and put it over the fire. You can bathe while I go out and check for further supplies. Later, I'll fashion some sort of drape around it so we have privacy. I'll probably want to use it later," he replied.

She brought over two big steaming pancakes, there was no butter or anything so they would eat them plain. He didn't care; it was hot food.

Miriam started eating. "How bad is it out there?" She could still hear the wind howling. "Did it stop or slow down yet?"

"Nope." He took a sip of coffee. "In fact, it's just as bad as yesterday. I think we got about two feet last evening and it is still snowing. I believe we are going to be here longer than I originally thought. That is why it is important to try to find a water supply of some sort. There are plenty of logs, I can split more if needed."

It seemed they were going to be alone together in this little cabin longer. At this thought, she blushed a bit. The bed had been warm and snuggly last night. She ignored the swirling winds that one could hear clearly on the second floor. She was so exhausted she must have slept as soon as her head hit the pillow. It was a real luxury to actually sleep in a *bed*. Usually it was rough cots, tent floors, and rucksacks. When the chill had started to penetrate the quilt, she had woken up only to find Trevor gone.

As he ate his breakfast, he wondered what was going through her mind. "How did you sleep?" he asked.

A smile bloomed on her lips. "I actually slept really well. I have not slept in a bed for - well, years it seems."

He chuckled. "Well, that is one benefit of being stranded, I guess."

"We were lucky to find this place," she murmured.

"Very lucky," he conceded. He finished up his food and moved over to the sink to quickly wash both of their dishes, leaving them to drain.

"I'm going to bundle up again and go outside. I'll bring in enough snow in the pails and heat it for you. Then I'll be outside looking around. I'll probably have to take the horse to get through the snow drifts." He donned his heavy gear.

"Thank you, Trevor. I appreciate that."

Smiling, he left the cabin.

<hr>

After Trevor got Miriam situated with the bath water he went to the shed and saddled up the horse. He whinnied in surprise and nudged Trevor with his nose.

"Sorry, buddy, but we have to brave the elements for a bit. Need to find some useful supplies if we can." He mounted the horse as the horse chuffed, his breath swirling in the cold.

Trevor directed him carefully out of the shed and around the cabin to the back. He had not had a chance yesterday to really check around the property. Slowly they moved through the snow and around the structure. All Trevor could see was a white landscape as more of the stuff continued to fall. He had wrapped a warm scarf around his neck and pulled up his coat collar, but it was still bitterly cold. He knew he needed to be as quick as he could in this weather.

Kicking the horse a bit, he trotted further around the property and squinted, trying to make out anything that might not be snow. About five hundred feet from the cabin, the forest started again. If they ran out of wood he would be able to chop down more if needed. Right now he was hoping to find some kind of water pump or something similar.

He was in luck. After further moving around the dwelling, in the back of the shed he could see something protruding through the snow and he dismounted to examine it.

Brushing snow and chunks of ice off, he found a crude water pump, frozen solid. He would need to bring some hot water out here and try to thaw it out and see if the thing still worked. He prayed that it did.

He had been gone a half hour. Trevor hoped that was enough time for Miriam to bathe and dress. He turned the horse around back towards the shed and dismounted once they were under its roof, patting the horse. He removed the saddle and gave the horse an extra ration of food, covering him again with the blanket. The horse settled among the hay with a satisfied grunt, glad to be out of the cold once more.

Trevor walked through the snow drifts, his tall boots protecting his pants from getting too wet. As he approached the porch, he knocked briefly on the door to give Miriam a heads up. She opened the door immediately and then closed it again tightly behind him as he entered.

She was wearing a warm black dress, a dress he had never seen her in before. It was snugger than her nursing dresses and showed off her curvy figure. Her blonde hair was still a bit wet from shampooing and waved down her back and breasts. She smiled up at him.

"Any luck?"

He reached down for the large water pail nearby the tub. He could see there was plenty of water for him to bathe later.

"Yeah, actually, I found a water pump near the shed. But it is frozen solid and I'll have to heat several pails of snow to try to thaw it out. That'll probably take me most of the morning." Grabbing up the pail, he looked down at her. "What are you planning to do?"

She gestured to the kitchen. "I'm going to arrange all of our rations with what I can find here. There may be some things here I overlooked yesterday. We need to have more in our diet than just beef tacky and beans. That will take a bit of time to get organized. I'll also keep the fire going."

Grinning down at her, he took the pail and braved the elements again. He knew he would be freezing for most of the morning, but it had to be done.

⊷━━━●━━━⊶

Trevor steadily worked on the pump, returning to the cabin to fetch hot water, then back to the pump to dump it. It took him ten trips with full buckets before the ice and snow started melting down the metal pipe. Trevor was exhausted and frozen but he finally found the round lever and turned it. At first, it just dripped the snow and water he had poured. He turned it further, pushing harder on it and finally a little stream of water emerged. He left it on and soon the pump gushed water. Relieved, he turned it off for now. He would need to keep it free of snow and ice, but for now they had water, which was essential. They could only use the snow for emergencies like last evening.

Taking the pail into the cabin, Trevor entered, setting the bucket down by the door. He looked like a snowman. He was frosted from head to toe.

Miriam gasped, coming over to help him out of his gear, noticing he was shivering uncontrollably. She quickly helped remove his shirt, directing him to the couch. She wrapped him up in several warm quilts, turning to put more logs on the fire.

"I'll get you some hot coffee. I'm going to warm up several pails of water so you can take a hot bath."

He moved up a bit. "I don't want you carrying heavy pails, Miriam. I can do that," he said.

She pushed him back down. "You have carried enough pails today. You are exhausted and chilled to the bone. Do what I say, Major!" she said sternly.

He relaxed back and she moved to the stove to brew hot coffee. Soon, Miriam was back with a steaming mug she handed to him. He accepted it and sipped slowly. Between the heavy quilts and the fire, he had stopped shivering. He watched her as she placed buckets of snow she had collected above the flames to warm up. She needed about four pails until the water was hot enough for Trevor.

She went to their supplies and found a heavy blanket. She fashioned a drape around the tub. It was a crude drape, but it would do the trick.

Returning to him, she insisted he bathe. He was actually falling asleep, he was so exhausted. Finally he pushed up and went to the tub. He could see the steaming water; she had lit a lantern and left it sitting on a chair, along with a bar of soap and some rough towels.

Flinging off his clothes, Trevor sat in the hot tub. He submerged his shoulders as he let the heat of the water relax his stiff muscles and chase the chill away. It felt wonderful.

⋖◦━━━━━◉◦━━━━◦▹

Miriam stayed by the fire, reading as she waited for Trevor. She wanted to prepare a meal for them, but that had to wait until he was finished in the tub. At first she could hear him bathing, using the soap and water but after a little while, there was only silence. After a half hour, she called him tentatively.

"Trevor?"

There was only silence and she tried again louder. "Trevor?"

Silence.

Rising, she decided to check on him. Fortunately, the water covered him and she kept her gaze strictly on his face. He was lying back against the rim, asleep. There were still some suds in the water and his hair was wet so she knew he had cleaned up and then nodded off.

Approaching him, she shook his arm slightly to wake him. After a moment, his eyes blinked open and he looked around sleepily, seeing her near the tub. "Miriam," he murmured.

"Trevor, you have been in here for over a half hour. Why don't you get dried up and dress? I'll make us a meal. It is past lunch time. I know you must be hungry."

"Yes, all right." He ran his hands through his wet hair as she stepped aside, going back to the fire to allow him some privacy.

After a few moments he came out, buttoning up his shirt. He had donned his pants and thick socks. He had tried to push his thick black hair out of his face. Smiling, Miriam offered him her brush and he used it, brushing his hair back. He needed to shave but he did not want to dig for his razor right now. He was simply too tired.

"Here," she handed him another cup of hot coffee. "Relax on the couch while I prepare a meal."

Gratefully he accepted the coffee and moved to the couch. He placed his mug down and threw a bunch of logs on the fire. Turning, he picked up his coffee and sank into the cushions.

Soon Miriam called him over to the table and Trevor took his mug and joined her. She had somehow found canned peaches. There were peaches, stew, and she had used the dough to make muffins earlier. He dug in. He was so hungry he could eat his horse. He snorted at that. He loved that animal; it had saved their lives.

At this sound, she arched a brow.

He glanced up at her, chewing his food. "I was just thinking I am so hungry, I could eat my horse!"

Her dark eyes studied him as she chewed her food.

"Not that I would! We have him to thank for getting us here," he remarked.

"Does your horse have a name?"

He looked up at her. "No, actually he doesn't."

"Well, since he has been such a loyal animal, I believe he deserves one, don't you?"

He couldn't help but notice how the lantern light caressed her beautiful face. Glancing away, he continued to eat. After a few moments, he answered, "I suppose you're right. What shall we name him?"

She shrugged. "He is your horse. I think you should have the honor of naming him."

Trevor mused over this. What would be a worthy name? "How about Prince?" he suggested.

Her smile widened. "I think that is a perfect name for him."

"A royal name for a royal animal," he deduced.

"Yes, quite. How is your food?"

"I don't know how you manage such miracles, but everything is great. Peaches?" he questioned.

"Yes. I found another pantry that has canned goods. There are more canned vegetables as well as various fruits. Whoever owns this place takes very good care to stock it."

"When we leave, I will leave gold coins to reimburse the owner for using this place. It's the least I can do," he answered.

She nodded. "We are using their food supplies, wood, and water. Yes, it is the least we can do."

"What would you like to do after we eat?" he questioned.

"Well, after I clean up, I was planning to read and tend the fire. The couch is big enough for you to nap if you would like to," she replied.

He sighed. "You don't mind, do you?"

"Of course not, Trevor. You have spent most of the day working in blizzard conditions."

"Okay." He stood, taking his plate to the sink. "Wake me up after two hours, though. I don't want to sleep any longer than that, all right?"

"All right. Why don't you grab some quilts? I'll take care of everything else."

He caressed her cheek briefly. "Thank you," he murmured, moving over to the couch.

Miriam could still feel the gentle touch of his long fingers and shivered a bit. It was not because she was cold.

She turned to her tasks as the man behind her settled on one end of the couch, pulling his long legs up, leaving room for her to sit.

After two hours, Miriam dutifully woke Trevor up. It was early evening and she planned to make them dinner. She informed him of that, taking a lantern as she went into the kitchen.

Trevor wiped sleep out of his eyes and went to pull on his boots to keep his feet warm. He moved to the fire, putting several logs on it. Tomorrow he would have to go to the pile outside and replenish their supply of wood. He watched the flames as Miriam moved about behind him, preparing food.

She called him in about twenty minutes and he joined her. She reheated the stew and there were some muffins. This time she added canned peas. It was important for them to eat vegetables. They both knew it would prevent scurvy if they were to be here any amount of time. Having fruit was good too.

"Tomorrow, I am going to drain some of the fruit juices and put them in containers for us. That way we will have something more to drink than just coffee and water."

"That would be good. I'll find a chest. I'll fill it with snow. We can put perishable items in it."

"Good idea!" she remarked. There was silence for a moment.

She spoke again. "You seem very good at this survivalist thing," she remarked, studying his handsome features in the flickering light.

"I told you, Miriam. Where I live, it is still pretty untamed. I taught myself how to survive or take care of others if the need arises." He chewed his food, his bright blue eyes meeting hers in the dim light.

She blushed, looking down at her food. "So you did." She paused. "What's it like where you live? I know you said it is rural. How many people are in your town? Can you describe it a bit more?"

He glanced up, continuing to eat. "Oh, there are tons of trees, a bit like where we are now. Mentor itself is a bustling little town. It is on Lake Erie, so there is a lot of boating commerce. There are ships, stores, a little church, an inn. And my medical practice." He shrugged. "A typical little town."

Once more he was being quite vague. She had a nagging feeling he was being disingenuous on purpose. She was silent, continuing to eat her food.

Trevor studied Miriam's face. He knew she expected more information but there wasn't a heck of a lot he could tell her without giving away his mission. He still did not know if it was complete or not.

The chip clicked on. *No, it is not. You will be given that information when your mission is complete.*

Surprise must have shown on his face.

"What?" she questioned.

"It's nothing. Nothing at all."

He continued to eat his dinner and she knew she would get nothing further from him. She continued her own meal in silence.

<hr />

The evening progressed much the same as the previous one. They both read and when they were tired enough they separated to sleep.

Once again Trevor settled on the couch with the quilts. He was very relieved they had found a source of water and he needed to make sure he kept the pump warm. He needed to bring in some more wood, he needed to kiss Miriam until they both melted…

The next morning, Trevor woke early again. Wiping sleep from his eyes, he could see the fire was low. Moving over to the woodpile (which he needed to add to today), he threw several big logs on until the fire flamed up nicely.

Shivering, he went over to the tub to wash up a bit. He knew it would be cold, and it was! He splashed his face, neck, shoulders, and arms before moving over to the couch to dress in his warm uniform. He would go out and split wood first. There still was a nice pile out there but he did not want to run low, so that would be his first chore. Actually, he had to check out the pump and keep it from freezing.

He hastily gathered a pail of snow and set it above the fire, waiting for it to melt before taking it over to the tub, adding some hot water for Miriam. It would be lukewarm, but it was better than freezing.

Panting a bit, he put on his heavy coat, gloves, and hat. He glanced briefly upstairs, but there was no sign of activity.

He opened the heavy door and could see it was still snowing. Not as heavily as yesterday, but a steady snowfall.

Moving around to the back, he could see the pump was not frozen up like yesterday. Making trip after trip, he brought in several pails of water to store in a large container, placing them in a small icebox he had fashioned. Then, it was off to chop wood.

As he closed the door again, he could hear Miriam stirring. Smiling, he left the cabin.

Miriam woke to the smell of the fire burning. Trevor must be up and about already. She stretched and reached for her warm robe and heavy socks.

Moving downstairs, she could see a roaring fire going. Glancing to the left she saw a bit of steam in the tub. She went to it, dipping her hand in. Yes, it was really warm and if he was occupied outside, she could take a quick bath.

She opened the heavy drape a bit. He was over by the woodpile, chopping wood.

Hurriedly she went upstairs to gather clothes, soap, shampoo, and her other effects. Returning downstairs, she undressed quickly, sinking into the water. It felt heavenly and she wanted to stay in and just soak. She knew he would be returning soon and she needed to make breakfast. He had been hard at work already.

Soaping up her hair, she scrubbed it carefully before dipping it into the water to rinse away all suds, squeezing her long locks tightly. She bathed her body quickly and exited the tub, grabbing up a towel. She rubbed her body and hair as dry as she could before dressing as fast as she could in the chilly air.

Sighing, she sat on a chair, combing out her wet hair. After preparing food, she would go over by the fire where the warmth could finish drying her hair.

<hr />

Trevor chopped wood for a good hour, wondering if Miriam had woken and bathed yet. He had about thirty logs split in half, adding to the dozen or so they had left. This supply would last at least three more days before he would have to chop again.

Wiping sweat from his brow, he put aside the axe, then stacked the wood. He was ravenously hungry from all of the work he had already done this morning. Perhaps she would have breakfast ready? He hoped so.

He moved up the steps of the cabin, knocking on the door.

Miriam opened the door to him, smiling. Today's dress was dark green with a lacy collar. He could see her hair was brushed and shiny. She must have bathed.

She ushered him into the warm cabin. "Come in, Trevor. I have breakfast for you. You must be starving."

He grinned down at her, removing his snowy coat, gloves, and hat. He laid the items on a little table by the door, stomping snow from his boots. "Sounds wonderful. What do we have this morning?" he inquired.

"I have hot porridge, peaches, a few muffins. And of course, hot coffee," she smiled up at him.

"All right, then. Just let me put more logs on the fire. I'll be right over."

Miriam went to pour them both mugs of coffee and took a seat at the table, waiting for him to join her.

He pulled out a chair opposite her, looking down at the steamy porridge. "Mmm! Hot food!" He dug in, his blue eyes looking up at her in amusement.

"Thank you for bringing in hot water to bathe." She paused. "Did you have a chance to wash up?"

"Just a bit. Washed face, shoulders. Just a quickie. The water was freezing!"

"Oh no!" she replied.

He shrugged, continuing to eat. "Maybe I'll get a chance later to clean up a bit more. I am a bit sweaty from chopping wood." He chewed his food, glancing at her face.

Miriam ate slowly, contemplating Trevor. Finally she spoke. "How is the weather outside? I don't hear any gale force winds."

"It is still snowing, but not as bad as the last two days. It's calmed down a bit, still a steady snowfall. I'd say we have about three or so feet out there."

Her dark eyes met his. "So, we will be here for awhile, until the snow melts enough for Prince?"

His brows knit into a puzzled frown, at first not understanding her reference. He then recalled he had named the horse Prince and smiled slowly.

Miriam could feel her stomach drop strangely and swallowed, quickly looking back down at her bowl.

"Yes, Prince won't be able to make it out for a while. If the snow continues, it will get even deeper. We'll just have to wait it out for now."

She ate her breakfast, thinking about his words. How would they spend their time? She did have books to read, there were chores for her to do around the cabin, cooking and cleaning. If they were here for weeks, though - what then? She was silent, eating her food.

Trevor helped himself to more coffee and a second bowl of porridge, glancing at Miriam. She was intently gazing down as she ate.

"What would you like to do today? I have to go out and attend to Prince for a bit, but that won't take long."

Her lovely eyes met his. "I was planning to clean up the cabin a bit, make up meals for lunch and dinner, store them." She shrugged. "Spend time by the fire, keep it going, that sort of stuff," she murmured, glancing back down.

Trevor finished up his breakfast and sipped at his coffee as he studied her.

At his silence, she looked up to see him contemplating her. She blushed as she noticed his scrutiny, looking back down at her food.

"I'm sure Toby has probably made it home by now," he said casually.

Her brown eyes met his. "Won't this storm have slowed them down too?"

"It seems to be localized to Virginia, not Pennsylvania. From where he and the Corporal left, it should have been a four or five day trip," he answered.

She sighed. "That is good. I hope he recovers quickly. He has friends in town who can help him out, thank the good Lord," she sipped at her coffee.

He waited for further comments but she just continued to eat. Usually she was more talkative. He watched her finish her breakfast and rise to take their dishes to the sink to clean up.

Trevor stood, looking over at her. "I'm going out to check on Prince now. Do you need me for anything?"

She turned to him. "No, no. I'm good. You do what you need to." She turned back to the sink.

"Miriam, is there something wrong?" he asked quietly.

Startled, she turned back to him. "No, nothing. I'm fine." She started scrubbing up the plates.

He sighed, moving to the door. He donned his heavy effects, moving outside to go to the shed.

As he closed the door firmly, Miriam turned back to stare at the door for a long time.

◄••─────••●●••─────••►

They spent the day tending to the fire, reading by it, and eating meals in the small kitchen.

After dinner, Trevor moved the drape around the tub after filling it with several hot pails of water. He took a quick bath and even brought his razor in to shave before a small mirror. He knew there was a larger mirror upstairs but he wasn't about to stroll around naked with Miriam around. He chuckled a bit at this thought and received a tiny nick. Dabbing it with a towel, he checked the spot in the mirror. Very small and it had already stopped bleeding. He finished up in the tub. Tomorrow, he would need to empty the thing and refill it with fresh water. That would be quite the chore but the water was several days old and needed to be refreshed.

Exiting the tub, he dried up quickly, using his comb to slick his hair back. He dressed and headed out to find Miriam reading on the couch. Grinning, he poured tiny shots of whiskey for them, offering her one.

Smiling, Miriam accepted it as they clinked tiny glasses, sipping the whiskey as they contemplated the fire. They talked casually about various subjects so whatever had been bothering her earlier seemed to have passed. Trevor reached for the quilts and covered them both up as they talked.

Soon it was time to retire. Trevor was exhausted after the busy day. He had another day of work ahead of him tomorrow.

Miriam climbed the stairs to seek out her bed. Trevor wrapped all the quilts around him after tending to the fire. He was asleep as soon as his head hit the pillow.

Miriam lay awake for a good hour, just contemplating the shadowy flames dancing on the ceiling, thinking about Trevor.

The third morning in the little cabin, Trevor woke and quickly pulled on his warm clothes. After attending to the fire, he turned, hands on his hips as he examined the metal tub. The thing was pretty full, it would be heavy to carry and empty. Fortunately he was in top physical shape and stronger than most men, especially in this century. It would be a huge chore but not an impossible one.

He opened the big door, using a log to prop it open as a swirl of snow entered. The snow was much lighter now; it looked like it might even stop today.

Shoving the tub across the floor, he finally moved it to the entrance way. He heaved it up. The dirty water splashed over the rail of the porch into the snow packed below. It made a slushy mess but he was not concerned about that.

Quickly he shut the door so the cabin would not become cold. He replaced the tub in its spot and stood, chest heaving a bit. Now he had to fill it back up with hot water.

He went to the water chest and filled about five pails, hanging each over the fire to heat. The tub was now full and steamy with clean water. It had depleted their water reserve so he would now have to go out to the pump to replenish their supply.

Miriam descended the stairs in her robe, her hair slightly mussed.

"I heard you moving about down here. You're already dressed and have been outside?" She moved toward him, pushing her hair back.

"Yes, I emptied the tub and put hot water in it. We will need more water so I'm going out to the pump to fill up more pails," he gestured toward the back.

"Hot clean water?" she said in amazement.

"Yep. Enjoy. I'll be outside getting water from the pump. Prince needs to be watered and fed so it will give you some time to enjoy a warm leisurely bath."

She smiled, delighted. "Thank you! I intend to fully enjoy it!" she answered.

Trevor grinned at her and went to get the large pail. "Well, off to pump water, visit Prince. It's snowing lightly and he could use a bit of exercise. I'll take him around the property to get out. Later on, if you would like to get out I can take you for a ride."

Her dark eyes met his. "That would be wonderful. I do have a bit of cabin fever."

Trevor nodded and closed the door, leaving her alone. Miriam went to get clothes and bathing items. Returning downstairs, she undressed, sinking into the warm steamy water. It felt heavenly and she settled in comfortably, letting the heat relax her as she closed her eyes.

⸺●◍●⸺

After twenty minutes or so, Miriam got out of the tub and dressed for the day before heading to the kitchen area. She prepared hot oatmeal with some jarred apples and coffee.

Wrapping her long coat around her, she went outside to let Trevor know breakfast was ready. She found him in the shed, quietly talking to Prince as he groomed him.

When he heard her approaching, he turned.

"I just wanted to let you know I have breakfast ready," she said.

"All right. Give me a minute and I'll be right in."

Nodding, she made her way through the snow back to the entrance. It was hard walking through the snow as it was so deep. It was snowing lightly, but the sun was trying to make an appearance. It would be a good day to get out and about a bit.

She stamped snow from her boots, hanging her coat nearby. Moving to the table, she poured out hot coffee.

Soon after Trevor entered and closed the door, shaking snow off of his outerwear as he removed it. Smiling, he moved to the little table to join her.

Looking down, he could see she had made oatmeal with apples. He sipped at the coffee first, grateful for the warmth after being outside.

As they started to eat, Miriam questioned him. "How did you get that heavy tub filled with water outside?"

Chewing, he glanced up. He swallowed and answered. "I shoved it across the floor, then dumped the contents over the porch railing. You should be careful around there. The watery mess will turn icy." He went back to eating.

Miriam was amazed that he could move such a heavy metal tub filled with water so easily and make it sound like it was no big deal. She knew it was. Many men (at least two) would be needed to move a tub that size filled with water. She shook her head in wonder. Trevor never ceased to amaze her.

"After we eat and clean up, I can take you for a ride on Prince, if you'd like. I took him out, but only for a trot. We can take a longer ride." His blue eyes met hers.

"Yes, that would be nice. I'll clean up real quick and bundle up."

"While you're doing that, I'll get him saddled and ready. I've already fed and watered him. I was grooming him when you came in, so he is all set to go."

"That's good. I'm looking forward to getting out for a while."

"Yes. You haven't been out since we arrived. The weather wasn't really nice enough until now," he remarked.

"You're amazing, Trevor. I just don't know where you find the energy to do the things you do." She spooned up some oatmeal as she studied him.

He glanced up. "What do you mean?"

She shrugged, smiling at him. "Carrying heavy tubs around, working on freezing pumps, bringing heavy pails of water back and forth all day." She waved her hands. "It's incredible. Most men would not have the strength to do the things I've seen you do in the past three days. However, you did perform miracles in the battles." Her dark eyes studied him intently as she ate.

Trevor took his time answering. Yeah, there were many things he could accomplish because he had been trained in just about any skill he would need in any given century. However, he could not tell Miriam that. Time to be evasive again with her - he hated that, but he could not reveal his mission.

He shrugged casually, not meeting her eyes. "I told you, I needed to learn certain skills to survive in the wilderness."

She studied his face. She knew she was getting another non-answer from him. For some reason, there were things he just did not want to reveal about himself

"Trevor, what are you not telling me?" She placed her spoon down, looking directly into his eyes.

His gaze met hers as he chewed his food. "Many things, Miriam. I am a secretive man. I've needed to be."

"Why?"

He sighed. "There are some things I don't feel comfortable talking about. Can we please just clean up and go outside?"

Miriam sipped at her coffee. She knew she could trust Trevor. He had saved her life and her brother's, but it was frustrating that he remained so mysterious.

She rose, stacking the dishes. "Very well, Trevor. I'll clean up quickly as you see to your horse." She moved to the sink and started washing up the dishes.

Trevor went to get his outer effects, glancing over at her slim figure near the sink as he pulled his coat on. Sighing, he opened the door to go attend to the horse.

⸻ ◉ ⸻

Twenty minutes later, Miriam joined him bundled up in her heavy coat, hat, scarf, and gloves. Prince whinnied as Miriam entered and she moved over to him, stroking his velvety nose with her gloved hand.

"He is a handsome specimen," she remarked.

Prince chuffed, nudging her gently.

Trevor grinned. "Yep, he's a fine animal. Let's take him out for some exercise." He mounted the horse, reaching down to pull Miriam up behind him.

She settled against him as Trevor led Prince out of his shelter, moving around the back of the structure.

She could see the snow had created a winter wonderland, the white landscape stretching to the nearby forest. There was a large clearing behind the cabin. Trevor drove Prince to a quick trot, running around the property quickly. Fresh air and snow kissed Miriam's face. The sun was even coming out. It glinted off of the snow, ice, and the snow-laden trees. She took a deep breath, enjoying being outdoors. It was still cold but not as bitterly cold as when they had arrived in the blizzard. Today it was pleasant to be outdoors, and she savored it.

Trevor glanced back. "Fine back there?"

"Yes," she answered. "This is wonderful to be outside. Everything is so beautiful."

"Yes, it can be lovely but it will also keep us snowbound for a while."

Miriam's euphoria suddenly vanished. This snow was keeping them here together for who knew how long? Judging by the depth, it would take quite some time to melt. Weeks? A month?

Trevor's voice interrupted her thoughts. "I'm going to take him through the forest. See what's around, if anything," he said.

"All right," she replied.

Prince picked a path carefully through the trees. Most were barren with just snow on the branches but there were some evergreens. Everything was frosted with snow. It was truly beautiful.

After about half an hour, Trevor turned Prince around back towards the cabin. Miriam enjoyed the ride, raising her face to the sky.

<hr />

Back at the cabin, they both dismounted. Trevor unsaddled Prince, giving him water and extra rations.

"I'll rub him down this afternoon after lunch," he remarked.

He turned to walk back to the cabin with her. They both took off their snowy outerwear.

Trevor went to the fire, tending to it so it blazed up again.

Miriam settled on the couch as she watched him, thinking about Toby. She missed him so much. She bit her lip as her eyes became moist. She did not want Trevor to see this.

She rose abruptly. "I'll get us some coffee to warm up," she moved to the kitchen area.

"Sounds good," he said over his shoulder, stacking logs.

Miriam returned with two steaming mugs, handing him one as they settled on the couch. She sipped her brew, studying the flames, silent.

Trevor also sipped his coffee but his gaze was on the lovely woman next to him. She was wearing one of her sturdy brown wool dresses to keep her warm. They had both removed their boots, their heavy socks keeping their feet toasty.

He wrapped a quilt around her shoulders but she moved it down. "I'm fine, Trevor. I'm warm enough," she remarked, her gaze staying on the flames.

There was silence for a while and Trevor sighed.

"Tell me what's on your mind," he said.

She glanced at him, rubbing a tear away. "I was just thinking about Toby. I miss him so much."

He placed his mug on a nearby table. "Come here," he said, wrapping his arms around her, cuddling her close.

Miriam set her mug on the floor, clutching Trevor as she buried her face in his chest. He was warm and she could feel firm muscles under his shirt. It felt so good to be held by a strong man. She snuggled closer, quietly crying.

Trevor stroked her hair gently, settling back in the couch, holding her close. He knew she didn't want to talk, just be comforted. He laid one hand on her head gently and stroked her back, just holding her and letting her cry.

After a while, she slowly moved away, swiping at her face, using her dress to dry her face.

"I'm sorry I lost it like that…it's just so hard sometimes—"

He interrupted her. "Shush. We all need to relieve stress from time to time."

They were still sitting close together and he took her hand, stroking the palm gently. "You needed a shoulder. Mine was available."

He smiled the smile that totally melted her inside.

She blushed, glancing away for a moment but she did not move her hand. He continued to stroke it lightly and softly - feather-light, she tingled - everywhere.

Miriam rose. "I think it's time to eat a mid-day meal. I know the fresh air has made me hungry," she remarked, going to the kitchen.

Trevor rose to place more logs on the fire then joined her in the kitchen. He set the table as she prepared food. They were both silent as they ate their food.

<hr />

After lunch, Trevor went outside again to attend to Prince. He needed to be rubbed down since he had exercised. Plus he knew Miriam needed some space for now. So he spent a couple of hours with Prince, grooming him.

He eventually went to check the water pump, shoving some snow away from it. When he turned it on, the water came out in spurts. Good, it was still working.

Trevor was cold and decided to head back to the cabin. It was late afternoon. The sun would set soon as it was late autumn. Were they into December yet? He didn't even know.

He entered the cabin and could see the fire was going; Miriam must have attended to it. She was sleeping on the couch, wrapped in quilts.

Trevor approached her. He could see the edge of the quilt had slipped a bit. He covered her gently, gazing down at her lovely features. She slept with her full lips parted, her long eyelashes casting shadows on her cheekbones. He stroked her hair gently, turning away. He would let her sleep and prepare dinner for them.

The smell of something frying woke Miriam. She slowly opened her eyes. It was evening; Trevor had lit some lanterns. She glanced about for him and saw him cooking in the kitchen area.

Shoving the quilts away, Miriam donned her boots and tried to pin her hair up a bit. She then moved into the kitchen to join Trevor.

He was frying beef tacky and heating canned vegetables. He'd also added some apples from earlier. The table was set.

Turning, he noticed her presence and smiled. "Dinner is just about ready. Have a seat," he invited.

"Trevor, you should have woken me. I can make dinner, you do so much else. It's the least I can do."

He brought beef tacky over to the table, forking out portions onto the plates. He then brought over the vegetables and fruit, pouring coffee. "It's no problem, Miriam. I do know how to cook too. Living alone, it is a skill one has to learn."

He seated himself and she did the same. She was not quite as hungry now as she had been earlier. She ate in silence.

Trevor broke the silence, talking to her about the war and other subjects that would not be touchy. They quietly chatted as they ate dinner.

After dinner, Trevor again bathed behind the drape. He put a pail of hot water in so that it was nice and warm. He bathed quickly, shaving and washing his hair. Retrieving his towel, he dried off and dressed, once again donning his tall boots.

He went over to the couch where he could see Miriam was reading. Smiling, he joined her, picking up his own book. They read in companionable silence until it was time to sleep.

Trevor curled up on the couch once again as Miriam sought out her warm bed.

26

Trevor woke early the next morning, moving to the window to part the drape. It was sunny again but he could tell it was definitely cold outside. The wind whipped the snow into whorls and cliffs, making it bitterly cold. He would need to attend to Prince right away and put a heavy blanket on him after feeding and watering him.

Everything was silent upstairs so Miriam was not yet awake. It was barely dawn. Trevor donned his heavy outerwear and warm boots before heading outside into the snow that came almost to his thighs. With this frigid weather it would take forever for the snow to melt. They had to be in December by now by his estimate. This was the fourth day in the little cabin but Trevor knew they could not leave shelter until the weather improved, and he had no idea how long that would be. This far south, it was bizarre to have this much snowy cold weather.

Shrugging, he entered the relative warmth of the shed where Prince was lying. He got to his feet as Trevor entered, the cold wind chuffing from his nostrils as he whinnied softly.

Trevor moved to his horse, patting him gently. "Hey, buddy," he said softly, "let's get you fed and watered. Then I have a nice warm blanket for you. You're going to need it today."

Trevor went about his chores as Prince whinnied again, moving his head up and down as though he had understood Trevor's words. Perhaps he had. He knew sometimes horses could be more intelligent than some humans.

He quickly tended to Prince. Afterwards he went to the pump to bring in several more pails of water. The sun was now completely up. He wondered if Miriam was awake yet.

When he entered the cabin, Miriam was just coming down the stairs dressed in her robe, hair slightly mussed.

Trevor glanced up at her as he removed his outerwear and she smiled at him.

"Out and about already?" She arched a brow.

"Yep. It's pretty cold out, I wanted to attend to Prince." He hung his coat, hat, and gloves on the hooks near the door, stomping snow off of his boots.

"I'll make some coffee real quick for you. Then I will make breakfast."

"Sounds good."

She moved to the kitchen area, preparing food as he attended to the fire.

When she called him over he settled across from her. Today's fare was again oatmeal but that was okay because it was nice and hot, as was the coffee. He quickly dug in.

Miriam spoke. "I guess I will have to use the drape to bathe today. I don't want you to go back out into the bitter cold." She could hear the wind swirling as it slammed against the window and roof.

He grinned up at her and her stomach flipped. *What* was it about him? That crooked grin made her heart melt. Stop it, Miriam, she warned herself. You and Trevor will be parting ways someday soon. This made her a bit sad so she ate her food, looking down.

"While you are doing that, I'll bring in more wood, tend to the fire. That way I'll only have to go out once more to attend to Prince."

She nodded in silence, continuing to eat her breakfast.

Afterwards, she moved to prepare her bath. Pulling the drape carefully around the area, she undressed, shivering in the cold. She submerged her shoulders, sighing. The water was warm; Trevor must have added a pail of hot water.

She started to wash as she heard him leave to collect wood.

Today she would not have time to enjoy the hot water. She bathed quickly so she could dress then let the fire dry her hair. She pulled on her dark green wool dress with warm socks. Combing out her long hair, she pulled the drape back, seeing Trevor reading by the fire.

"The tub is free if you would like to use it." She moved toward the couch.

Setting his book aside, he stood, glancing down at her. "That's a good idea. I could use a bath."

She could see he had a roaring fire going. She settled down with her own book as she heard him moving about in the tub.

⊰━━━━━━●━●━━━━━━⊱

The next few days passed uneventfully. They did get more snow, but only inches instead of feet. Still, it added to what was already on the ground. Trevor thanked the gods that they had found this place. Otherwise, their lives would have been in danger. The weather continued to be cold but he was able to take Prince out for rides. Miriam came along so she could get some exercise and time outdoors too.

They were always half frozen when they returned but their jaunts did allow them some sunshine and Prince needed the exercise.

For now they had enough supplies for about another month. After that, if they were still here, he would have to hunt for food. Thanks to the pump outside, they would have plenty of water.

As Trevor groomed Prince after another trot, he contemplated again how long they would be here. Perhaps the chip could help out.

How long will we have to stay here? I know I have to stay with her until I can get her home safely.

He waited a moment for an answer. After a minute passed, he got an answer.

You must stay until your mission is complete. You are far from that task right now.

Trevor frowned. *I thought my mission was to keep her safe. Once I return her home, my mission should be complete, will it not?*

Several moments passed.

No. You will be given that information when your mission is complete. For now, you stay with her.

Trevor covered Prince, heading back to the cabin with his brow quirked, puzzled. Why would his mission not be complete then? He didn't understand, but he knew for now this would be all the information he would get.

He entered the warm cabin, shaking off the cold.

⊰━━━━━━●━●━━━━━━⊱

Miriam put her book down as Trevor entered. They had been here over a week, but the weather was still bitterly cold.

She rose quickly. "I have some coffee heated. Let me get you some."

She went to fill a large mug, bringing it over to Trevor on the couch.

He accepted the coffee silently, staring into the fire. Usually, Trevor was chatty. After a few moments, Miriam figured maybe something was wrong.

"What is it, Trevor? Is something wrong?" she asked.

His blue eyes met hers as he sipped. "No, no, there's nothing wrong." Sitting back, he cradled the mug in his large hands, his gaze moving back to the fire.

She settled next to him with her own coffee. She was tired of reading; it was sunny today. She was going to suggest taking a ride with Prince, but she could see Trevor had something on his mind.

"Trevor, *talk* to me. I can see you are uneasy about something."

He met her dark eyes. Remember Trevor, she is smart, and attuned to your moods by now. He needed to be careful.

He shrugged casually, sipping at his brew. "I was just wondering how long we will have to stay here. We have enough rations for a while, but not for the entire winter…" his words drifted off.

"Do you think we will be here that long?"

"It's hard to say. If the weather stays cold, obviously the snow won't melt enough for Prince. It is too snowy to risk leaving yet. If I have to, I can hunt for food." Shrugging, he continued to gaze at the fire. "I guess we will just have to see what happens."

Miriam contemplated his words. She had been thinking the same thing, wondering how long their exile here in the little cabin would last. Fortunately they had found shelter, food, water, and firewood, the necessities. They were even able to bathe, thanks to the tub. Yes, it was roughing it, but for now they were comfortable, warm, and had each other for company.

She answered him. "I am not worried about it, Trevor. For now - we are snowbound. We will have to make the best of it."

He met her eyes. "Yep. We'll make the best of it - together."

27

Mid-December arrived. Toby was putting up a Christmas tree he had chopped down from the back property. He had a little fire going to keep the front room warm. He placed the tree in a corner by the fireplace, stepping back.

It looked fine tucked into the little corner; it just needed some candelabras and ornaments which were waiting on a nearby chair.

Stoically he decorated the tree even though he was far from being in the Christmas spirit. He had received word three weeks ago that his sister and Major Tompkins had disappeared from the Army unit when a vast snowstorm hit the area. The unit waited several days but after not finding them had no choice but to push on to pursue General Lee, eventually leaving the bad weather behind.

Toby glanced over at one of the front windows. He lit a candle for his sister every evening so that she could find her way back home to him. Knowing she was with Major Tompkins gave him great confidence they would survive. He did not know why, he just knew. So, he did what his sister would be doing. He carried on. With help from neighbors and friends, he was able to put in a late harvest. It should yield at least enough food to last until next spring, with maybe even some leftover to sell.

As he started placing ornaments on branches, he heard a soft knock on the door.

Curious as to who would be out so late when it was so cold and snowy, Toby went to the sturdy door to open it. Dr. David Irvin was standing on the little porch, snowflakes falling gently on his hat and coat. Grinning, Toby motioned him inside. David stomped snow from his boots carefully before entering.

"Hello, Toby!" He hung his coat and hat on pegs in the hallway as Toby closed the door against the cold.

"Hi, David! Come in by the fire. What are you doing out on such a cold night?"

Toby knew the doctor had returned from the war at the beginning of December, his enlistment being up. They kept each other company, both worried about the same woman.

David turned to him. He was wearing a flannel shirt with black slacks. He put his hands near the fire to warm them, then answered the younger man. "I thought you could use some company tonight. I know I could," he turned to Toby.

"Can I get you something warm to drink? Coffee, maybe a brandy? I think I got some around here somewhere..."

"A brandy would be fine if you can manage it and you join me."

Toby turned to go into the kitchen pantry in the back. He was pretty sure he had a bottle tucked there.

While Toby went to fetch drinks, David noticed the Christmas tree Toby was in the process of decorating. He knew the younger man put it up with hopes that he would see his sister soon. He sighed as he heard Toby returning.

"Yep, found it just where I thought it was. Let me get a couple of glasses." He went to the big dining room chest, removing crystal flutes. He brought them over, carefully pouring out brandy for the two of them.

"Here ya go," he handed one to David.

David clinked his glass against Toby's. "Merry Christmas to you, Toby."

Toby smiled, then gestured for the doctor to sit in the comfortable chaise placed in front of the fire. Toby joined him.

"I can see you are decorating your tree," David remarked.

"Yep, I was just starting the ornaments when you knocked," Toby took a slow sip of brandy as did David.

David eventually stood, placing his glass on the side table. "Let me help you with that. I have a small one already up. Yours is quite beautiful."

Toby stood too, moving to the ornament box. The candelabras were already glowing on the tree.

As David proceeded to help decorate the tree, he noticed Toby's candle in the front window. He placed one there every evening for his sister. They both missed her terribly. David was not even sure she had survived the snowstorm, and sometimes sadness overwhelmed him. He didn't share his thoughts with Toby yet. He wanted the man to at least have the joy of Christmas in his heart.

"How are you doing, Toby?" he asked casually as he placed homemade glass ornaments on the tree.

Toby was placing an angel his sister had made long ago on the top bough. He glanced over at the doctor. "I'm doing all right, I guess," he said.

"I miss her too, you know. Especially this time of year," David said quietly.

Sighing, Toby stepped away, reaching for more ornaments as he sipped a bit of brandy. "I miss her every day, but I know someday, somehow, she will return."

David faced him, deciding he had to be truthful with Toby. "Toby," he hesitated, "I want you to prepare yourself for the fact that Miriam... well, she may not come back," David had tears in his eyes.

Toby shook his head. "No, I don't believe that."

"Toby, how could she still be alive after all of this time?"

"I don't know, doc. I just know here," he gestured to his head, then to his heart, "and here, that she is. I just know." He shrugged, turning back to the tree.

David wished he could be as confident as Toby seemed to be. For both of their sakes, he hoped Toby was correct and his doubts were unfounded.

They continued to decorate the tree, making small talk and sipping brandy.

<hr />

Christmas day dawned bright with light snowflakes falling on new snow. As Toby walked through the town he glanced around. Everything was beautiful covered in a white frosting. The church spire pierced the winter sky. Services would begin in a couple hours.

Toby was on his way to David Irvin's home with a present for his friend. In the general store he had found some cigars he knew David would enjoy. He had also brought a fine brandy he had splurged on for the two of them.

Glancing away from the church, Toby foraged through the snow to a large white Victorian home with a single shingle out front which read in bold black lettering "Dr. David Irvin, Medical Doctor." David's home featured a wide white porch and several stairs leading up to the black door that had an elaborate gold knocker on it.

Toby climbed the stairs and knocked on the door sharply. Soon he heard David moving toward the door, opening it. The two were planning on attending church mass together, but first they would exchange gifts.

David was still wearing his maroon silky robe over long warm pajamas. Grinning, Toby stepped into the elaborate foyer, removing his outerwear as he placed a pair of slippers on his feet.

"Merry Christmas, doc David!" He came over to give the other man a warm hug.

"Merry Christmas, Toby!" the doctor replied, returning the hug.

David gestured him over to the fireplace in his living room, located beyond double French doors. His home was decorated lavishly but comfortably. It was larger compared to the Klarks' house so that David could see patients in his home. The walls were decorated with a cream moiré wallpaper. He chose wine and crimson for furniture with lots of wooden accents. The home was lovely and cozy. Toby spent a lot of time here in front of the elaborate fireplace just chatting with David.

Today, David had a few gifts under his tree. Toby went to place his own gifts among them.

"Welcome! Come by the fire. We will chat for a while. I have coffee and croissants for us to enjoy," David gestured to his table where a silver platter was laid out.

Toby helped himself to coffee, placing a croissant on a plate. He settled back into crimson cushions as David did the same.

"Cold out there?" David asked casually as he poured out coffee, sitting back.

"It's snowing lightly, but I bundled up, so the short walk wasn't that cold," Toby sipped at the hot rich coffee.

David nodded as he sipped his brew.

"With the freshly fallen snow, our little town looks quite beautiful, especially with all of the lights and candles in the window displays."

"Yes, everyone is trying to forget the war, so they have tried to keep the Christmas spirit alive. As you and I have done."

"I did it mostly for Miriam."

"Yes, I know Toby," David replied quietly.

Toby sighed. "Do you think she knows it's Christmas?" Toby knew his sister was very religious, as he was.

165

David met his eyes. "I do not know, Toby. Somewhere in her heart, she probably knows." David's gaze moved to the fire.

They finished breakfast, then opened gifts.

David was delighted with his cigars and brandy, profusely thanking Toby. Toby carefully unwrapped a couple of gifts. The doctor had given him a new warm winter coat. It was of fine quality. He also received a pair of new winter boots. Toby knew the man had spent quite a bit of money on his gifts and blushed slightly. "David, you never should have–"

The doctor interrupted him. "Bosh! I have money. I want to spend it on special people in my life. Please accept and wear it in good health." He knew Toby was almost healed up from the wound he had received which had brought him home in November.

Toby smiled, placing the items back in the boxes, putting the wrapping paper over them. He placed them back under the tree.

David stood, clapping his knees. "Please excuse me for a moment as I go upstairs to change for services."

"Of course, doc. I'll help myself to more coffee."

"Please do," David replied as he climbed the elaborate wooden stairs.

<hr>

The church was decorated with Christmas trees with red ribbon and simple pine boughs. The stained glass windows threw colors over the worshipers as they sang Christmas hymns, listening to the service. Toby and the doctor stood in the middle of the crowd. It seemed the entire town had turned out for services. Children and babies moved restlessly as the adults prayed and sang.

After services, there was a Christmas festival for everyone to enjoy in the church social room.

Everyone gathered to enjoy Christmas punch, cookies, and sweets, visiting with neighbors and loved ones. Toby and David joined in, chatting with neighbors and friends, both remembering the woman they loved and missed.

She was with them in spirit.

Life went on in the little cabin in the forest.

They had enough supplies to last for several more weeks; they had been stranded now about three weeks. Trevor was thinking soon he would have to take Prince into the surrounding woods, maybe try to get a deer to supplement their supplies. He pumped water and chopped wood daily. Miriam kept busy cleaning and preparing meals. Their days fell into a certain rhythm. Afternoons and evenings were spent talking by the fire. Actually, Miriam did most of the talking while Trevor listened.

He learned she was an emotional, sensitive woman as well as intelligent. She was also religious and tried to talk to him about the subject. Trevor would always change the conversation deftly, not wanting to discuss this particular topic.

Today he was out chopping wood early; it was sunny but extremely cold. His breath hissed out as he stacked logs to take into the cabin. Miriam was still sleeping when he had come out, but that had been a good hour ago. He figured she would be up soon making breakfast. He was hungry.

He grabbed the logs up in his strong arms, heading for the door. Opening it abruptly, he forgot to knock because his arms were full.

Glancing around he saw Miriam in the tub, the drape down. She was sitting upright bathing, her beautiful breasts exposed. Before she gasped and could put her arms over her chest, he got a quick view of perfect round globes with pink nipples erect, pert.

She quickly submerged her body in the water, cheeks pink.

Trevor muttered an apology, throwing the logs to the floor as he quickly exited the cabin. Obviously she needed more time this morning.

He went to the shed to saddle Prince and take him out for a long run, trying to erase the sight of how lovely she was - everywhere!

———————•◉•———————

Miriam was so embarrassed she had not finished up by the time Trevor entered. She must have slept in a bit later than normal and had felt comfortable leaving the drape down, feeling she had enough time. Since she had clearly been wrong about that, she started moving faster, washing her hair and rinsing it out before quickly toweling off.

She reached for her brown dress, donning it with thick black stockings and low boots. She braided her long blonde hair to the side. Looking in the small mirror, she decided that would have to do.

Miriam found breakfast rations and began preparing the food. She had the meal ready swiftly with the table set, coffee all ready to pour. She sat down at the table and waited. And waited...

———————•◉•———————

There was a tentative knock at the door. Miriam rose to open the door to Trevor, who did not meet her eyes. He took his outerwear off, hanging it by the door.

He turned to her and she gestured toward the table.

"The food has been ready for a while. Would you like me to reheat some stuff?"

He moved to the table. "No, it will be fine as long as the coffee is nice and hot."

"Yes, it is," she answered, pouring coffee into mugs, taking her seat.

They both dug into the meal, carefully looking down at their plates, both trying to ignore what happened earlier.

Miriam cleared her throat, her dark eyes looking up. "How is the weather?"

"The same as usual, sunny but very cold. I figure we are well into December."

December. It must be around Christmas time. There were plenty of evergreen trees around. There was a spot right by the window that would be perfect for a Christmas tree. She hesitated, wondering if he would want to take a trip out to the woods to cut one down to bring back.

"December, around Christmas time?" she asked.

Her question startled Trevor. Yes, Christmas was December 25th, was it not? It was probably that time of year or close to it.

"Yes, probably," he answered indifferently.

She hesitated, then went ahead. "Would you mind the two of us taking a trip into the woods with Prince to cut down a tree for Christmas?"

Trevor was startled but then he remembered just how religious she was. It would mean a lot to her to get a tree and decorate it - and wasn't it the tradition to give gifts? He did not have a gift for her but he could certainly give her the gift of a tree.

"Sure, Miriam, we can get a tree if you like," he answered, his blue eyes meeting hers. "We can go right after breakfast if you want. It will give us time to find one and haul it back here with Prince."

Her smile lit up her whole face. His gut plummeted. Watch it, Trevor. Yes, she's gorgeous, beautiful, and kind. Everything a man could want in a woman. She was also about five hundred years older than him.

"Wonderful!" she responded, finishing her meal.

Trevor ate the rest of his food in silence.

They bundled up in their warm outer garments and boots for their trek outside.

<hr />

Prince picked a path carefully through the woods, the same path they had taken many times so it was pretty smooth and packed for the horse.

They reached a clearing ringed with evergreens. They had their choice of any tree there.

Dismounting, Trevor helped Miriam down from the horse as she gasped, clapping her gloved hands together.

"Oh, this is just so perfect," she extended her arms, twirling to encompass the clearing. Her blonde hair flew under her knit cap. She smiled, turning to him as she grabbed his arm.

"Quick! Get the saw! I can't wait to choose!" She was excited, happy. Trevor smiled down at her.

"Yep. Let me grab it." He had strapped it to the saddle, bringing along a length of rope to drag the tree back to the cabin.

As she walked among the trees, Miriam lifted her face up and gasped. "They are all so tall!" she exclaimed.

Trevor followed her closely. "Remember, we have to get one that will fit through the door," he noted. "There are various sizes but we have to keep that in mind."

Miriam was excited, having fun just walking through the forest, amazed and awed at the beauty all around them. Snow-covered boughs drooped to the ground while higher ones branched out above them, snow-laden with icicles here and there. They gleamed, winking in the sunshine.

Trevor had the rope looped over his broad shoulder. He carried the saw in gloved hands carefully; he'd made sure it was sharp before leaving. Glancing about, he could see there were many trees to choose from. He would leave that particular task up to Miriam. He knew she would enjoy doing so.

She stopped at a tree that was slightly taller than Trevor. Since he was six feet four inches, the tree had to be about seven feet. That would make it about one foot too tall for the door. Looking at the trunk he could see it was high, so if he cut up higher it should work.

Miriam turned to him with beseeching eyes. "This one..." she said tentatively, gently touching a pine bough. Snow trickled down.

"I think I can get it to fit through the door. Stand back a bit," he warned.

She did so, backing up several feet. Trevor went to work on the trunk, sawing back and forth. The tree swayed as he cut it, snow falling all around the ground and onto Trevor.

It was surprisingly easy to cut down; it fell in a matter of minutes. It fell in a straight line, right at Miriam's feet as she jumped back.

"It's perfect!" she exclaimed.

Carefully he placed the saw on the ground and picked up the rope, tying it to the trunk of the tree. Once that was accomplished, he grabbed the rope and saw.

"We can go back to Prince now. I will tie the tree to the wagon."

"Don't you need help?" she asked.

"No, I've got it, Miriam. Not an issue," he assured her. He picked up the rope, slowly turning the tree towards the path of their footprints.

They backtracked to Prince, soon arriving back at the clearing. Trevor sheathed the saw, then proceeded to tie the tree to the sled securely, knotting it tightly.

When he was finished, he mounted Prince, reaching down for Miriam to help tug her up behind him. Turning Prince toward the cabin, the tree slid behind them as they headed back. Miriam had a big smile on her face.

◆━━━━━●◉●━━━━━◆

Arriving back at the shed, Trevor instructed Miriam to get a large tub of warm water for the tree. He would strap it down where she wanted to place it.

Happily she went inside, removing her outer garments. She heated a huge pail of water. When it was warm to the touch, she found a large steel tub, placing it in the center of the room. Just then she heard Trevor knocking.

She opened the door to him, seeing nothing but evergreen boughs. Trevor's voice could be heard outside.

"I have to push the thing all the way inside in front of the fire so you need to move to the kitchen area," he informed her. "Let me know when you're there."

She quickly moved to the table. "All right. I'm at the table," she called.

Trevor heaved, pushing the tree all the way inside the cabin until it was touching the far wall. He entered and tried to see if he could close the door. No, part of the stump was still blocking it. He glanced up at Miriam who had her hands clasped to her lips in joy.

"I have to go get the saw, shave a few more inches off so we can fit it, to be able to close the door."

"Fine!" she responded as he left.

She moved over to the freshly cut evergreen, touching the stiff pine needles. It was cold from being snow-covered, but she knew it would look lovely in front of the window. She had some candles she could display, but no ornaments. Perhaps she could make some out of supplies. She had been secretly knitting Trevor a sweater out of some material she had managed to squander from the Army. It was navy blue, which would look fantastic with his blue eyes.

The man she was thinking of entered, quickly going to work with the saw. Soon enough, he had shaved off several inches. He tried pushing it into the room again. This time it slid in completely, leaving wood shavings at their entrance.

He looked up. "I'll have to clean up the wood shavings, then I'll put up the tree."

"Never mind that for now, Trevor. I'll do it after we put up the tree." Miriam could not wait to see it upright.

"Fine." He could see the tub waiting filled with water. "Miriam," he said in chagrin, "you should have left the heavy water for me to carry!" He frowned.

"It's all right, Trevor. I managed it."

Sighing, he went to the center of the tree, grabbing and pulling it upright. Slowly the tree moved upwards until it was standing straight and tall. The top bough brushed the ceiling slightly, but that was not a problem. Trevor moved the tree over to the tub, placing it in the middle. Holding the tree upright, he glanced over his shoulder at the woman behind him.

"Is this where you want it?" he asked.

"Yes, that's perfect!" she declared, smiling up at the evergreen.

"All right. Can you come here and hold it upright so I can get ropes to strap it to the tub?"

"Of course." She took his place, putting her hand through the pine boughs, grabbing the center trunk firmly. "I've got it," she told him.

Releasing it, he glanced down at her. "I'll go get some ropes from the shed."

He left her holding the tree upright. Soon he was back with several lengths of rope for the task, closing the door to keep the heat in once more. He removed his coat and gloves, then went about the task of securing the tree with four ropes.

When he felt it was secure enough, he informed Miriam to step back, grabbing the tree first to make sure it did not fall. She released the tree, stepping back. When she was clear he slowly stepped away.

The tree stood securely, the boughs spread and giving off a fresh pine scent. It brushed the ceiling, tall, filling the area in front of the window perfectly. It actually now hid the small window, making the room a bit dimmer even in sunlight.

Miriam approached slowly, stroking one of the pine boughs, feeling the prickliness of the needle. "Oh, Trevor. It is wonderful!" She turned to him. "I could not ask for a more wonderful Christmas gift. Thank you!" Her brown eyes were soft and moist.

"Merry Christmas, Miriam!" He grinned down at her.

Swiping at her tears, she came to him, hugging him briefly, feeling strong muscles under his warm shirt. She stepped away, blushing.

"I'll see to our mid-day meal," she moved toward the kitchen area.

Trevor glanced at the fire and then at the wood shavings by the entrance. He would attend to both as she prepared food.

◆━━━━●●●━━━━◆

Miriam could not wait to decorate their tree. She had already put several candles out in the kitchen area as well as on the side table near the couch. The pine scent was lovely. She just loved the smell emanating from the evergreen.

She informed Trevor in the afternoon she wanted to go out back to look for possible decorations. Pine cones and such, if she could. Trevor said he would accompany her. They put on their outerwear and boots again.

Walking in the deep snow, they headed towards the woods behind the cabin, not needing Prince for this particular chore. Their clothes would get wet from snow but they could change, drying out clothes near the fire.

Miriam managed to find some pinecones on the ground near an evergreen and gathered several in a sack she had brought. It was still clear but cold; however, moving around kept them warm. She glanced around the woods, seeing if there was anything else she could use. Several wood boughs had dropped in the woods from the weight of snow. She snapped off several sticks, a dozen or so, knowing she could use them with some scrap material to make crude ornaments.

She stood, facing Trevor who was watching her curiously.

Smiling, she met his eyes. "These will do just fine."

"Are you ready to head back?"

"Yep!"

He reached for the sack. "Here, I'll carry that for you."

"No, I'm fine, Trevor. I have it. It is not heavy," she assured him.

He shoved his gloved hands in his pockets. "Let's head back in then."

Smiling, Miriam turned to follow their footsteps back to the warm little cabin.

◆━━━━●●●━━━━◆

That evening, Trevor read after bathing as Miriam fashioned ornaments on the sticks, sewing fabric to make bright flag ornaments. The fire crackled as they spent time in companionable silence.

173

Later on, Trevor tossed and turned as he inhaled the scent of pine, remembering Miriam's lovely breasts, trying not to think about it. He finally drifted to sleep with her beautiful face on his mind, then in his dreams.

29

The next morning, after bathing and eating, Miriam placed the flag-like ornaments and pinecones on the evergreen, decorating it for the holiday.

When she was through, Trevor could see the bright colors were festive against the dark green of the tree. The pine cones offered natural color. The entire effect was cheerful. Once she lit the candles later on it would light up their tree. He could see how much fun she was having decorating as he sipped coffee after fetching water and firewood.

He checked his chip. *When is Christmas Day?* After a few moments, he received a response. *It is in two days. Christmas Eve is tomorrow night.* Satisfied with this response, he knew Miriam would probably want to know this information.

As they were eating their mid-day meal, he casually informed her, "You know, Christmas Eve is tomorrow night." His blue eyes rose to hers.

Miriam looked startled. "How did you know that?"

"I have a pocket watch and it has the days on it," he said quietly.

Miriam arched a brow. "I have never seen this pocket watch."

"That's because it is a pocket watch. I don't usually have it in view."

"Oh," she murmured, taking in this information. That meant she needed to finish Trevor's sweater tonight while he was sleeping. She knew this would not be difficult since it was almost done. She would put it in a box with string, placing it under the tree Christmas morning. She smiled thinking about giving Trevor a special Christmas gift. Had anyone else ever given him one? She suspected not.

They continued to eat their mid-day meal in silence.

Afterwards, they bundled up. Trevor took her for a ride on Prince, as it was sunny outside although still extremely cold. The fresh air and the beauty of the landscape always lifted her spirits. She raised her face to the sky, letting the sunlight kiss her face.

After their jaunt, they shook off their outer garments. Miriam made hot fresh coffee.

As they enjoyed their coffee, they sat near the fire, talking.

Late that afternoon, the wind started howling around the little cabin again. Trevor went out to the little porch to check on the weather. Sure enough, it was snowing. Not the blizzard they had traveled through, but a steady fluffy snow hurled around by the wind.

Closing the door snugly against the elements, he turned to Miriam. "It's snowing again," he informed her, going to the fireplace to throw extra logs on.

She rose and started lighting candles and their lanterns against the dark afternoon. It was as dark as sundown, although that was still about an hour away.

"I'll put the soup on so it will be hot in time for dinner," she stood, placing her mug on the table.

"All right," he replied, picking up his own mug. He contemplated the flames and their pretty Christmas tree as he waited for dinner.

Soon enough, Miriam called him over to eat. They both enjoyed the hot vegetable soup she had made along with homemade muffins. Everything was hot and tasty, and Trevor was hungry.

Miriam ate in silence, occasionally glancing at their Christmas tree.

"Thank you, Trevor, for getting a tree for us. I really appreciate it."

Her dark eyes met his as he glanced up from his food. "You've already thanked me, Miriam. It is my Christmas gift to you." He shrugged. "I don't have anything else to offer for the holiday."

"It is the *best* present I could ever receive," she emphasized. "I absolutely love it. It makes the cabin so cozy and festive." She continued to eat soup as she studied him.

He met her gaze, smiling, and her heart fluttered. All he had to do was smile and she was a puddle. *What* was up with that? No other man had been able to make her insides melt with just a simple smile. She tried to ignore the fact that she was greatly attracted to Trevor. What woman wouldn't be, with his handsome features, gorgeous eyes, and fine physique?

Tamping down her thoughts, she looked back down at her bowl.

"I am so glad you like it, Miriam," he replied as he ate his dinner.

After dinner, Miriam hurriedly cleaned up. She washed and dried dishes, putting them away as Trevor attended to the fire.

Their usual routine was to chat by the fire or read after dinner. Since she saw Trevor pick up a book, she did the same as they snuggled by the fire.

Miriam enjoyed looking up at the tree, lit up by the candles and the festive ornaments gleaming. Smiling slowly, she looked back down at her book.

◄ ⦿ ⦿ ►

That evening, as she could hear Trevor sleeping soundly below, she finished knitting his sweater for him.

Finishing up, she inspected it. She knit a high collar to keep his neck warm. It was cozy and soft. She stroked the material, knowing it would look marvelous on him.

She packed it away in a box, wrapping a red ribbon she had found around it, putting the box under her bed for now.

She snuggled under her quilts, dousing the lantern as she listened to the wind howl around the roof.

She drifted off soon, thinking about tomorrow which was Christmas Eve. As she slept, it wasn't visions of sugar plums dancing in her head; it was dreams of a handsome man with deep blue eyes and raven black hair.

Christmas Eve dawned sunny with a light snow falling.

After bathing, Miriam put on her heavy garments to take a stroll around the property. It was not quite as cold as it had been in the past several days.

Leaving the small porch, she could see Trevor chopping and stacking wood for the day. She smiled, moving toward him and joining him.

Trevor glanced down at her as he placed a log on the pile.

"What brings you out so early?"

She took a deep breath, inhaling the fresh air. Snow lightly fell on her knit hat and hair. "I wanted to take a bit of a walk, get some fresh air." She looked down at the pile of logs stacked neatly. "I can help you stack the logs," she offered.

"No, it's fine, Miriam. I've got it," he replied.

"Trevor, I am quite capable of stacking firewood, I do it all the time at home. Plus, I could use the exercise." Her dark eyes met his.

"All right. I'll chop, you can stack," he moved over to the logs he had to split. There were about a dozen or so.

They worked together in the light snow. As she stacked the wood, Miriam warmed up further. It felt good to be outside, moving around.

When they were finished, Trevor insisted he would carry in the wood stack. Miriam told him she wanted to stroll around the property for a while. He warned her to stay close to the cabin and not enter the woods.

She assured him she would comply as he started carrying wood inside.

Miriam moved around to the shed where Prince was munching on hay Trevor had provided. She could see a large dish with water.

As she entered, Prince whinnied. Approaching him, Miriam stroked his velvety nose softly. "Hello, big guy," she greeted. He nudged her, chuffing. Her hand stroked down his silky mane and Prince nudged her again affectionately. "You are a handsome one, aren't you?" she murmured before stepping back. "But I am interrupting your morning meal. You go ahead and eat, Prince."

Prince nodded his head, going back to chomping on hay. What an intelligent animal!

Smiling, Miriam moved back outside, taking a long walk around the yard. Her clothes were getting damp from the snow, but when she returned she planned to take a long hot bath.

A half hour passed. Entering the cabin, Miriam stomped off snow from her garments and boots. Trevor was by the fire, sipping coffee, contemplating the flames.

Miriam removed her outer garments, hanging them by the door. Turning to Trevor, she smiled. The hem of her dress and undergarments were wet from the snow.

"I am going to get a new outfit, take a hot bath," she said.

"Fine. While you are doing that, I am going to take Prince into the woods. I have been thinking about what we could have for a Christmas meal... I think I can bag a deer. We can use the venison for meals for weeks. I plan to field dress it in the woods and pack the various meats in a big ice chest I will put outside the door. It will stay cold there." He stood, glancing down at her. "That will give you some time to take a nice leisurely bath."

She smiled. "I think that is a perfect idea. I have vegetables I can add for our Christmas meal, plus muffins. I think we even have rations for me to make plum pudding for dessert." She knew she would be cooking the rest of the day after her bath, but that would help fill up time. She was excited about Christmas day.

Trevor moved to the door to put on his winter gear. "I have a shotgun out in the shed. I will probably be gone a couple of hours."

"All right. I'll bathe, then make muffins and plum pudding. Tomorrow, I will make the venison roast and vegetables for our Christmas feast."

"Sounds good, Miriam. I'll see you later on." He exited the door as Miriam climbed the stairs to change out of her wet clothes.

Miriam put about five pails of hot water in the tub. It was steamy and hot. She took her time bathing, letting the hot water relax her. As it started to cool, she started washing, soaping up her hair and body, then rinsing thoroughly.

Emerging from the tub, she quickly dressed. It was chilly so she would feed the fire before she started baking.

Donning a black dress trimmed with a white lace collar, she pulled up thick black tights, adding sensible black shoes. She dried her hair quickly by the fire, brushing the long tresses out until they were dry. She left her thick hair down, pushing if off of her face.

Miriam headed towards the kitchen, inhaling the piney scent the tree was giving off. She paused to check the water level, adding more water to the tub. Finishing the task, she went to the kitchen to check the pantry for the supplies she would need.

She was going to make the muffins first. She searched out the dough mix. They were getting low on it but she did not care. It was Christmas. She would use it to make the muffins and the plum pudding.

Smiling, she set about baking, lighting the coal stove before rolling out the dough on the table with a wooden spindle.

<hr />

Trevor returned to the cabin. He could smell muffins baking. Miriam was in the process of mixing sauce for plum pudding.

Smiling, she glanced up at him. "Were you successful?" she asked.

"Yep. Found a big buck about a half hour out. Took him down quickly. It took me some time to field dress him. I am going to start cutting the meat up in the shed. It will take me awhile." He grabbed a muffin because he had not eaten a mid-day meal. He poured himself a cup of coffee to warm up. They always kept a pot on the stove.

"If you are hungry, I can fix you something," she remarked.

"No. This snack will hold me for a bit."

She smiled, going back to her task as he went outside again, firmly closing the door behind him.

The task ahead would be a bloody one. He fully intended to bathe after putting all of the meat in the chest. They would be well-stocked for a good month. The way the weather had turned out, he knew they would need it.

Whistling to himself, Trevor headed to the shed. He reined Prince outside to a post with water because he did not want the horse witnessing the upcoming task.

◂•————————•◉ •————————•▸

Trevor packed the last of the meat in the chest, using a towel to wipe off as much blood as he could. Fortunately most of it was on his hands, not his outerwear. He went to fetch Prince, giving him extra hay and fresh water. Prince whinnied, lying down in the warm hay, content to rest for now.

Trevor pet him, then turned to go to the cabin.

Entering, he could see Miriam was done baking and reading by the fire. She had a good blaze going. Trevor removed his heavy garments, stomping snow off of his boots as he tugged them off.

Miriam placed her book in her lap, smiling at him. It was now late afternoon, pretty close to suppertime.

"I am going to take a bath. Feel pretty grimy after putting the meat together."

Trevor went to the fire, placing a large pail of water over the heat. Then he went to a chest where he stored his clothes. He removed a green plaid flannel shirt, warm black pants, socks, white undergarments. Taking the clothes to the tub area, he pulled the drape around, covering the area.

He returned to the fire. When the water was sufficiently hot, he poured it into the tub. He had emptied the thing a few days ago, so it was still pretty clean. He knew they would both want to use it Christmas morning.

"Well. I'll see you in a few minutes," he informed Miriam, who had picked her book back up.

"Take your time, Trevor," she responded.

Trevor removed his clothes, sinking into the hot water, letting it relax his muscles after all of his chores today. After a while, he started bathing, soaping up everywhere, dipping his head to scrub at his hair too. Rinsing off, he grabbed a towel and dried off, pulling on his clothes.

Returning to the fireplace, he used the towel to continue to rub at his black locks. He combed his hair back off of his face.

He glanced over at Miriam. She stood, putting her book on the side table.

"I'll make dinner now. You must be starving."

"Yep. I could certainly eat."

"I still have soup left from yesterday along with muffins. I'll go heat it up. I'll get you some coffee now." She moved to the kitchen area.

"Sounds good!"

Trevor lit the candles and lanterns as sundown approached.

Glancing outside, he could see it was snowing lightly. It looked pretty in the glow of the outside lantern. He closed the door, going to set the table for dinner.

When the soup was hot, they sat down to enjoy their dinner. Trevor had two portions as he was so hungry. When satisfied, he helped Miriam clean up the dishes.

They moved to the fireplace. Trevor went to his chest, removing his whiskey. Finding two glasses in the kitchen, he returned to Miriam seated on the couch.

"Since it is Christmas Eve, I think it only appropriate we have a toast or two." He poured out whiskey in both glasses, handing one to Miriam.

After corking the bottle, he settled next to her. They clinked glasses. "Merry Christmas!" he said.

Miriam smiled at him. "Merry Christmas to you, Trevor." She slowly sipped at the whiskey. It was strong but smooth, immediately warming her belly. She took slow sips as she looked at the man seated next to her.

"So, it is Christmas Eve. What shall we talk about?" she asked.

Trevor was silent for a moment, studying the fire, sipping whiskey. His deep blue eyes met hers in the firelight. "What about home? Do you miss Toby?" he asked quietly.

Miriam gave a deep sigh. "Yes," she murmured, "especially now, around the holiday. We always exchanged gifts, went to church services, socialized with friends. Then we would come home to a big meal I cooked and enjoy a libation, like now."

A wistful smile crossed her face as she gazed at the fire.

Trevor sighed. "I don't when or how, but someday I will reunite the two of you," he promised solemnly.

She met his eyes, those gorgeous long-lashed eyes. It was unfair for a man to have such beautiful eyes. She chased away her thoughts. "How long do you think we will be stranded here?"

"With the weather as cold as it is, it won't melt for a while. I would say at least another month. We are heading into January and that is the coldest time of the year."

"You mean it could get *colder* than it already is?!"

"Yep. This weather might seem mild in a week or two. We could see zero or sub-zero temperatures if this type of weather front continues." He sipped his whiskey, meeting her eyes.

Miriam looked aghast. Then she remembered Januarys in Pennsylvania. Yes, it could get quite cold there too, but this far south in Virginia? To her, that was just strange. Somehow she felt it was fated that she and Trevor were trapped here. For what purpose? She did not know yet; perhaps she never would.

She went silent, sipping her drink, contemplating tomorrow. She was really looking forward to Christmas morning.

After they both bathed, she planned to bring his gift down to him, then prepare their Christmas meal. Even though she was not at home with family and friends, she was with Trevor. He was very special to her. She tried to ignore the reasons why.

Trevor topped off their glasses again and they sipped, chatting before turning in for the evening.

31

Christmas morning dawned bright with sunshine.

Miriam quickly pushed back her quilts and pulled the gift package for Trevor out. She was hoping to get it under their tree before he woke.

Hearing silence, she figured he might still be sleeping. As she crept down the stairs, she could see him on the couch, one arm flung wide with his head turned into the cushions. It was barely light outside yet.

Quickly, she placed his gift under their tree. Turning to the embers in the fire, she quietly placed enough logs on it so that it flamed up.

She could see the quilts had slipped a bit on the man lying on the couch, so she gently covered him back up.

Miriam returned to her bed, waiting until she heard him moving about. They would both need to use the bathtub. She planned to make pancakes with fruit this morning. Later, she would make the venison roast.

She dove under her warm quilts, chasing away the chill from being downstairs. She snuggled up to her pillow, eventually drifting back to sleep.

◄━━━━━━━━●◉●━━━━━━━━►

Trevor's eyes fluttered open. Lifting his head, he could see someone had tended to the fire because it was burning cheerily.

He swiped black hair out of his eyes, slowly pushing the quilts away. Had Miriam been up already? He always rose before she did. Looking outside, he could see it was clear and sunny. It was well into the morning. The sun was bright, reflecting off of the snow.

Wiping sleep from his eyes, he went to put coffee on. Then he returned to attend to the fire. After dressing and coffee, he would go out to split wood as was his usual routine first thing in the morning.

Curiously, he glanced upstairs, but he heard no movement. If Miriam had been up, she must have gone back to sleep.

Shaking his head, Trevor finished his coffee, dressing to go outdoors to attend to Prince and split logs. He also needed to bring in the venison roast so it could thaw out for dinner later. He headed outside, clicking the door shut behind him.

Miriam woke when she heard the door closing. Trevor must be up.

She grabbed the special velvet green gown she had been saving for today, as well as her warm black tights with boots. After bathing, she would make breakfast.

Returning downstairs she could see Trevor had attended to the fire. She heard him chopping wood out by the woodpile.

Making sure the drape was secure around the tub area, she added a couple pails of hot water before bathing quickly. Toweling off, she dressed before going by the fire to dry her hair out as she brushed.

Miriam headed to the kitchen, finding her supplies for breakfast. As she did so, the door opened. Trevor entered wearing his heavy coat and clothes.

"Ah, you're up," he remarked, placing a pile of wood near the fireplace. He stood, dusting off his hands. "Bathed and dressed already." He admired the green velvet dress. It showed off her curves nicely.

She smiled at him, busy preparing breakfast. "Yes. Merry Christmas, Trevor!"

"Merry Christmas to you!" He glanced at the tub area. "Mind if I clean up a bit before breakfast?"

"No, of course not. In fact, the water should still be warm."

"All right, good." He went to get warm clothes. Today a red flannel shirt and dark pants with his boots. Taking the items into the tub area, he hung the drape around before disrobing.

Miriam smiled again, drinking her coffee and finishing preparing breakfast for them as he bathed.

It wasn't long before Trevor joined her, his dark wet hair making his blue eyes even bluer, bright against the black wet hair. He had donned a red flannel shirt with warm pants. He looked scrumptious. Miriam tried to concentrate on her pancakes and coffee instead of how delicious the man looked.

"Were you up earlier?" he questioned her.

"Yes. I was up a little before dawn, came down and attended to the fire," she glanced at the tree where she had placed his gift. It was exactly where she had left it. He must not have noticed it yet. She turned her attention back to her meal.

"I have already finished my morning chores. What would you like to do this Christmas morning?" Trevor sipped at his coffee as he studied her.

"Well," she paused, sipping from her own cup, "I have something special for you under the tree. When we clean up, I would like for you to open your Christmas gift. Then, if you like, we can take Prince out for a run. When we return, I will start preparing our Christmas dinner. I noticed you put the roast in the sink."

"Yep, I brought it in earlier." He turned his head to look at their tree, noticing a box tied with bright red ribbon. Turning back, he chided her a bit. "Miriam, I was not expecting a gift. I don't have one to give you in return."

"You already gave me my gift. Our beautiful Christmas tree," she remarked, finishing up her pancakes.

Trevor's blue eyes studied her as he chewed his food, touched that she had thought enough of him to get him a gift. He wondered how she had managed such a feat way out here, with hardly any provisions

"Well, thank you very much for thinking of me."

She blushed a bit. "I hope you like it."

"I am sure I will." He finished up his food, sipping coffee and then pouring more for the two of them.

Miriam started collecting the dishes, washing them up quickly. She couldn't wait for Trevor to open his gift. She dried the dishes and put them away in the cupboards, wiping down the table as Trevor watched her, sipping coffee.

Finishing up, she turned to him. "All done?"

He rose from the table, taking his mug with him. "Yes."

She took his hand, quickly leading him over by the fire and the couch opposite it. "Sit here," she instructed.

He complied, placing his mug on the side table while Miriam went to their tree. The sun lit up the tree from the window a bit, shining on the ornaments Miriam made.

Picking up the box, she walked over to Trevor, handing it to him. "Merry Christmas, Trevor," she said as she sat beside him, excited.

Trevor smiled slowly. "I think this is the first Christmas gift I have ever received."

Her brows lifted. "None of your patients ever gave you a gift?"

"No, not really. Sometimes they would give me food or other items in gratitude, but never a Christmas gift."

"Open, open it!" she exclaimed, a big smile on her face.

Trevor slowly opened the box, removing the red ribbon as he lifted the lid. Nestled in the box was a navy blue sweater with a high collar. Gasping, he lifted it out of the box. He could see she had made it long enough for his height. The material was soft and heavy.

His eyes were wide as he turned to her. "However did you get the material to make this? I assume you made this yourself?" he asked in amazement.

She grinned broadly. "Yes, I did. I would secretly knit upstairs in the evenings. I got done just in time for the holiday. I had some material from the Army. They will not miss it. Do you like it?"

Trevor hugged her close to his chest, kissing the top of her head. "I love it!" he exclaimed. "It will keep me toasty when I have to go outside for chores and to wear around the cabin." His eyes were tender as he placed it in the box. "Thank you so much, Miriam. This means the world to me," he said quietly.

She blushed. "I am so glad you like it."

"Where did the fancy velvet dress come from," he gestured at her dress. "I know that did not come from the Army," he added.

She met his eyes. "I did bring some of my own clothes from home - in case there was not a need to wear my nursing uniform. Now, in hindsight, I am glad that I did," she answered.

Grinning, he placed his gift aside. "When you are ready and bundled up, I will take us out to get some fresh air. The snow has stopped. It is crisp and cold, but sunny.

She smiled. "That sounds like a plan."

Prince took them on a jaunt through the snow-covered forest. They were bundled up against the cold. The fresh air felt good on their faces. They took a longer ride than usual, enjoying being outside in the wintry landscape.

The horse was enjoying the extra exercise, prancing merrily through the snow and whinnying, glancing back at his riders.

After a while, Trevor turned him back to retrace the hoof prints leading back to the cabin. It was about mid-day and he knew it would take Miriam some time to put their dinner together.

A half hour later, they had arrived back at the cabin. Dismounting, Miriam headed inside as Trevor tended to the horse, rubbing him down well after the long ride. He brought fresh water and hay to the horse. Prince whinnied in joy, chomping on hay as Trevor patted him, then covered him with the blanket once again. Most likely the horse would rest through the afternoon. In the early evening Trevor would come out again to attend to him.

He returned to the cabin and saw that Miriam was busy in the kitchen. She had the coal oven fired up as she prepared the venison. Trevor turned to the fire to attend to it, stoking a good roaring fire.

After that, he turned to Miriam. "Do you need any help there?" he asked.

"No, I'm good, Trevor."

Trevor lit the candelabras on the tree and a lantern on the side table. He picked up his book, deciding to read while Miriam worked.

⊲ ∙∙∙∙∙∙∙∙∙∙∙●∙●∙∙∙∙∙∙∙∙∙∙∙ ⊳

They had muffins and fruit for a quick snack late in the afternoon when Miriam joined him. Afterwards, they chatted by the fire as the sun slowly set.

Soon, it was time for Miriam to finish making side dishes for dinner. She set the table, lighting more lanterns as Trevor attended to Prince.

Eventually Trevor joined Miriam in the kitchen. They ate their Christmas dinner in the flickering light of candles Miriam had placed on their table to make it a bit festive.

The venison was delicious the way she had prepared it. There was a mixture of vegetables and muffins as sides. She surprised him with plum pudding for dessert. He had never had it before; it was sweet and rich. He enjoyed every morsel, praising her on the fine meal she had prepared with their limited supplies. Trevor then helped Miriam wash and dry dishes, putting them away for her.

Finishing up, they went to the fire. Once again Trevor fetched his whiskey bottle, pouring out two glasses for them. They slowly sipped the liquor by the fire as she related Christmases past to him.

Trevor thought it was the best Christmas he had celebrated. He was pretty sure it was the *only* Christmas he had celebrated.

As December turned into January it became bitterly cold. The wind picked up and it snowed just about every day. Trevor went about his chores but instructed Miriam to stay inside. He made sure Prince was bedded down and covered from the cold. He had to use hot water pails to unfreeze the pump so they could still access water.

By the end of his daily chores outside Trevor would be freezing. He would come inside looking frosted like a snowman. Miriam made sure there was fresh water in the tub so he could take a hot bath to warm up. She kept the fire going for him and always had quilts ready for him. He would accept coffee from her gratefully and then settle by the fire.

Evenings were also very cold. Miriam could hear the wind whip around the roof of the little cabin. Although they always had a fire going at night, most of the heat traveled upstairs. Trevor had to depend on quilts to keep him warm.

As the month waned, Miriam contemplated the bed. It was large enough to fit two adults. If Trevor shared the bed with her, they would both be warmer through body heat. That was a dangerous thought, the two of them sleeping together. Not that she thought Trevor would take advantage of the situation - she was afraid that *she* might! It was still something to keep in mind, she thought as she drifted off to sleep.

The next morning, as usual, she bathed and then prepared breakfast while Trevor was chopping wood.

When he finally came in from chopping wood and attending to the horse, she gasped. He looked half frozen; even his dark brows had frost crusted on them.

She quickly went to him to help him remove his heavy garments before bringing him by the fire. She wrapped quilts around him, bringing him a hot steaming mug.

"Here," she said, handing him the mug, "dry off and warm up before breakfast. In fact, I can bring it over here for you. I have some hot oatmeal."

He nodded, too cold to even speak yet.

As Trevor sipped his coffee, huddled before the fire, Miriam brought over a hot bowl, placing it on the table.

"When you are ready," she indicated, then went to throw more logs on the fire so it blazed up.

She went to grab her own mug. They sat in silence for several moments. Miriam wanted to give him some time to warm up before speaking to him about what was on her mind. She really felt it was unfair that he had to brave the elements and also sleep downstairs when the bed would be warmer for both of them.

Trevor finally stopped shaking from the chill. Reaching for the oatmeal, he slowly ate, sipping at his coffee. Miriam took his mug and refilled it for him. He smiled in thanks, continuing to eat his meal as he gazed into the flames. He had loosened the quilts a bit and was no longer frosty. She felt he needed to take a hot bath. She had already made sure there were five hot pails added to the tub. It was ready whenever he decided to use it.

"Trevor," she said tentatively, waiting to see if she had his attention.

He didn't answer for a moment, continuing to gaze into the fire. He had finished his oatmeal, setting it aside as he sipped at his mug.

Miriam tried again, placing one hand gently on his arm to gain his attention. "Trevor, I would like to talk to you about something," she said quietly.

Slowly blue eyes met hers, his brow quirked. "Yes?" he asked.

She hesitated, deciding to go ahead. "I think it would be best for both of us if you joined me in the bed upstairs in the evening. It is way too cold at this point to sleep alone. Body heat is essential in weather like this, especially with you doing chores outside in the bitter cold." Her brown eyes met his directly.

Startled, Trevor studied her more closely. "I'm fine, Miriam. Really, I can-"

She interrupted. "No, you are not. You are freezing every morning you come in. It takes a good half hour before you are even ready to bathe. I can tell it is taking a toll on you and I *need* you. And so does Prince," she pointed out.

Trevor contemplated her words. It *would* make sense for the two of them to share the bed for warmth. But... given his attraction to Miriam, it could lead to trouble.

"Miriam, do you really think that is a good idea?" he said quietly.

Looking away from him, she blushed. "I know you have doubts about this, as do I, but I really think it is in both of our best interests."

Trevor was silent for a while, mulling over this. Whenever he was in doubt, he always consulted the chip. *What about this idea? What should I do?*

After a moment he received an answer. *It is part of your mission.*

Sleeping with her is part of my mission? he asked in surprise.

Yes. The answer came back immediately and he was startled.

It must've shown on his face because she questioned him, "What?"

He slowly met her eyes. "All right. Tonight I will join you upstairs when we retire."

Miriam did not know if she was relieved, apprehensive, or happy. She felt a mixture of emotions at his answer.

She smiled tentatively. "In the meantime, if you are through with your coffee, the water is nice and hot for you."

Trevor peeled off the quilts and slowly stood.

"Good. I am going to take a long, hot bath. If I fall asleep, wake me."

"Hopefully you will not," she took the dishes into the kitchen area as Trevor wrapped the drape around the tub, undressing.

<hr />

They spent the day by the fire, reading. Trevor had to go out one more time to attend to Prince but he was out only briefly this time. When he returned, he was not as frostbitten.

They read, then chatted together. Trevor had removed their Christmas tree weeks ago. He used blankets to help cover the small window. Even though there were heavy drapes, the cold still penetrated. He did his best to make sure the window was well insulated. It kept the little cabin darker, but they used candles and lanterns. So far they had enough of each to keep the cabin lit, the fire helped too.

When it was time to retire, Trevor waited as Miriam changed into her nightgown and brushed out her hair, or whatever she did before bedtime.

She called him up when she was ready. He made sure the fire was set for the night with the screen secure around it. He wore his long-sleeved undershirt and a pair of loose pants to sleep in.

He slowly climbed the stairs and could see she was already in the bed, snuggled to the far side where there was a small table with a lantern on it. He noticed there was a book. Did she read in the evenings? He was exhausted and would probably be asleep as soon as his head hit the pillow.

Miriam made sure there was enough room for Trevor, covering them both up with the warm quilts.

"Good night, Trevor," she murmured, reaching over to douse the lantern, plunging them into darkness with only the fire flickering downstairs.

"Good night, Miriam," he said quietly, turning on his side, snuggling into the bed and pillow. It felt so nice to sleep in a bed. He closed his eyes, asleep almost immediately.

Miriam snuggled into the bed but she was awake for quite a while, listening to Trevor breathe as he slept.

Finally, she slept also.

⋆━━━━●◉●━━━━⋆

The next morning Miriam woke up to find herself alone in the bed, with the quilts tucked securely around her.

Trevor must be outside already doing chores.

Sighing, she quickly got up to gather clothes and bathe. She wanted him to have a hot meal when he came in. As she did so, she could hear the wind swirling around the cabin.

Winter continued to be snowy and cold. It was still necessary for them to stay in the little cabin in the woods.

33

It was the third evening of them sharing the bed. So far, except for the extra heat, that was the only benefit of sleeping together. Trevor was always exhausted, falling asleep right away. Miriam would snuggle next to him for body heat, then fall off too.

Tonight, after dinner, they were chatting in front of the fire as the wind continued to blow. Miriam was introspective as she watched the flames.

What would happen when Trevor finally took her back to Chambersburg? She had no doubt that he would eventually get her there safely. What then? Would he be leaving to rejoin the Army? Or returning home to Ohio?

"Trevor," she said tentatively, "what will happen when I am finally home?" She paused to meet his eyes. "What will you do then?"

Trevor was a bit surprised by this question. He assumed once he returned her home his mission would be complete, but now he was not really sure of that.

He hesitated, then answered her. "I guess my mission will be complete. I'll be moving on to my next mission." He shrugged his broad shoulders, his deep blue eyes meeting hers.

Miriam glanced away to the flames. "What about us? Will I ever see you again?" she murmured.

Trevor sighed deeply, settling into the cushions. "I don't know, Miriam. I honestly don't. I know I must keep you safe and I plan to do that."

"You have already done that. When I am home safe, what then? I guess I am asking, what are your plans? Will you return to the Army or return home?" She sipped at her coffee, waiting for his reply.

He met her gaze directly. "I really don't want to go back to that hell-hole called the war. I have seen too much suffering and dying. Perhaps I'll return home, perhaps not."

This was an ambiguous answer. "You still did not answer my question about us," she blushed a bit, looking down at her lap.

He was silent for a moment, then he reached out to softly touch a tress of her hair, stroking lightly. His touch was gentle, but made chills run up and down her back.

Removing his hand, he said quietly, "I am not sure what will happen there, Miriam. I think we should let the future take care of itself. I do care for you a great deal, but I don't have much to offer you."

Startled by this remark, her dark eyes met his. "You have a great deal to offer, Trevor, and you know it."

"I guess I am saying I don't know if I can offer you a future or not." He shrugged. "The future is too uncertain; so many things can happen."

Miriam ruminated on his answer. He was right, of course. One could not predict the future. They could become separated again because they were still in enemy territory here this far south in Virginia. They could return as civilians and maybe be left alone by the Confederates... or maybe not. For now, they were safe in their little cabin, at least until the snow melted enough for Prince to carry them both back to Pennsylvania. It was probably at least a ten-day trip back or more, depending on road conditions.

Miriam was quiet, sipping her coffee, watching the flames.

Trevor occasionally glanced at Miriam as she fell silent, gazing at the fire. He knew his words had not satisfied her, but what could he say to her without giving away his mission? At this point, he was still unclear about his mission; he knew only that he must stay with her and protect her. So far, that was exactly what he was doing. Somehow, he sensed now that there was more to it than that.

He accessed the chip to try to get more information. *Is there more to my mission than just keeping Miriam Klark safe?*

There was a brief silence. He waited. Finally it clicked on.

Your mission is stay with her until you return her home. At this time, you will not be given more information. It is not time yet.

He looked away from Miriam, perplexed again, not wanting her to see his expression. *I can't complete my mission if I am not given all information pertinent to doing so.*

You have all of the information you need at this time.

Once again, it clicked off.

Trevor tried to put the question from his mind, talking casually to Miriam about different subjects until they retired.

As per their routine, Miriam would groom, getting ready for bed, then she would call him up. Trevor would climb the stairs and slip under the quilts next to her. She would douse the lantern and settle in.

Tonight he could hear her sleeping before him. He usually fell off to sleep first.

He was bothered by a nagging feeling; he did not know quite what it was. There clearly was something more he was supposed to do in this century involving Miriam. He was astute enough to figure that out even though the chip would not give him an answer.

He glanced over at the curvaceous woman next to him covered with quilts. The moon pierced the window coverings a bit to light up her figure and light hair.

She was beautiful, intelligent, had a sense of humor, and was kind. She was a nurse, a healer, caring for others. He knew he could fall in love with her easily if he allowed himself, but he knew that was not his fate. His destiny was to return to the future for his next mission when this one was complete. Therefore, he would never see her again.

Trevor's thoughts kept him up for a while before he drifted off to sleep.

Miriam breathed easily, slowly, as if she were sleeping. She knew Trevor was awake, watching her. She pretended to be asleep, but she could feel his gaze on her and wondered what he was thinking. Perhaps he was thinking about their earlier conversation?

Eventually sleep arrived and she drifted off...

In the morning, Miriam arose to find Trevor up and about as usual. Last night was an enigma she could not solve, so she would take each day as it came. She would try her best to help take care of them both while stranded here in the cabin in the forest.

T he January winds continued to blow bitterly, with snow usually arriving each evening. They didn't receive a lot, just flurries, but it added to the several feet already lying around.

The little cabin kept them safe and warm. Trevor always had the fire going briskly. He chopped wood every morning and returned to stack it neatly by the stone fireplace.

He bundled up heavily outside, but he was still icy cold upon re-entering the cabin. Miriam always had a warm blanket with a hot tub ready for him. There was always hot food, for which he was very grateful.

They continued to sleep together in the evenings for warmth. Trevor usually woke before Miriam, finding her wrapped in his arms.

Trevor always quickly dressed and went downstairs for coffee. He tried to ignore the physical attraction he felt for the woman, but it was no good. Especially now, with the two of them sharing a bed, holding each other at night. He knew there was passion bubbling underneath, just waiting to be released. Dangerous territory, Trevor reminded himself.

<hr />

Miriam was making breakfast as Trevor came in from outside after attending to his horse and chopping wood. As usual, he was frosty from head to foot.

She approached him, offering to help him remove his effects, but he waved her away, so she moved to the kitchen, bringing him a big mug of steaming coffee.

Accepting it with a nod, Trevor hung up his outerwear to dry on the pegs near the door. He moved to the couch to settle in. She had a nice fire going and he could smell pancakes sizzling.

Miriam called him over for breakfast and he moved to the table. Yep, she had made pancakes, adding canned sliced apples. A few days ago, he had been fortunate enough to find a bushel of apples tucked away in the back of the shed. They were frozen, but he had brought them in, putting them above the fire to defrost. It would supplement Prince's diet; he needed more than just hay to continue to be healthy. So far, the noble horse seemed to be holding up just fine. It was important his animal remained healthy so eventually when the snows melted, he could carry them back to Pennsylvania.

After a bit of silence, Miriam addressed him. "What are you thinking about?" she asked quietly.

His blue eyes met hers. He swallowed his food, reaching for his mug. "I was just thinking about Prince and how important it is to make sure he makes it through this harsh winter too."

As he sipped, she answered, "Yes, it is very important so that eventually, we can leave."

"Do you miss home?" Trevor looked down, pushing his food around as he waited for her reply.

She was pensive for a moment, then answered him. "Yes. I miss Toby so much sometimes it hurts."

He glanced up to catch her gaze; her eyes were a bit moist.

Trevor reached out to pat her hand gently. "I promise you I will get you home to him," he assured her. He started to move his hand away but she grabbed it back, squeezing tightly before letting go.

"Thank you," she murmured.

Miriam was quiet, then leaned back in the chair. "How far into January do you think we are?"

Sighing, Trevor pushed his empty plate away, sipping at his brew. "By my calculation, I would say about mid-month. This weather will stay bad for a while before it gets better."

"We have been here several months already."

"Yes, we were lucky to find food, shelter, firewood, and provisions. This could have been a whole lot worse."

"Yes, I know."

Miriam somehow felt it was fated they were here together at this time. She did not know why she thought this; it was a feeling deep down. Why?

Why were they meant to be together here? Through the grace of God, they were safe and healthy. There had to be a reason for everything that was happening. She also knew she was attracted to Trevor on a level she had never felt for *any* man, and that thought bothered her.

She stood, clearing their dishes, taking them to the sink.

"Why don't you use the hot tub while I clean up the dishes," she remarked over her shoulder.

Trevor was surprised at the abrupt change in her mood, but went to go get his clothing and bathing supplies.

<hr />

He dressed in warm clothes, joining her by the fire. She was working on quilting with some spare material. She usually spent her days quilting if she was not cleaning or cooking. If it was not too cold, they would take Prince out for a trot. He would groom the horse in the afternoons.

Thus, the days passed by with a rhythm to them. It was the nights that were not so easily handled.

Shrugging off his thoughts, Trevor picked up his book as they both relaxed, listening to the January winds blowing around the cabin, snug by the fire.

<hr />

Trevor made venison steaks for dinner, adding some vegetables. They ate in light cast by their lantern and the candles Miriam had placed about.

Their meal was quiet. Trevor admitted to himself that he was exhausted. Today it had been particularly cold out with the winds whipping the snow around. Even bundled up, he had shivered hard and did not stop until being inside for about a half hour. Even though it was only dinnertime, he was ready to sleep. He knew Miriam would not be ready for several hours yet.

Miriam noticed how weary Trevor was. It had to be hell, being out in this weather every day doing his laborious chores.

She spoke softly. "Trevor, why don't you go upstairs to bed early? I'll clean up our dishes and see to the fire. I probably will read for a little while before I come up."

He straightened, watching as she removed their plates and cups. "You don't mind, do you?"

"Of course not. Being outside in the bitter cold every day must make you weary. Sleep. I'll be up in a bit."

He stood slowly, taking a lantern upstairs. He approached her, kissing the top of her head gently. "Thanks. Good night," he murmured, turning to go to the stairs.

Miriam watched him, standing by the sink for many moments, introspective.

• ◦ ———————— ◦ ● ● ◦ ———————— ◦ •

After making sure the fire was going cheerily with the screen firmly in place, Miriam climbed the stairs with her own lantern.

Looking over at the iron bed, she could see Trevor sprawled in the middle, covered in quilts, his chest rising and falling as he slept. His black hair was tousled, falling into his eyes.

Quietly, Miriam went to get her nightgown, disrobing in the semi-darkness. Shivering, she quickly donned her flannel nightgown and warm socks.

Placing the lantern down, she crawled into the bed on her side where Trevor encroached. She pulled quilts over her, hearing him murmur as he turned away, lying on his side.

Curious, Miriam leaned over him, studying him. He had a bit of beard growing on his chin and cheekbones. Those perfect, sculpted cheekbones. His long eyelashes lay against his face; his black hair blended with the night. His firm muscles down his back were visible. She could not resist an urge to stroke softly, barely touching him, whisper light.

His muscles were lean, firm, his skin was supple for a man. He had a clean, masculine scent she found very sensual.

Quickly she moved away to her side of the bed, covering herself, dousing the lantern. Stop it, Miriam! The two of you will be going separate ways when the snows melt.

Miriam lay awake for a long time as she listened to the wind swirl around the cabin, her thoughts on the man lying next to her.

35

Pink and lavender hues leaked through the window and over the blanket, gently touching Miriam's face. She had a restless night. Peeping at the window, she figured it was about dawn. Trevor was probably up and downstairs.

Turning in the bed, she could see his long body still covered in quilts, facing her, sound asleep. Surprised, she laid back down quietly, pushing his hair gently off of his face. He continued to sleep, and she stroked his bearded cheek, emboldened. She had a strong urge to kiss those very kissable lips, but she knew that would wake him. She was content just to study him as he lay asleep, unaware of being observed.

She moved up on an elbow, gently moving his hair back. He was always up before her, even at dawn. She recalled just how tired he had been yesterday.

Rising, she decided to let him sleep. She would take a quick bath, then prepare breakfast for them. The first thing, as always - put on a pot of coffee.

She gathered her warm black dress, underclothes, and her black tights. Moving downstairs in the rising sunlight, she tended the dying fire, stirring up the coals before stacking logs. Soon she had a pretty decent fire going. She filled several pails of water to heat. She tried to be as quiet as possible so she would not wake Trevor.

No sound came from upstairs yet. She moved the drape around the tub area, quickly disrobing. The water was soon warm enough. She bathed, washing her hair swiftly. She wanted to be done before Trevor came downstairs.

After donning her clothes, she went to the fire with a mug of coffee to brush her hair out and dry it. The sun was well up now. She judged it to be around 7:00 a.m. from the position of the sun.

Still not hearing movement upstairs, she went to heat beef tacky with apples for breakfast, pouring herself a second coffee.

"Why didn't you wake me?"

Miriam jumped, startled, putting one hand to her chest as she turned to see Trevor buttoning up his flannel shirt. His hair was disheveled.

He moved like a cat, silent. She had not heard a sound until he spoke.

"Trevor - you startled me!" she exclaimed.

He gave her his crooked grin. *That* always made her weak in the knees.

She turned back to preparing the food on the stove as she answered. "I could see you were still sleeping and you were very tired last night. So, I got up, bathed, tended the fire, and now I am making breakfast. Why don't you eat before going outside? I have hot coffee ready too." Was she babbling? No, she wasn't. Was she?

Quickly she laid out plates, filling them with food before placing the pans back on the stove. She poured out coffee for Trevor as he took his seat opposite her. Those deep blue eyes pierced her intently as he studied her.

He looked down at his food as she slowly released her breath, eating her breakfast.

"It sounds like the winds have died down," he said idly as he ate.

She had not noticed. "Yes, you are right," she murmured.

"Have you checked outside? Is it still real cold or snowy?"

She glanced up. "No, I was busy with the fire and then heating water-then-" she waved her hands at the food, her words fading.

"All right. I'll check after I eat and bundle up. Have to feed and water Prince too. If it is not too bad, do you want to go for a ride?"

"Not today. I have a lot to do inside," she glanced down, eating slowly.

Trevor was surprised by this remark. Usually she liked to be outside to get fresh air and exercise.

"Fine. I'll be out for a little while. Then I will take a bath."

"I will have hot coffee for you," she promised.

"Great." He went back to eating his breakfast.

<hr />

Trevor went out to attend to his chores while Miriam tended the fire. She would keep busy quilting, preparing meals for later on. She stored them in the ice chest outside. The cold air wafted in. It was cold, but not bitterly cold like the last several days. She did not see any sign of Trevor; he must be in the shed with Prince.

After storing the food, she closed the door.

The *last* thing she wanted to do was be holding onto his body as they rode his horse. Not with all of the carnal thoughts she was having lately. Why exacerbate the problem?

Pulling her quilting materials out, she settled on the couch, occasionally getting up to tend to the fire.

Trevor enjoyed being outside today. The air was brisk, fresh, for once not bone-chilling cold. Bundled up, moving around, he actually was quite warm.

He decided to take Prince out for a trot. He packed his shotgun in case he needed it for game or defense.

Prince chuffed as he mounted, happy to get out to stretch his legs after being inside for days.

The two explored the nearby forest. There were several paths packed down a bit from previous visits, although there was a fresh covering from the recent snow. The sun glinted on the snow and ice. It was a perfect day to be outside.

Trevor was curious about why Miriam preferred to be inside today. It was not like her. In fact, she had been acting a bit odd the last few days.

Shrugging off his thoughts, he kicked Prince into a gallop, racing across the fields.

About an hour later, Trevor returned to the shed, rubbing Prince down. By his estimate of the sun, it was about mid-morning, ten or eleven.

Finishing up with Prince, he headed to the door of the cabin, stamping snow from his pants and boots. Entering, he could see Miriam on the couch working on her quilt.

As he came in, she looked up, smiling. Trevor returned her smile, seeing she had a nice fire going. He removed his outer gear, placing another log on the fire.

"Well, bath time," he said, gathering the items he needed.

"I will heat lunch in about an hour. I made soup earlier."

"All right, good. Something nice and hot!" He smiled at her, pulling the drape around.

She went back to quilting, content to have him back. She smiled.

⊲⊷⊷⊷⊷⊷⊷⊷⊶⊷●⊷⊶⊷⊷⊷⊷⊷⊷⊷⊶⊳

Trevor joined her by the fire shortly after with a mug of coffee. "Can I get you coffe?" he asked.

"No thanks, Trevor. I'm good for now," she replied, looking down at her materials.

Trevor could see she was using a lot of green with some white and a trace of pink in what looked like a star design. Once through, she would have a very nice quilt. He continued to study her as she worked, content to sip his coffee, watching her and the fire.

At his silence, Miriam glanced up. Trevor was looking down at her quilt with a slight smile on his face.

"What?" she inquired.

"Nothing. Just watching you work. That is a fine looking quilt you are making. I like the colors and design so far. You are talented at that."

"Most girls are taught to quilt at a very young age. My mother taught me."

"Tell me a bit about your mother. Do you look like her? What was she like?"

"My mother?" She glanced up to meet his eyes. Glancing down, she replied. "My mother was a strong woman, also a healer. She would help Daddy out in his medical practice. I wanted to be like her, that is why I became a nurse, I guess," she shrugged.

"What was her name?"

Trevor seemed very curious about her past. "Her name was Mary, and yes, I have her dark eyes, but my dad's light hair. Toby looks more like Mom than I do, I think." At the mention of her brother's name, she looked a bit sad.

"After the mid-day meal, let me take you out for a bit. If you don't want to ride, we could walk. It's a real nice day out there. We should enjoy them when we can," he remarked, studying her as he sipped coffee.

205

"Yes. Walking would be good exercise, especially if the weather isn't too bad."

"It's nice, brisk and sunny." Trevor stood, "I'll go get the soup, put it on to heat."

"You don't have to do that, Trevor, I can-"

"It's not an issue, Miriam."

He put his mug in the sink, going outside to the porch where the ice chest was located. Finding the pot of soup, he brought it inside to heat up.

Trevor was right. It was wonderful to be outside after being cooped up in the cabin for several days. Miriam enjoyed the long walk around the property. The sun shone down on them as they paced through the deep snow. It was invigorating. She breathed in deeply, seeing her breath come out in puffy clouds.

Miriam smiled, turning to her walking partner, bundled up as she was. He had a pistol on his hip. She decided it was for safety purposes although the animals mainly stayed in the forest; they did not venture close to the cabin.

Snuggled inside her heavy coat with gloves, her scarf, and warm hat, she was toasty, and the exercise felt wonderful. She picked up the pace but Trevor kept right up with her. She started to run in the snow, giggling. Trevor loped beside her, grinning, his long legs keeping up easily.

After a bit, she slowed down, then stopped, catching her breath, her heart racing. It felt so good; her body was humming. Glancing next to the man beside her she could see he was barely winded as he glanced down at her, smiling.

"That felt good!" she exclaimed.

"Yep, yes, it did."

Laughing, she bent down to grab some snow, molding it into a ball, throwing it at his chest.

Not to be outdone, Trevor reached down to build a bigger snowball, lobbing it at her legs. He was careful not to hit her face, neck, or chest.

Laughing and playing in the snow, they used up all of their energy.

Around late afternoon, when their shadows were getting long on the snow, they headed back to the cabin. They shook snow off of their clothes and boots. Both would need to change into warm clothes and spread their apparel near the fire to dry.

<hr/>

Miriam insisted on making dinner, as he had made lunch. She brought in the venison roast she had prepared, adding vegetables with it. She lit candles and the lanterns as the sun went down, setting the table for dinner.

The delicious aroma of cooking meat filled the little cabin, making Trevor ravenously hungry. Exercise and his chores had made him tired and hungry. Not weary like yesterday, but a good tired. His body felt rejuvenated after being outside today. He could tell by Miriam's pink cheeks it had helped her too.

Soon she called him over for dinner. He joined her as they casually chatted.

Afterwards, Trevor helped clean dishes, then attended to the fire. He read a book, as did Miriam.

Maybe the book would distract her enough so she could sleep tonight. After the exercise today, she was hoping sleep would come quickly.

<hr/>

They went through the usual night routine. When Trevor entered the small bedroom, Miriam was tucked in on her side, wearing a white flannel nightgown trimmed with delicate lace.

Glancing away quickly, Trevor removed his clothes except for pants and warm socks. He moved under the quilt, looking over at Miriam.

"Nice and snug?" he asked, facing her under the quilts, meeting her chocolate eyes.

"Umm hmm," she answered. She yawned a bit.

"Tired after today?" he murmured.

Miriam was a bit surprised. Usually when he came up, they did not talk. Trevor usually went right to sleep, then she would follow.

"I guess. The exercise and the fresh air helped," she murmured back softly.

He reached out a hand, gently stroking her cheek. Miriam bit her lip in surprise, feeling herself melting inside.

"Good night, Miriam," he said softly.

Turning away, he pulled the sheets and quilts over his shoulder, settling in the bed.

Miriam quickly did the same, dousing the lantern, still feeling his gentle touch on her cheek.

Miriam had sweet dreams that night.

36

The morning sun softly peeped around the drape to touch Miriam's features gently. Trevor leaned up on an elbow as he examined the lovely woman lying next to him. She breathed evenly, her full lips parted slightly. He moved her blonde hair off of her cheeks, smoothing it back. She murmured quietly. He froze, not wanting to wake her.

After a moment, she whispered his name, still sleeping.

Surprised, he waited several moments but she turned to the opposite side of the bed, continuing to sleep.

Trevor studied her curves outlined underneath the quilts. He knew he should get up; he had chores to do and things that needed his attention. Right now he just wanted to gather Miriam into his arms and kiss her, not stopping until she kissed him in return.

Crazy thoughts, Trevor, he told himself. *Why* was he having these thoughts? Well, face it, you're a man stranded with a beautiful woman. It would be crazy if you *didn't* have these thoughts.

He continued to assess her, gently pulling her toward him, ignoring the alarm bells screaming in his head.

She murmured quietly as he laid back, holding her in his arms. Tucking her head into his chest, he cuddled her close, pulling the quilts around them. The sun was barely up; it was dim in the little room. He could hear the embers of the fire popping downstairs, as it needed attending. It could wait. Everything could wait.

Miriam slowly woke, realizing she was snuggled against Trevor. She could feel his chest rising and falling as he slowly breathed.

Cautiously she moved her head up to see blue eyes studying her and raven hair tossed by sleep.

"How long have you been awake?" she said quietly.

He shrugged. "A bit, not that long," he answered, stroking her hair back.

At his touch, she felt heat in her cheeks and elsewhere. Steady there, Miriam!

She gathered the quilts to her breasts as she slowly sat up, brushing her hair back.

"Would you like me to make breakfast now?"

"No."

She waited, but he continued to study her. "What is it?" she asked.

He shrugged, not seeming to be in his usual hurry to get up to start the day. Puzzled, she frowned a bit, studying his features in the dim light.

"Trevor..."

"Come here," he said quietly.

"What?"

He reached up to gather her back into his arms. Surprised at this action she looked up into his face. Trevor studied her intently, his deep blue eyes dark, intense.

Before she could speak further, he bent down to deftly catch her lips. He kissed her very slowly, softly, tracing her mouth and lips. She murmured, lying back against the pillows as he moved above her, fingers diving into her hair as he deepened the kiss.

He kissed her so lightly, teasingly, and Miriam felt her head spin as she returned the kiss. She had never kissed like this before- slowly, passionately- with her whole being.

He came up for breath, his fingers still buried in her blonde tresses. "I want you," he said quietly, brushing tendrils of hair off of her cheeks.

Miriam's fingers reached up to move black hair off of his brow and face. "Yes," she answered. It seemed their entire relationship had led to this moment. It seemed good and right.

She sat up, slowly removing her white nightgown, baring the gorgeous breasts he still remembered from that day when she was bathing.

He could see her beautiful body now in the early morning light. She had high breasts, delicate, full, with pink nipples that were erect either from cold or passion. He didn't care which. Gently, he fingered the nipples, his palms rubbing them, making them stiffer yet. She cried out softly.

He stifled her cry with his mouth, lying on top of her as they hit the pillows once again. He continued to kiss her as his fingers and thumbs worked her nipples, teasing, pulling. He bent down to take one in his mouth, sucking, nipping, hands massaging her breasts.

Miriam grabbed his dark hair, sobbing softly, arching her back off of the bed as she pulled his head closer. Kaleidoscope colors flashed in her head. She nearly fainted, it felt so delicious. She never knew the meaning of passion and she realized now just how sensual she really was. She was moist between her legs and could not wait-

At the next moment, Trevor was shoving the waist of her gown up, baring her pubic mount. His mouth dived into the slick blonde curls, exploring the silky folds everywhere. Miriam gasped as she felt a pop of release from below. Oh my God, I just had a small orgasm, she thought.

She didn't have time to ruminate on it, because Trevor slid his hard organ between her legs, making the sexual act complete. She cried out again, this time in both pleasure and pain.

Trevor felt the hard hymen as he tore through it with his penis. Glancing down, he gently soothed her, not moving for a moment, letting her get used to the sensation of being filled by him. "Easy, easy," he murmured, then he moved his hips up and down, up and down, loving the slick folds enveloping his cock.

She gasped as he slowly rode her, his eyes closed in bliss, grabbing her hands with his, pressing them hard back into the pillows. Miriam arched her back. The pain was still there, but not as bad, and she could feel pleasure returning.

Trevor reached down to softly tease her down there so that she would get wet and the pain would ease. His long finger deftly felt around, finding the hot spot and stroked, stroked as his penis moved in and out. He felt her tense and then come right against his hand and he groaned.

"Oh baby, you don't realize how sexy you are, do you?" his husky voice murmured as he continued to move into her, then out.

"This- this can't be happening-" she gasped.

"Oh, yes it is," he grunted, continuing his thrusts, closing his eyes. He knew it would be good with her, but *just* how good, he never dreamed.

Shutting thoughts out, he continued to move, waiting for her, grabbing her buttocks. Driving harder, faster as he felt her begin to move with him.

She grabbed onto his broad shoulders, lifting herself against him as he stabbed into her. Throwing her head back, her long blonde tresses fell to her buttocks, brushing his hands as she screamed and came hard. She tightened around him, squeezing, squeezing every drop out of him.

Trevor grunted, then groaned, spurting into her and not moving until she was full of him.

Finally, he moved onto his side, bringing her with him, cuddling her close. They both were covered in a fine sheen of sweat even though the room was freezing.

Gasping, he cuddled them both back under the quilts as they caught their breath.

Finally he glanced down at the woman in his arms.

"I'm going to go attend to the fire, put several pails of water into the tub so we can bathe."

He rose, tucking the quilts around her. She got a magnificent view as he rose naked and went down the stairs.

She was still gasping for breath and moved the quilts closer, content and satiated.

• ◉ •

Trevor was chilly and grabbed his pants as he loaded logs onto the fire. After they roared up, he filled several pails of water, moving the drape away. They would not need it today, he chuckled to himself. He planned to wash her thoroughly… everywhere.

Jogging up the stairs, he found her wrapped in her warm white robe. She blushed.

"I was cold," she murmured, seeing he had donned his pants too.

He smiled slowly and she could feel her body respond. Stop it, Miriam, she chided herself.

"Well, let's get you downstairs into the hot tub so you can warm and clean up."

As she rose, he noticed the blood spots on the sheet. He quickly threw a quilt over it, knowing he had to change and clean the sheets. Thankfully, there were spares.

"Why don't you go down and get started? I'll join you shortly."

"All right," she murmured, carefully going down the wooden steps.

As she moved downstairs, he removed the stained sheets, bundling them up, returning from the chest with clean ones. He quickly made up the bed with pillowcases, replacing the quilts and smoothing everything out. He could hear Miriam as she bathed downstairs and he moved down to join her.

As he entered downstairs, he could see she was submerged in the water up to her chin. Her cheeks were pink from the water. Her long hair was wet and pulled off of her face. She smiled slowly as he shucked his pants.

He joined her in the hot, steamy water. "Now, where were we?" he said as he moved to cup her face in his large palms. She moaned as he bent to kiss her lips.

⬩━━━━━●◉●━━━━━⬩

After bathing, Miriam grabbed her robe and quickly dressed upstairs, pinning her hair up.

Returning downstairs, she prepared to make breakfast for them as Trevor bundled up and headed outside. It was still bitterly cold but he needed to bring in firewood and attend to his horse. Miriam made sure she had strong hot coffee ready for him.

As she made food, setting the table, she glanced at the tub, ruminating on last night and this morning. She smiled softly. She was still a bit sore between her thighs but the hot water had helped soothe that. She blushed. She and Trevor were now lovers, not merely acquaintances or work partners but also intimate lovers.

She was quite content as she made sliced apples and heated beef tacky. As she cooked she tried to ignore the thought that she had never been happier.

⬩━━━━━●◉●━━━━━⬩

Trevor chopped and stacked wood near the woodpile, breath chuffing out into the frozen air. As he did the mindless chore, his thoughts roamed.

Now that he and Miriam had become lovers, he wondered what the future held. He knew when the weather broke he would need to get her home to her brother. Then- what?

You will be expected to return for your next mission once this one is complete.
Startled, he internalized his thoughts as the chip clicked on unbidden.
What about Miriam? I just leave her? he asked.
Yes, you leave when the mission is complete.
Is that now, or in the future?
First, you must return her home, then you will get further instructions. That is all for now. The chip clicked off.

Trevor shook his head, stacking wood.

The weather was still snowy and cold, so it would be awhile before they could venture away from the cabin to travel. Until then, he had Miriam to keep him company.

Picking up a large stack of wood in his arms, he pushed open the cabin door, dumping the wood. He stomped snow from his boots and brushed it off his clothes.

Miriam looked up when she heard Trevor open the door. A swirl of snow followed him in. Grinning, he removed his snowy outerwear, hanging them on the pegs. He tugged off his boots and then rubbed his hands together to warm them, smiling at her.

"What's for eats this morning?" he asked

Miriam was finishing setting the table. "I have hot coffee, sliced apples, and hot beef tacky," she informed him as she poured out a large mug of the steamy brew for him.

He joined her at the table. They dug into the food, both hungry.

Miriam carefully avoided his eyes as she ate her breakfast, her cheeks pink. Trevor noticed her reticence and smiled, knowing the reason for it.

"It is a bit chilly out there. I recommend we stay inside. What would you like to do?" he lifted a dark brow, studying her face.

Now she was really blushing! "Well, I have some sewing to do, a bit of cleaning, meal preparation-" she stuttered.

"Miriam, I do not expect to have sex, twenty-four/seven. You're safe for a while." His blue eyes were amused.

"How long is a while?" she flung back tartly.

Ahh, there was that spunk he admired!

He shrugged broad shoulders. "We'll see, won't we?"

Blushing again, she finished her meal, collecting the dishes to wash, relieved to see Trevor retrieve a book and sit near the fire. Now, *why* was she relieved?

⁕

Evening came and Miriam warmed up vegetable soup she had made the other day. She called Trevor over to eat. They settled at the table, sipping coffee.

Trevor spooned up soup, glancing over at his dinner partner. They had spent the day reading (and Miriam also sewed) so it was a quiet indoor day.

"The soup is delicious," he complimented her.

She shrugged a bit. "Something I had left over; plus it's hot." She looked down at her dinner, avoiding his eyes.

Trevor idly studied her as he picked up his coffee, slowly sipping. "Something wrong?"

Startled, she met his gaze. "No. Nothing." She continued to eat, glancing back down.

"Miriam, I know you by now. You are not usually this quiet."

Her dark eyes met his. "Just nothing to talk about," she said nonchalantly.

"Oh no?" his blue eyes met hers in some amusement.

She blushed. "I didn't think one *talked* about that."

"Sure, you do," he assured.

"What is there to say?"

He leaned forward and whispered, his voice husky. "That it was awesome and I can't wait for this evening. Supposed to be cold. We'll have to snuggle."

The wind swirled around the cabin loudly as if to emphasize his point.

She arched one blonde brow. "I am sure you had much more in mind than just snuggling." She met his eyes directly as she took a bite of her food.

Trevor chuckled. "Eat your dinner, darlin'." Smiling, he went back to his soup.

• • •

It was a frigidly cold January night but Trevor was true to his promise. He pulled Miriam close, starting to kiss her everywhere. Languid, slow, sliding kisses, and Miriam was a puddle.

As he moved over her she flung her arms around him.

They lay buried in the warm pillows and quilts, making slow sweet love.

37

The bitter cold wind whipped around the big Victorian house in the center of town. Toby and David Irvin sat before a blazing fire enjoying a libation after seeing patients for the day.

The weather remained snowy, with temperatures below freezing. Most people stayed in their warm homes. On this snowy evening, as the wind blew and whirled snow around, lights glowed behind windows and doors, people snug in their homes for the evening.

Toby was a farmer and since there wasn't much he could do during the winter season he was helping out David in his medical practice, assisting him. He knew he came nowhere near his sister's expertise, but he helped as much as he could and was learning. Toby had already laid up stores and supplies to plant in the spring when he had returned from the war last fall.

The War. It still raged on; his sister was missing along with Major Tompkins. The only ray of hope he had was that she was with the Major. It gave him comfort. Although he knew David was skeptical about her chances, Toby never stopped believing that one day she would return to them.

David glanced over at the younger man, taking a sip of brandy. "You're introspective tonight, young man," he remarked.

Toby's gaze left the fire to meet David's. He shrugged. "Just thinking about my sister..." his words trailed off.

David adjusted his legs, propping them up on an overstuffed ottoman placed before his big chair. Toby sat opposite on the chaise. "Your sister has been missing for months-" David hesitated, unsure what to say next.

Toby studied David. "You think she's gone, don't you?"

David shrugged, glancing at the fire. "I really don't know, Toby. I hope not, but the circumstances-" he hesitated. "This storm has been very bad, and it seems they even got hit much further south. I hope she found some shelter. If not," he hesitated again, "it's hard to say."

Toby sipped at his brandy, contemplating David's words. "Yep, I know all of that David but here—" he indicated his chest, "I know she's safe. I don't know how I know, I just do," he ended quietly.

"I hope you are right, Toby. I truly hope you are." He paused. "How about a little dinner? We worked hard today." David rose, summoning his housekeeper, Anna.

The two men moved to the dining table, which was already set for them.

"Yes, sounds good. I could use a hot meal before heading home."

"Why don't you stay tonight? The storm is really bad this evening. That way you won't have to worry about traversing it tomorrow morning. There are spare clothes for you in the extra room."

Toby had stayed on other occasions throughout the cold weather. He grinned. "I just may take you up on that, David," he said as he sat at the table.

David smiled, following suit as Anna brought in serving dishes. Anna had a cozy little apartment upstairs and was always available to help out.

The three enjoyed the meal as the snow blew around the big house, swirling down the deserted cobbled street.

<hr />

The storm had let up a bit at dawn. The sun was even trying to make an appearance.

After cleaning up and eating, the two men got ready for the day. They received patients in David's two medical rooms located in the back of the spacious building.

There were many cases of whooping cough and the flu due to the bad weather. A few accidents also came in, along with several sick babies. The two men worked side by side, trying hard not to think about a woman they both missed and cherished.

<hr />

By the time they saw their last patient, the sun was starting to set. Toby insisted on heading home because the weather had improved enough for the short walk. Besides, he wanted to get his own fire going, heat his place, and make sure he had enough firewood to get through the season. It was about mid-February now. He would need supplies for at least another month.

He carefully unlocked the door to his home, shivering. The place was cold and deserted, with drapes closed on all of the windows. He lit a lantern and went to the fireplace. He quickly threw kindling on, lighting it. After he had a small flicker of flames going, he put on some larger logs. He prodded the pile with an iron poker until the flames caught and flared up.

Removing his coat and boots, Toby went to the pantry to see what he could rustle up to eat. He didn't feel it was fair for David to constantly be feeding him. He found some beef tacky along with grits, heating them over the stove, making hot coffee too.

Taking his meal into the main room, he sat before the fire, reminiscing about his sister as he ate his meal, not realizing his eyes were tearing up.

<hr />

Toby was back to work early at David's place and the doctor greeted him heartily. Their patient load was a bit light today, so Anna was able to make a noon meal for them.

Toby enjoyed ham, eggs, and toast with good strong coffee. It was such a luxury for them both to be able to take a break from their duties.

They chatted casually about their patients and caseload. David again thanked Toby profusely for helping out.

Toby waved this away. "It's the least I can do, doc. You've been so good to me this winter, feeding me, housing me, good company too. Don't know what I would have done without you," he ended quietly.

"I feel the same way, Toby. You have been a good companion and aide. I sorely miss her too, you know." David added some gravy to his ham as he looked up.

Toby was sipping his coffee. "I miss her all of the time. Especially at night when I have more time to think."

"Well, spring should be upon us in a month or so. When the weather breaks… well, you never know. Since the war is still raging…" David let his sentence hang.

"Yes, I don't even want to think about that. Can't think about that right now. I just want her to be safe and sound, wherever she may be."

David sighed deeply. "There are church services tonight. Are you attending?"

Toby looked up. "I always do."

"If I'm not too late working, I will join you."

Toby smiled, then went back to his lunch.

That evening, Toby joined David in the large church, singing from hymnals and praying along with the other congregants.

Please bring her home safe to me, My Lord. I miss her so much and need her back. I love her and I need her. Please keep my sister safe and return her to me.

David glanced at Toby as the younger man bowed his head. David added his prayers to Toby's, praying for the woman he was in love with.

38

L ife went on in the little cabin in the woods. The weather continued to be cold but they kept the fire stoked. Prince was taken out every day for a run. The two would enjoy the frosty air. Trevor assured her they were well into February and the weather should break within weeks. What would happen then, Miriam wondered. She tried not to be introspective, take each day as it came; enjoying the time she had alone with Trevor because she knew it would not last.

Today they were exploring the crisp cold forest, Prince picking a path carefully through the snow-laden trees. The sun was shining today; one could actually see some of the snow softening. It was not quite as packed as it had been. The days were longer now too with more sunlight, which also helped melt the landscape a bit more.

Miriam was silent as she enjoyed the pleasant ride, her arms loosely clasped around Trevor's waist. She caught a blur of red over her shoulder briefly, noticing a cardinal. She knew spring could not be too far off. Once the snows melted, Trevor would be returning her home.

Miriam contemplated that thought. Yes, she missed Toby and friends in town, but the time she had spent with Trevor here in their little cabin had been magical. She had known from the start it would only be temporary. Someday she would return home, but so much had changed. They were now lovers, the cabin a quiet sanctuary away from the world. Shelter from the war, from all of their problems and cares. She was not quite sure what Trevor's plans were once they returned. He had not elaborated on them. Miriam wasn't sure she wanted to know. She would always hold this time and place dear in her heart no matter what happened. She had fallen in love with Trevor, but she somehow felt he did not feel the same. Not having a lot of experience with men- or love, for that matter- it was hard for Miriam to divine what he was thinking or feeling.

She shrugged her shoulders under her cloak, deciding to take each day as it came.

◆━━━━━●●●━━━━━◆

When they returned to the cabin, it was about mid-day. Miriam set about making them a meal as Trevor saw to his horse.

He returned within several moments. Miriam served porridge she heated up along with coffee.

They both settled at the little table after Trevor tended to the fire. Miriam scooped up porridge slowly, her gaze drifting to the fire.

Trevor noticed her silence and cleared his throat. "Something you want to talk about?" he asked

Startled, Miriam's eyes met his. "I was just wondering…"

He waited a moment, then prompted her. "Wondering what?"

She sighed. "How much longer we will be here. How soon do you think the snows will melt?"

His blue eyes rose to meet hers. "With the amount we got, even with the increased sunlight, I'd say at least several more weeks. Probably beginning of March or so, depending on warming trends." He ate porridge as he studied her face. Was she anxious to leave?

"Oh," she glanced back down at her food, continuing to eat.

Trevor crossed his hands under his chin, leaning forward. "Got cabin fever? Or just miss home?"

Miriam looked up. She shrugged. "Not really. I mean, I do miss home, but I don't have cabin fever at all. Our outings have helped in that regard. And…" How could she articulate she liked being here alone with him? Her words trailed off.

"And?" He waited for a further comment.

She decided to be honest with him. "And… I like being here with you. Our own little haven." She blushed, looking down.

Trevor noticed the pink cheeks, smiling slowly.

"I must admit, I far prefer being alone here with you than out on the battle fields killing or potentially being killed." He picked up his coffee, took a sip.

His words startled Miriam. Her widened eyes rose to his.

Trevor could see the surprise on her face. "Why does that surprise you?"

Miriam took a moment to answer him, pushing her porridge around in her bowl. She met his gaze. "I wasn't sure how you felt about me, how you felt about being here."

"Miriam, look at me," he said quietly.

Her dark eyes met his once more.

"We got stranded together; neither of us had a choice in the matter. We were lucky to find this place. Somehow- you know as well as I do- it was fate that it happened. It was *meant* to happen."

Once again, Miriam was taken aback. So, Trevor suspected the same thing she did, that somehow they were supposed to be stranded together.

He continued. "Over the past several months, we have grown closer. It would be odd if we didn't. Now that we have become intimate, my feelings for you are much more intense. I will be sad when I have to take you home, but it is inevitable. When the snows melt, we will have to leave. You will be reunited with Toby." His eyes delved into hers, waiting for her reaction.

Miriam looked away a moment, contemplating his words. He admitted he had intense feelings for her. He had not specified exactly what those feelings were, but did she really need to know? He was a tender and caring lover. Through his kiss and caress she knew just how much he cared for her. Her instincts had not failed her.

She reached across the table, clasping his hand. "Trevor, if I had a choice of who I would want to be stranded with in the wilderness, you would be my choice," she said softly, squeezing his hand.

He returned the squeeze, smiling that wicked grin of his. "Finish up your porridge, darlin'. Then I think it's time to snuggle for an afternoon nap."

Miriam knew what that meant, blushing. Her body tingled in anticipation.

———•◉•———

Evening came. They were lying in the bed, snuggled in quilts after a sweaty bout of sex. Miriam leaned on one elbow, tracing the muscles on Trevor's chest with one finger. His black hair was tangled and wet, sticking to his forehead, his blue eyes shadowed.

"You have a magnificent body," she whispered.

He slid his finger down into the cleavage exposed above the sheets she clasped to her breasts. "Yours isn't too shabby either, m'lady," he answered.

She smiled tenderly. "No matter what happens in the future, I will always have these memories to sustain me."

Trevor was silent, knowing they would not have a future, and that saddened him. He shook off this thought, leaning over her, pressing her back into the pillows. He kissed her tenderly, slanting her face up so he could take her lips completely, swallowing up her soft moan. His lips left her mouth and traveled to her eyes, her brows, tracing softly to her ear and neck.

Miriam gasped at the sensations created, grabbing fistfuls of thick black hair. She brought his mouth back to hers as he entered her again, his hips bucking against hers.

They both forgot everything but the physical act of love as they moved together under the quilts.

39

The winter continued to wane. Sunnier days arrived, melting the snow lying about. Their jaunts in the woods were easier for Prince to navigate as much of the pathways melted into slushy snow and ice. Snow dripped from the trees in streams, plopping to the ground to create icy whorls. The scenery was still beautiful even though it was now changing.

Trevor surmised they were almost into the beginning of March. Spring was just around the corner. Looking around, he figured in a few weeks it would be clear enough for him to return Miriam home to Pennsylvania, to her brother.

He was alone in the woods with Prince, taking him out a bit further to see how the terrain was. Miriam was at the cabin making their meals. Even with the food he provided by hunting, their supplies were getting low. It would be necessary to move on anyway. They would need enough supplies to sustain them on their two-week journey back.

Trevor kicked Prince into motion, going further into the woods, tentatively picking a path. This far away from the cabin there could be Rebel patrols; he had to be careful. He wore civilian clothes and not his uniform for just that very reason, but still there was need for caution.

He dismounted, patting his horse. Prince responded by chuffing and nodding his head. Trevor walked a few feet away, crouching down and observing the snow trails. Everything here was smooth, pristine, indicating no one had been in the area. Satisfied, Trevor stood, his eyes rising to the sky. It was crystal clear blue with the sun directly overhead. It must be about noon. Miriam would be expecting him for a mid-day meal.

Trevor mounted his horse, directing him back the way they came.

Sensing food and water were to be offered soon, Prince picked up the pace, carrying them both back to their home.

◆━━━━━●◉●━━━━━◆

Trevor saw to his horse, feeding him, watering, and rubbing him down. Prince moved toward a bed of hay and laid down for an afternoon nap.

Smiling, Trevor moved through the snow, which now came to just about his ankles. He remembered when it came to mid-thigh. The temperatures were milder; it was pleasant to be outside. Taking a deep breath of the fresh air, he entered the cabin, noticing Miriam over in the kitchen area. She was frying up what looked like beef tacky with some jarred beans. Trevor hung up his coat on the peg, stamping snow from his boots as he removed them.

He moved to the table, smiling as he rubbed his hands together. "Ah, another beef tacky meal! Yum!" he declared.

Miriam smiled as she placed food on the table for them. "Yes, once again. I do have some venison left for dinner so we can have that." She forked up food, glancing at the man opposite her.

The outdoors had weathered his face a bit, giving him some color, intensifying the blue eyes. His black hair was disheveled from the wind, dipping over his forehead. He was so gorgeous she wanted to just jump across the table and attack him. Shaking off her thoughts, she questioned him. "Any activity out there?"

He glanced up to meet her eyes. "Nope. I went out further today too, several miles. Wanted to make sure there weren't any Rebel troops or stragglers nearby. For now, it looks all clear."

She nodded, continuing to eat. She knew it would be soon they would be saying goodbye to their little retreat. It would be dangerous to be back on the road during wartime, but she trusted Trevor to keep them both safe.

"I figure when we are ready to leave, we'll use the less traveled paths. It may take longer to get back, but it will be safer," he said.

Her dark eyes delved into his. Yes, it would be safer. She knew they would be traveling as civilians. Hopefully they would not be bothered by either Confederate or Union forces. At least, that was the hope. They would travel as husband and wife, as farmers. She ate in silence, wondering about the man across from her. Although she spent many months alone with him and they were now intimate, he was still such a mystery to her.

<hr />

Trevor brought in more firewood and they both read by the fire after their meal. A couple of hours later, he suggested they go out for a late afternoon jaunt before dinner and sunset. Miriam agreed, bundling up. These days it was not necessary to wear quite so many layers.

They both mounted Prince, galloping across the fields toward the woods, eager to get more exercise. After roaming the forest for a couple of hours, the couple returned at sunset, watching the golden rays set behind the frosted and melting trees together.

<hr />

After dinner, they read again for a while. Trevor decided to consult the chip to see if he could get more information about when they would be leaving the cabin and the safest way to do so.

When will it be safe to leave here? He questioned.

In a moment, he received an answer. *You can see the snows are melting. As you have determined, it is the beginning of March. In ten or so days, it will be safe to leave. Head northwest, avoiding main pathways. Use the compass you have been supplied with. It will lead you to your destination.*

Trevor sighed, glancing into the fire. Ten more days. Better make the most of it, Trevor.

"I'm a bit tired. What do you say we retire?"

Miriam closed her book, giving him a mischievous grin. "Tired already?"

"No, I just can't wait to hold you," he admitted. He put down his book. Taking her into his arms, he carried her up the steep wooden stairs.

<hr />

When they made love it was slow, tender, each touch a soft caress, each kiss languid. Trevor kissed each inch of Miriam's soft skin, lingering over her breasts and stomach, making her moan with pleasure. His long fingers parted slick lips, delving below, stroking her gently, carefully, sinking his fingers into the silky folds that were drenched wet for him. Slowly, he pressed himself inside her until he was buried to the hilt. He lay on top of her, silent, still. He felt every inch of him surrounded by her. Leaning down, he kissed her deeply, fingers diving into her hair. He moved in and out, closing his eyes in bliss. Throwing his head back, he groaned. He picked up the pace until eventually he was riding her hard, as hard as he rode his Prince until she screamed and he finally spit his seed deep into her body.

Covered with sweat, Trevor moved to her side, wrapping them both tightly in the sheets as he breathed heavily.

They made love all through the night, sleeping close to dawn. There wasn't a reason to wake early anyway. They could sleep as long as they wanted to. For now.

40

As the snow continued to melt, Trevor made preparations to leave soon. He made sure to hunt for enough provisions to pack away in the icebox. For water, he would need to fill large jugs from the pump. Fortunately, the pump had supplied water throughout the winter; the snowy environment probably helped. There were enough canned goods left to supplement their food supply. He would have to make sure he took plenty of hay for the horse.

He and Miriam spent their days preparing for the long trip home, packing up food, clothing, and other supplies. They would be camping out on the way home. It would be much rougher conditions than their little cabin, but in the end, Miriam would be with her brother.

Evenings were spent snuggling and making love. Miriam knew in her heart that once she returned home, she would probably never see Trevor again, so she cherished these moments alone with him.

⋅⋅⋅⋅⋅⋅⋅⋅⋅●◉●⋅⋅⋅⋅⋅⋅⋅⋅⋅

Mid-March arrived and the snow only appeared in patches on the landscape. When they traveled, they would not need to worry about leaving a snowy trail. Early crocuses and new green grass pushed up through the melting snow. Birds returned. There was a freshness to the breeze after the long cold winter.

Trevor and Miriam packed up all of their supplies after a hardy morning meal. Prince was well-fed and watered. He snorted as Trevor attached the supply wagon, making sure it was snug and tight.

Stepping away, he patted Prince, looking up into the horse's dark eyes. "Ready for a long trip, Prince?"

Prince nodded, nudging Trevor's shoulder with his velvety nose. Grinning, Trevor stroked his nose, then patted it.

"I have a few more things to see to. I'll be right back."

He turned to go into the cabin. Miriam was busy putting the rest of their food supplies into several sacks, as some would need to be handy and available while traveling. She glanced up as Trevor entered.

"Just about ready," she said.

She was wearing a lighter grey cloak than her heavier dark one. The temperatures were quite mild, so the weather shouldn't be a factor unless they ran into rainstorms.

"Let me help you out there," he offered, approaching her.

"No, really I've got it, Trevor. I'll take these out to the wagon." She picked up the sacks, heading out.

Trevor went over to the fire, making sure it was dead and cold. He had tamped it down last night. Making sure all embers were dead, he put his hands on his hips, glancing around the little abode. He would miss this little place greatly. He had many fond memories of it.

Going to the kitchen table, he laid down several gold pieces and several hundred Union dollars. He knew it should more than reimburse the owner for their use of the food, wood, hay, and shelter. God bless whoever owned this place. Without them, they would not have survived.

Trevor briefly checked upstairs. Miriam had left everything tidy and neat, the bed perfectly made up with clean linens. Descending the stairs, Trevor closed the door, making sure it was latched tight. Then he turned to join Miriam who was waiting near Prince.

"All set?" he questioned.

"Yes," she smiled tentatively, then her gaze moved to the little log cabin. "I will miss this place," she remarked.

Trevor's eyes followed hers, gazing at the quiet little abode. "I will too, but it is time to move on," he said quietly.

He mounted Prince, reaching down for Miriam's arm, seating her behind him. He waited for her to get settled.

"Ready?"

She put her arms loosely around his waist. "Yes. I'm ready," she declared.

Trevor gave Prince a gentle kick. As they moved into the forest, Miriam turned to gaze at the little brown cabin until the trees finally enveloped it. Her gaze moved forward as Trevor used his compass to direct them to Chambersburg.

The first day of travel was uneventful. They did not meet any other travelers or soldiers on the back road.

At sunset, Trevor built a fire. They roasted some venison, adding canned vegetables. After dinner, Trevor doused the fire, not wanting to attract any attention. They used lanterns in their tent and snuggled together in their bedrolls. They fell quickly off to sleep, both tired from traveling all day.

It took about a week for his compass to tell him they were no longer in Virginia but headed to Maryland. That was still Rebel territory, so they kept to backroads. Trevor estimated if the weather continued to be fair, they should reach south central Pennsylvania in another seven days.

Sighing, he kicked his horse into gear. They were both weary of the travel, although never once did Miriam complain.

Travelling through central Maryland, they encountered a wild rainstorm. Clouds had been roiling overhead since early morning. By early afternoon the rain was coming down in sheets. It was impossible to see on the trail.

Trevor picked a path into the forest, where they quickly set up camp. He erected their tent, then attended to his horse. As he brought their lantern and supplies inside, he could see Miriam huddled on a bed roll.

Trevor placed the lantern in the center of the floor and took out some food rations, handing Miriam a portion. She accepted it silently as they both listened to the rain pelting the tent from every side. The sound was deafening as the water relentlessly poured from the sky, the occasional growl of thunder sounding further off.

As he bit into his food, Trevor glanced around at the darkened day. "The way it's coming down, I don't think we'll be able to move much today. Probably have to stay here until the storm lessens."

He sat across from Miriam as she glanced up.

"Yes, it sounds pretty bad, like it could last for days."

"Spring rainstorms like this tend to come quickly and go just as quickly. I figure we'll be able to move out by tomorrow. The roads will be muddy for Prince." His blue eyes studied her.

She licked her fingers daintily. "Where are we at now?"

"Somewhere in central Maryland. By my estimation, we should reach your town in about five more days, given good weather conditions."

Five days. She would then be reunited with Toby. The thought made her happy but she also felt sad. She knew she would not see Trevor again. He would be rejoining his unit in the Union Army.

"Five days...so close..." she murmured.

"You will be happy to see Toby, won't you?"

"Yes, yes, of course. I've missed him so."

Trevor ruminated over her answer. He knew they would be parting ways soon. The chip would let him know if his mission was complete. What then? He had no idea.

He poured out hot coffee from the tin pot for the two of them. They settled in to eat and snuggle from the pouring rain.

<hr />

Trevor went out briefly to check on Prince, feeding him. When he returned he was sopping wet. He changed into dry clothes. They both ate cold rations for dinner by the lantern light.

Later that evening, after making love, they listened to the rain slash against the canvas tent. Eventually Trevor fell asleep. His chest rose and fell softly as he held Miriam in his arms.

Miriam turned to study his face as he slept in the low lantern light. His dark hair was tangled and she gently pushed it back. He murmured a bit, but did not wake. She caressed his fine features, noticing the long eyelashes brushing chiseled cheeks. She wanted to capture this moment forever, keep it buried in her mind and soul so when they were apart his face would be forever a part of her. She would always carry a part of him; that would never change. For that, she was so grateful.

Leaning over, she softly kissed his lips, then snuggled against his strong body. She relaxed and eventually slept too.

<hr />

Trevor was correct. The morning sun shone brightly the next morning as they packed up their camp. Soon they were back on the roads. As predicted, the paths were muddy and difficult for the horse to traverse, slowing them down. Miriam wrapped her arms around Trevor's waist, glancing at the scenery. She wasn't in a hurry.

<hr />

With the spring rains arriving and the snow gone, Toby was able to put in a good crop. It was early April, warm enough to start digging.

He purchased a large amount of corn seed, pumpkin seed, tomato and sunflower seeds. This would yield a plentiful crop for the two of them.

As Toby diligently used his digging tools to plant, he mused on that thought- the two of them. He never doubted his sister would be returning to him. He knew David had given up all hope, but he hadn't. He knew in his heart his sister was alive and would return. Standing, he wiped sweat from his brow, looking up toward the clear blue sky.

Yes, she was out there somewhere with Major Trevor Tompkins. The two of them would return. Someday.

Toby went back to planting corn seed, working diligently and carefully. He expected a bumper crop this year. When through here, he would get water from the pump and thoroughly sprinkle the seeds. Hopefully with spring upon them, they would get plenty of rain.

After working hard all day, Toby decided to go to the local tavern to treat himself to dinner and an ale. He cleaned up, walking several blocks into town. Neighbors and friends all greeted him. Toby smiled and waved back.

Entering the tavern lit with candle lanterns and oil chandeliers, Toby approached the long polished wooden bar. Several other patrons were at the other end and greeted him. Toby smiled and waved as the barkeep came over.

"Hello there, Toby. What can I get you tonight?" he said affably.

Toby smiled. "Hello, Tom. I think I'll splurge and get some dinner tonight. What's good?"

Tom grinned, wiping the mug he was holding. "Got some real nice roast chicken with some potatoes and vegetables to go with it, along with some muffins."

Toby gestured to the mug. "Sounds good. I'll top if off with an ale. I'll grab a table nearby."

"All right, Toby. You got it. Coming up." Tom poured a tall mug of ale, handing it to Toby.

Accepting it, Toby found a cozy table for two in a far corner. He watched as the blonde barmaid served another table. She had a cute face, Toby thought.

The door opened. David Irvin entered, going to the bar, not noticing

Toby in the corner. Tom came right over to greet him and David ordered a whiskey. Tom carefully poured out the drink in a glass as David removed a light jacket.

The men spoke briefly before Tom gestured to Toby's table.

David turned, brows arched, said a few more words to Tom who nodded as David made his way over to Toby.

"Hello, Toby. Guess you decided to come for a libation too," David remarked as he settled across from Toby with his drink.

Toby smiled. "Yep. Worked hard today planting corn. Decided to treat myself to a nice dinner. You?" he sipped from his mug as he studied the other man.

"I just came for a drink. Anna usually makes dinner, but since you're here, I'll join you. I'll just have her reheat for tomorrow. So, planting already, huh?"

"Yep. The weather has been fine. I want to get as much done as possible before the summer weather is upon us. Warms up quick after April."

"Usually," David replied.

They both fell silent for a moment, then Toby spoke. "Been busy at your practice?" He had not seen David for a few weeks, as he had been busy planting and tilling his property.

"Yes, we've been quite busy. I am still trying to find an assistant to help out. It is tough, but I make do."

The barmaid brought over steaming plates for the men, serving them quickly. Smiling, she placed a basket of muffins down for them. "Refills?" she gestured to their drinks. Both ordered refills.

They dug into the delicious food. The tavern was well-known for its generous good food, a rarity in wartime.

Soon they were talking casually about David's patients, friends in town and general topics. Both were careful not to mention the woman they longed to see again.

42

Miriam was so weary of traveling on horseback. It seemed the trip home was taking forever. However, every mile brought her closer to Toby so she was happy to be returning. Trevor made sure they took breaks during the day to walk and exercise a bit, knowing it was easy to get saddle sore from the long ride back to Pennsylvania. Even knowing she would be home soon did not console her. She knew she would be saying goodbye to Trevor and that broke her heart. She let herself become too close to him, falling in love with him and that was foolish. They had no future together.

At mid-day Trevor dismounted from Prince, helping her down. They made a little fire, having some hot rations for lunch. They ate silently, musing on the journey. So far, after the rainstorm in Maryland, the trip had been uneventful. The weather continued to be fair. They actually saw other travelers on the road. Fortunately they had not encountered any Confederate troops in Maryland. Trevor assured her there was no need to worry as they were now in Union-occupied Pennsylvania.

"How many days until we reach Chambersburg?" she asked quietly, swallowing her food, her dark eyes on his.

Trevor shrugged a bit, kicking a pebble. "It won't be long now. Two, maybe three days." He avoided her eyes.

"Then you will return to your unit. Is that right?" She studied him closely.

He sighed deeply. "Yep, that is the plan. I will need to pick up my orders in Chambersburg to see where they send me next." He paused. "The important thing is to get you back home safely." He glanced at her as she ate her food.

"I never doubted that you would," she said.

"We've been very lucky. Finding the cabin when we were stranded, not meeting any enemy troops now or then… could've been a whole lot worse."

"Yes," she murmured, sipping coffee.

After a moment, she spoke again. "I will miss you so much, Trevor."

Trevor met her eyes. "I will miss you also, Miriam. More than you know. But you will be safer at home with Toby, out of this madness called war."

She sighed, looking away, continuing to eat her lunch.

Trevor held Miriam in his arms as she slept. After making tender love, she had drifted off. He lay awake because he realized this was their last night together. He had not told Miriam yet just how close they were to her town. They should arrive in Chambersburg by tomorrow afternoon if his estimations were correct. So far, they had been.

Looking down at her snuggled into his chest, he gently stroked her honey hair that glinted in the faint lantern light. She slept quietly, breathing evenly. He caressed her face lightly so he would not wake her. He wanted to keep the memory of her lovely face alive in his mind and soul. Would he remember her once he returned to his own time? He knew he could probably access the chip and get an answer, but he didn't want to know. He wanted to always feel the way he felt right now. Bathed in soft light holding close the woman he had protected for so long, stroking satiny skin and realizing he cared for her deeply. It would never work. He wouldn't even be born for about another three hundred years. This time in the past would be her future, not his. Pain stabbed at him as he realized this.

He pulled her closer, snuggling them into the bedroll and finally closed his eyes.

It was mid-afternoon. Toby was diligently planting tomatoes, having finished the corn just yesterday. The weather was fair. Actually, it was quite hot out here in the sunlight. Toby swiped sweat from his brow. He would put in several more rows, then quit for the day and make himself some dinner. He managed to bag a deer several days ago, so there was plenty of meat. He had made venison stew with quite a bit leftover.

Bending to his task, he glanced up at the sky, estimating the time. It was probably close to three or four. The sun would set in about three or so hours.

Toby was several acres away from his small home, but he could hear horse hooves in the distance. A small cloud of dust formed in the clear afternoon. The sounds seemed to be heading towards his house. Quirking his brow, Toby shaded his eyes, but he could not make out much.

Squinting, he could now see a single horse nearing his home, carrying what looked like two people.

Toby dropped his digging tools, high-tailing it to his house, running briskly despite the heat of the day.

Trevor dismounted at the entrance to the small porch, reaching up to help Miriam down. She was wearing a light cotton yellow dress with a white bonnet. Dust swirled around them as Prince whinnied softly, glad the journey was at an end for now.

"I need to water Prince first off. Where is your pump?"

"It is around back." She glanced around. "Toby should have heard us arriving." Her gaze went to the front door which remained closed.

"I'm sure he is around. I'll get some water. I'll be right back." Trevor went around the back of the structure as Miriam removed her bonnet, tossing out her blonde curls.

She fanned her bodice, sweating lightly in the heat as she looked around the property for her brother. She could not wait to see him again. As they got closer and closer to town her heart had sped up in anticipation of seeing her little brother again.

Looking out towards the fields, she could see a figure rushing toward the house and knew instinctively it was Toby.

She ran out into the fields to meet him, finally arriving where he was, flying into his arms. She hugged him tightly as Toby clutched his sister to him, eyes closed, thanking God.

Trevor watched the reunion of the two out in the sun-drenched fields as he watered his horse. He had done it. Miriam was home safe with her brother.

The two of them turned arm-in-arm, slowly walking back to the house to greet him.

Toby gave Trevor a huge smile. He wrapped his arms around the taller man tightly. Stepping away, he clapped Trevor on the back.

"Thank you for everything, Trevor. I cannot express how very grateful I am. Welcome to our home. I'm sure you're both hungry and thirsty. Let's go inside."

Toby linked arms with the two of them as he pushed the door open.

Smiling, Miriam entered her home for the first time in three years.

◈◈◈

A small fire crackled in the fireplace as the three enjoyed venison stew with some wine Toby had tucked away. Miriam and Toby talked non-stop about *everything*. They had so much to catch up on. Toby was interested in her story about how she and Trevor had found a tiny cabin for shelter from the snowstorm. She filled him in on all the details- how they celebrated Christmas, how safe and desolate the area was. The war seemed far off and was hardly mentioned.

Glancing around the little home, Trevor noticed a nice dinette buffet holding china and crystal. Although small and basic, the home had two nice couches and chairs along with the dinette table. It was a comfy little home, nicer than he had expected for this time era. The food was filling and the company congenial. Trevor was enjoying their conversation. He was content to be off of Prince for the evening, but knew he would need to depart in the morning. He didn't mention this to either of them. They were so happy being reunited; he didn't want to spoil the moment.

After dinner, Toby and Miriam quickly cleaned up the dishes. They all settled near the fire to sip more wine and converse more. Toby told Miriam all of the news from town, catching her up on neighbors, friends, and of course, David.

◈◈◈

When it was time to retire, Toby made up a nice comfortable bed for Trevor. He piled pillows and quilts on the couch with a small fire still crackling.

"Hope you'll be comfortable here, Trevor. If you need anything, I'll be right upstairs in my room." He gestured at wooden steps leading upstairs where Trevor assumed there were two bedrooms.

"Thanks, Toby. I'm sure I'll be fine. Between the long ride and the excellent wine, I'm pretty tired." Trevor smiled down at the younger man as Toby smiled and put his hands in his pockets.

Miriam leaned up, kissing Trevor on the cheek. "Good night, Trevor. We will see you in the morning," she murmured softly.

With one last glance back at Trevor, she followed Toby up the stairs carrying a lantern. There were candles lit on the side table for Trevor. He stripped down to his underwear, then blew the candles out. He settled on the sofa, asleep almost immediately.

Although Miriam was so happy to be in her familiar bed again, she laid awake for a very long time.

Dawn crept around the edges of curtains, stroking Trevor's face softly. Disoriented, he rose slightly, looking around. Groaning, he laid back, remembering they were now at the Klarks' home. The sofa felt heavenly after sleeping on the ground for two weeks; he was reluctant to move.

He didn't hear anything from upstairs yet, no movement at all, but then it was very early. He knew he needed to take Prince and leave today. The thought made him sad.

He accessed his chip to get information. *Is my mission complete?*

After several moments, he received an answer. *Yes, it is.*

Now what? He asked.

Now you return.

Return? How?

Take your horse when you are ready. And you will return.

Trevor ruminated over this answer. He could leave now. Pack up, saddle Prince, and go. Sighing, he knew he couldn't do that. He couldn't leave until he said goodbye to Toby, but especially to Miriam. He knew how she felt about him. He cared deeply for her too, but it was his destiny to return to the future where he belonged. Hers was to stay here with her brother, and possibly David Irvin.

Trevor rose, finding a small sink. He quickly cleaned up, grabbing his trousers and shirt. As he was buttoning it up he could hear footsteps on the stairs.

Glancing up in the dim light, he could see Miriam making her way downstairs in a white lacy nightgown. She pushed back her hair, smiling at him.

"Good morning, Trevor," she said softly. "I see you're up and about already."

Trevor moved to the sofa to fold the quilts neatly, placing the pillows on top. He turned to her and smiled slowly. She looked lovely in the early morning light.

"Yep. Actually just woke up a few minutes ago. Used the sink quickly too."

"I'll make some pancakes. We have honey to go with them and milk, or do you prefer coffee?" She moved to the kitchen area near the dinette table.

"Pancakes sound wonderful. Hot black coffee for me, please." He sat at the table as he watched her move around, getting an iron pan to put onto the cast iron stove. She lit it, starting to mix pancakes and ladling them onto the hot pan.

She turned to him, placing dish settings for three. "Toby will be up soon, I'm sure," she remarked.

"Toby is up, for sure," a voice heard from the stairwell said.

They turned to see Toby approaching, buttoning his shirt with his russet hair mussed. "So good to have you back again sis, cooking a homemade breakfast." He leaned down to kiss his sister's cheek then sat opposite Trevor.

"Good morning, Trevor."

Miriam brought over three hot coffees and the men accepted them.

Trevor sipped the hot brew, grinning at Toby. "Good morning to you, too."

"How'd ya sleep?"

"Very well. Went out as soon as my head touched the pillow. Sleeping on the ground for two weeks can do that to you."

Miriam busily cooked, her back to them as the men chatted. Soon she brought food over for the three of them. She served steaming pancakes, placing a jar of honey in the center of the table. Everyone dug in, enjoying the hot meal.

"Are you planning to work in the fields today, Toby?" Miriam asked.

"Nah. Of course not! Not with you home. Everyone will want to see you. We will have to visit in town, maybe have lunch at the tavern to celebrate. Sound good, Trevor?" Toby's eyes turned to the man opposite him.

Trevor was silent several moments. He needed to tell them he had to leave today. Somehow the words wouldn't come. How could he phrase it?

Miriam knew he had to return to his unit, but she probably expected him to stay for awhile. It was obvious Toby did.

He gulped coffee, then carefully placed it down, meeting curious gazes. His eyes met Miriam's. "I'm afraid I can't stay."

"What?" Toby gasped. "Why not? You are released, aren't you, Major?"

"Please, call me Trevor. No, I'm afraid I am not. I have to return to my unit today," he said quietly, now looking down at his pancakes.

Miriam was silent, continuing to eat her breakfast, somehow not surprised by this announcement. "When?" she simply said.

"Well, I can certainly spend a certain amount of time with you today, but by this afternoon, I will have to be on my way."

"So, you can visit in town with us?" Toby asked.

"Briefly," Trevor said succinctly.

"David will be eager to see you both," Toby remarked.

At this comment, both Miriam and Trevor were silent, finishing the early meal.

As Miriam and Toby readied for the day, Trevor went out back to tend to Prince. "Well, we have another journey ahead of us today, my friend. Are you up to it?"

Trevor rubbed the horse down. He stroked Prince's nose as his horse gently bumped his shoulder. "I'll take that as a yes." Trevor's large hand stroked the bare back of the silky horse, brushing out his mane neatly. "You must look handsome for the return." Trevor quietly murmured to his horse who whinnied and chuffed.

As he stood, he could see Miriam striding towards him wearing a pale blue dress with a white collar, her blonde hair tied back with a ribbon. The sunlight picked out honey glints in her hair.

"I thought I would find you out here, attending to Prince." She moved closer to stroke the horse, who whinnied and pranced for her. "I will miss you, my friend," she said softly.

At these words, Prince laid his head gently on her shoulder, leaning down as Miriam touched her cheek to his white mane, her hand buried in it as her cheek caressed him. Trevor watched the two silently until she gave Prince a final pat, stepping away.

"We are ready to head into town, if you are. It is a short jaunt, a few blocks away," she informed him, looking up into royal blue eyes.

Those eyes. She would miss those eyes the rest of her life.

"Sure. I've attended to Prince. We can leave when the two of you are ready."

"Toby is waiting out front," she told him, waving goodbye to Prince.

The two moved around the house where Trevor could see Toby waiting, wearing a red shirt with slacks, his thick russet hair neatly combed back.

"Hello there, Trevor!" he greeted.

"Toby," Trevor responded, glancing at the dirt road that led into town. "Where is our first stop?"

"Well, since it's early morning, thought we could call on David first. His house and practice are in the middle of town, about five blocks or so." Toby pointed directly ahead.

"Lead the way," Trevor said, falling into step with them.

As they moved into town, many friends and neighbors gasped. Recognizing Miriam, they came over to greet her. They stopped several times to chat, taking a good half hour to actually reach David's house.

David's house was a large white Victorian with lattice woodwork running the entire width of the spacious porch. Trevor noticed the sign hanging from a shingle: Dr. David Irvin, MD. Smiling, he walked up the steps as Toby banged the brass knocker a few times.

The door was opened by an older woman with a sweet smile. She greeted Toby but upon seeing Miriam, she let out a delighted squeal. She held her arms wide, hugging the young woman tightly.

Miriam returned the embrace. "Hello, Anna. It is wonderful to see you again."

Anna stepped back to look up into Miriam's face. "It is *so* good to see you!" she exclaimed in a slight German accent. "You look so well. And you are safe! Oh my goodness, the Lord be praised!" She ushered them into the foyer of the roomy house.

"What's all the noise about, Anna?" Trevor could hear David's voice further in the house before he appeared between French doors to the right of the foyer.

When he saw Trevor standing with Toby and Miriam, David's silver brows arched. "Miriam!" he gasped.

He immediately went to her, scooping her up in his arms. He squeezed her tightly as everyone looked on. "Oh, thank God! I had all but given up- oh, thank you, God!" he gasped again.

David stepped back to examine Miriam. "Are you well? How did you ever survive? Oh, where are my manners? Come in, come! Anna, please put out the closed sign for now." He ushered his guests into the spacious living room.

They entered the room. Trevor noticed the tasteful décor: the lavish white fireplace (now dormant), the cream moiré wallpaper, the lush red carpeting, a lovely sofa and chairs placed about with crystal lamps.

David ushered Miriam and Trevor to a teal upholstered sofa as he and Toby took plush pale blue wing chairs opposite.

Anna was quick with a silver tea service, placing china and a teapot down, smiling the whole time. "Would you like refreshments also?" she asked the guests.

"Thank you, Anna, but thanks to Miriam, we had a hardy breakfast," Toby replied.

Smiling, Anna retreated to the back of the house. David kept studying Miriam, amazed and grateful she had returned. He knew he had Major Trevor Tompkins to thank for that miracle.

"I am so happy and grateful to see you both again." David's silver eyes moved to Trevor. "I cannot thank you enough, Major Tompkins," he said quietly.

"Please, call me Trevor." Trevor now wore his blue Union uniform. He sipped at his hot tea, inhaling the delicious scent.

"I had all but given up hope-" David began.

"I never did," Toby said emphatically. "I knew someday you would return, sis. I never stopped believing that."

Miriam smiled at Toby. "Somehow, I expected that." Her gaze turned to David. "David, you must have more faith."

"Oh, believe me, I prayed night and day. But to have them come to fruition… God's gift and plan. Welcome home!" He raised his teacup in a slight toast, the others followed suit.

"So- where to begin? I have so many questions," David said. "What happened after the snowstorm?"

Miriam settled in to tell David about their adventures, leaving out the fact that she and the Major had become lovers.

At mid-day, after seeing several patients, David joined them at the local tavern for lunch. He insisted on buying. They found a round table on the far side, settling in. The blonde bar maid came over to take their food order, placing a basket of muffins on the table. The men ordered ales and Miriam ordered tea. Smiling, she departed.

They chatted casually about friends in town. Both Toby and David caught Miriam up on local happenings.

"I am still looking for an assistant for my practice, Miriam, if you are interested. I can't find anyone and I could really use your skills," David said.

The barmaid returned with their beverages, saying food would be out soon.

The men sipped at their ales as Miriam answered. "Toby may need me around the farm a bit; I've been away for so long." Her dark eyes met her brother's in the dim light.

Toby set down his mug. "Sis, I've got everything totally covered. Only have a few more days of planting to do, then just harvesting in the fall."

"In that case, I would be more than happy to assist you, David." She paused. "Trevor has to return to his unit this afternoon," she informed David and Toby.

David's brows arched. "Already? You've been given orders this soon?"

"Yes, I am to pick them up today and continue on. Today will be the last day I am here." Trevor traced the rim of his mug, looking down.

"I am quite surprised by that. Usually they will give an officer several days to get his affairs in order," the doctor said.

Sighing, Trevor lifted his mug to sip. "Not this time."

"Well, we must celebrate while we can. A shot of whiskey all around!" David declared.

Trevor smiled. "I must decline since I am returning, but thank you for the thought."

The barmaid brought steaming platters of food over, serving everyone. The group dug into their food, chatting casually together, enjoying each other's company while they could.

<hr />

In the afternoon, David returned to his practice. The Klarks and Trevor returned to the Klark residence. Miriam was going to prepare dinner, but that could wait until Trevor departed. She wanted to spend as much time with him as she could.

Toby said he had some work to do out in the fields so that Miriam and Trevor could be alone. He again exuberantly thanked Trevor for returning his sister safe and sound. Saluting the two, he headed out into the fields as Trevor and Miriam lingered on the steps of the porch.

Trevor had already saddled Prince, bringing him around to the front. He cropped grass as the two sat on the porch steps.

The sun was getting lower on the horizon. Trevor surmised it was probably almost dinnertime. Time for him to go. Time to leave.

He turned to Miriam, brushing a stray strand of blonde hair back, tucking it behind her ear as her brown eyes met his. A slight breeze ruffled his black hair. His deep blue eyes were serious, sad. Miriam's eyes teared up as she realized the time had come.

Trevor took her in his arms, gently rocking her. "Don't cry, baby. This is farewell, not goodbye. I will see you in my dreams," he said softly, tucking her face into his chest.

Miriam sobbed, clutching his arms tightly. "I wish you didn't have to go," she cried.

He stroked her hair. "I know. I wish things could be different, but they're not. You have a future here; I don't."

She looked up to gaze into his face.

"Your place is here. Mine isn't," he continued to stroke her hair.

"Why not?" She swiped at tears, intently gazing into his eyes. "There's something you're not telling me. At least tell me before you go."

You cannot reveal your true identity, the chip warned.

"I wish I could, but I can't. Miriam, this is hard for me too. I want only the best for you. I can't give it to you." He paused. "I love you. Keep that sentiment in your heart when I am gone." He stood, and she did too.

He put his arms around her, drawing her to him as he kissed her deeply, thoroughly, making her moan softly.

Trevor turned abruptly, going to his horse as Miriam descended the final steps. She watched as Trevor mounted Prince in the late afternoon light, the sun haloing around him.

He looked down at her standing there in her pale blue dress, her honey hair pulled back with tears streaming down her face.

"Remember, I love you."

He turned Prince onto the pathway, galloping out of sight, leaving only a cloud of dust behind.

Miriam watched his dim figure until it was swallowed up by the afternoon. She turned to enter her home, still crying, grateful that Toby was out.

Trevor was gone. She would never see him again.

he weeks passed by. Miriam helped David in his practice, trying not to miss Trevor but it was so hard. They had been together daily for months. Not seeing him at all broke her heart. She carried on stoically, as there was no other choice. At least her work distracted her.

Miriam had a secret that she had not shared with anyone, not even Toby. For now, she held it fast, for it comforted her in these days when she was lonely. Even surrounded by family and friends, she was so alone.

David was so happy to have Miriam assisting him once again. He was able to see more patients, and with her skill set the time flew quickly.

Over the weeks, he noticed she was quieter than usual. He knew she was missing Trevor. The day he left, no one had seen him at all. It was as if he just disappeared.

Something else was bothering Miriam. He knew her well enough to know that.

After they closed for the day, he would invite her to stay for dinner. She usually returned home to be with Toby, but he felt it was important to speak to her.

When David asked Miriam to stay for dinner that evening, he could see that she was a bit startled, but she agreed.

David had Anna make a roast with accompanying sides. She served them quickly, lighting candles and lanterns. Smiling, she retreated back upstairs to her quarters.

David poured out some ruby red wine for them, handing Miriam a glass. She accepted it, sipping slowly.

David studied her across the dining table. Tonight she was wearing a pink gingham gown with her long blonde hair flowing around her shoulders. In the candlelight, she looked lovely but surreal, present but also distant.

He shook off this weird thought, addressing her as they began their meal.

"Miriam, there is a reason I suggested we have dinner together this evening," he began.

She was cutting her roast, glancing up to meet his gaze. "Oh?"

"Yes, I felt it important that we speak. Something is bothering you." He held up a hand briefly. "I know you are missing Trevor, and I totally understand that. I think, however, there is also something else bothering you."

Miriam was startled by this remark. Did he know? Had he guessed?

She reached to take a tiny sip of wine. "Whatever do you mean, David?" She arched a brow.

David folded his hands under his chin and met her eyes directly. "I think there is something worrying you. You seem- sometimes- to be distant, far away in your thoughts." He waved one hand. "It has not affected your work, you are always attentive and excellent, but there is something... I can't quite put my finger on it," he ended, studying her.

Miriam breathed a slow sigh of relief. So, he didn't know.

She shrugged. "I'm just glad to be out of the war. After the horrors I've seen, that we have both seen..." her words trailed off as she picked at her food, glancing back down.

David was silent for several moments. Somehow he didn't think he was getting the truth out of her.

"Miriam, do you trust me?"

Startled a second time, her eyes searched his. "Of course, David. Why do you ask?"

"Because there is something you're not telling me." He paused, then decided to go ahead. "Miriam, you know how I feel about you. I am in love with you."

At these words, Miriam placed her fork by her side, placing her hands in her lap, not meeting his eyes.

"Miriam?"

Big dark eyes met silver grey. "Yes, I know," she murmured.

Sighing, David wiped his mouth with the linen napkin, sipping more wine as he studied her.

"I have an important question I want to ask you. I've been meaning to for quite some time," he said quietly.

Miriam waited and he paused.

"I would like you to be my wife, Miriam. I would be honored and proud to have you as my partner for life." His grey eyes were serious, moist as they met hers.

Miriam gasped, her hands flying to her mouth. Surprised but then again, not surprised. Slowly, she lowered her hands and met his gaze, carefully picking up her wine glass.

Finally, she answered him. "I cannot."

David quirked his brows. "Cannot? What do you mean?"

She had to tell him the truth. Oh Lord, please help me.

"David, I am pregnant. With Trevor's child." There, it was finally said. She felt relief and apprehension.

At these words, David laid his napkin down, approaching her chair. He knelt down on one knee and took her hand gently.

"Miriam, I suspected that. How could you be alone for months with such a man and not become lovers? It does not change how I feel about you. I love you. He is gone and I am here."

He took both of her hands, turning her to face him directly.

"Please accept. I know you don't love me now, but that could change, my dear. I promise to claim the child as my own, and we will raise it as ours."

At his words, Miriam gasped, eyes widening. "David, I cannot ask that of you, I cannot-"

David interrupted her. "Miriam, will you be my wife?" he asked again.

Tears appeared in her eyes and she sobbed softly. "Oh, David, I don't know what to say, I-"

"Just say yes," he said quietly.

She stood to embrace him. "Yes," she whispered.

David leaned down to gently kiss her, smoothing her tears away.

"It will be all right. I promise you, everything will be fine. I give you my word," he whispered softly.

They embraced in the candlelight, their two shadows mingling as one.

EPILOGUE

April, 2037

Dr. Michael Tompkins Irvin (descendant of Trevor Tompkins and Miriam Klark) discovers the cure for cancer.

THE END